BROTHERS OF THE BADGE

ALASKA STATE TROOPERS, FBI AGENTS, AND U.S. MARSHALS PROBE AN INFORMANT'S DEATH

Ron Walden

Alaskan True to Life Crime Writer

ISBN 978-1-9-726318-2
eBook ISBN 978-1-95-726319-9
Library of Congress Catalog Card Number: 2015932338

Acknowledgements

Brother of the Badge is inspired by the friends I associate with in my daily life. Many of my friends are retired troopers and policemen, firemen and correctional officers. All of these men and women have stood between the good and evil elements of life during their entire careers. I am proud to be in a league with these fine people. I thank them for all the stories, both real and those remembered with a twist, told at the coffee shop each morning. If you see any of them, please raise a coffee cup as a salute to them for the service they have given you and your community.

I thank my friend Charlie Weimer, Vice President of First National Bank of Alaska. I imposed on him for information about the banking industry and foreign banking practices. We have been friends for more than 30 years. I can always count on him for good advice.

Thanks also to the staff and management of Mykel's Bar and Restaurant and Soldotna Inn Hotel for allowing me to use them as one of the locations in this work of fiction. I thank the owners and manager of the Ido Café for allowing me to use their café and their manager as a model for the location and waitress in *Brother of the Badge*. Again, the story is fiction, but these people are wonderfully real people.

Finally, I thank my son Scott for keeping me out of trouble with my computer. I am a dinosaur without computer skills. His hours of labor and repair have made *Brother of the Badge* possible in spite of me.

Most of all I thank my loyal readers and friends for their support.

Chapter 1

Alaska in springtime is a magical place. Leaves are budding out, young moose calves are emerging from the woods and fishing for salmon and halibut is exciting. The temperatures are warming and tides tapering off a little. Cook Inlet has the second highest tides in the world making tidal change a notable event. The speed of the tidal change is amazing causing a tidal rip filled with debris and drawing all types of fishes to the center of the inlet to feed. Sports fishermen as well as commercial operators are out in force searching for the bounty that arrives in early June each year.

Retired State Trooper Alan Pulis and his old partner and friend, Bill Gant, were on their way to Anchor Point to launch their 24 foot Hewescraft boat for a day of halibut fishing. They had been friends for more than twenty five years. Both were now retired and were partners in ownership of this saltwater fishing boat. The two men met when Gant was a rookie cop and Pulis was his Field Training Officer. It was a friendship lasting through the careers of both men. In the early years they worked together often and were friends off duty as well as at work. Pulis had been a trooper two years longer than Gant and over the years they had been assigned separate posts and later reunited in another station. The Troopers learned to trust each other in many dangerous situations.

In the early years both men were married and spent a great deal of time together with their families. Alan Pulis and his wife Cybil had two children, a son Raymond and a daughter Lucile. Both were now grown and moved away from home. Last year Cybil was diagnosed with cancer. Within months she was totally bed-ridden. Alan devoted his entire energy to caring for her. The children made trips to Alaska to help him care for their mother, but with families of their own they would only stay for short periods of time before returning to their respective homes. Cybil weakened and finally succumbed to her disease nearly a year and a half ago. Alan was heartbroken and lost interest in life. The children offered to take him into their homes, but he refused the offers.

Bill Gant was married to a stunning beauty in those early days. She was dissatisfied with her lonely life as the wife of a trooper. The stressful confrontations became too much for the two of them and she filed for divorce after three years. Gant never remarried. He was popular with the ladies, with his good looks and dynamic personality but never became permanently involved with anyone. Alan and Bill remained friends during these trying times. Alan buoyed the spirits of his friend Bill when he was troubled by his divorce and Bill did the same for Alan while Cybil was ill. Each stood by the other in their times of need, making theirs a solid and lasting friendship. Partnership in the boat seemed a natural thing to do when the opportunity came about.

A retired schoolteacher had purchased the boat originally. When he became disabled he put it up for sale. Alan learned of the boat and approached Bill Gant to partner with him in something the two of them could enjoy. They would be able to fish whenever they wanted and share the expenses. Since they usually fished together it was a natural. They bought the craft and for the past two years have been on the water fishing and enjoying retirement.

This early June morning they were on their way to Anchor Point to launch. It was early, but in June the sun is only out of the sky for about three and a half hours. The air was warm and clean. The sky was blue and the wind was calm. All this made a promise of a great day of fishing. The two men sipped hot coffee poured from a thermos, saying little while they motored down the highway keeping an eye out for moose that may cross the road. They had seen a few cows with calves, but none on the roadway.

"Hey, Bill, I have a trivia question for you."

"And what would that be?" asked Gant before taking another sip of his coffee.

"Today is the 8th of June. What happened here in Alaska 102 years and two days ago? It was an historic event. It made the news all around the world." Pulis raised his coffee cup to beg an answer.

Gant pondered the question, "Let me see, uh, Oh, I've got it! That was the last time you caught a fish."

"Wrong, besides I always out-fish you. Come on, be serious a minute. This is a real question."

"Well let me see. That would make it June 6, 1912, right?"

"Right, now what was it?" Pulis snickered knowing he had stumped his partner.

"OK mister know-it-all, I give up. I have no idea. What happened on that date?"

Alan paused and sipped his coffee for effect. When he knew he had pressed Gant as far as he would stand he said, "On the afternoon of June 6, 1912 there were two simultaneous volcanic eruptions. Mount Katmai volcano and nearby Novarupta exploded and showered ash and rock for 60 continuous hours. It covered the city of Kodiak, 75 miles East, with five feet of ash. Mount Katmai was blamed, but later it was determined the two mountains erupted in unison. The eruption turned a mountain larger than Mount St. Helens in Washington into, what is now known as, The Valley of Ten Thousand Smokes."

"And just how did you come up with this information? I know you didn't read a book," joked Bill.

"I'm surprised you haven't heard about it. It was in all the papers. Of course TV hadn't been invented yet. Maybe that was it." Alan laughed as he teased his friend.

"Is it going to be this way all day?" asked Gant. Both men laughed. "I put the herring in the blue cooler. Lunch is in the red one. I guess it's my turn to pay for the launch fees. I hope you filled the gas tanks." Again they shared a chuckle.

The launch site in Anchor point is a unique experience where you unhook your trailer and park the truck, get inside the boat, raise the motor leg and wait for the beach tractors to hook up to your trailer and back into the surf. Good weather and little wind made the launch easy and pleasant this morning.

Alan backed the boat a short distance and turned toward the open water. He idled the motors a short time to warm up before putting them into gear to motor toward the fishing spot marked on the Global Positioning System (GPS). The sea was nearly flat with only a small sea-swell. They made good time to the fishing spot - a small underwater mount-marked on the map.

Bill stepped onto the gunwale and made his way to the bow of the boat to drop the anchor. The depth finder indicated 126 feet of water, but the tide required at least 400 feet of anchor line. He dropped the Davis anchor and paid out 600 feet of line before tying it off the bow cleat. The tide was still incoming for another hour. Putting out a fishing line now meant very heavy weights in order to keep the bait on the bottom where the fish could get at it. They decided to bait up and wait for the tide to slow. Several minutes were used to prepare bait and rods before they relaxed to wait on the tide.

Alan returned to the cabin to get them each one final cup of coffee before the tide slowed. They stood on the aft deck, leaning against the rails. Bill faced west toward the shore of the Kenai Peninsula while Alan faced the opposite shore. Neither man spoke, only drank his coffee and admired the early June morning. Sea birds circled and a large sea otter floated nearby. The sky held a few puffy white clouds. The only sounds were the water, the birds and far-off boat motors of other fishermen heading to their favorite spot in Cook Inlet. Alan watched the nearby rip tide filled with kelp and other debris as it passed the boat. Suddenly he set his coffee cup on the rail and entered the cabin. He returned with a pair of binoculars and lifted them to his eyes.

"Hey, Bill. Take a look out there in the rip. It looks like a life jacket floating there." He handed the glasses to his partner. "To the left, out in the rip, can you see it?"

Gant scanned the rip a moment. "Oh, yeah, I see it. It's getting closer to us. Damn, Alan, it looks like there's something in it." He handed the binoculars back to Pulis.

"I see what you're talking about. It's coming pretty fast." He thought for a second before making the decision, "Hook the buoy to the anchor line while I start the engines. I think we had better take a look."

Bill stepped over the rail and began to make his way to the bow. He turned to speak with Alan, "Be careful in the rip. I see a lot of kelp and trash out there." He continued to the front where he clipped the anchor line to a large orange buoy, then tossed it over the nose of the boat. He picked the boat hook from the roof of the cabin on his way back to the rear deck. As he untied the long handle boat hook he heard the engines start and the boat began to move to the west toward the tidal rip.

Alan dodged all manner of flotsam as he maneuvered toward the bright orange life vest floating in the mess ahead. He managed to dodge the large rafts of kelp as well as a tree floating there before approaching the life vest. Bill was on the rear deck with the boat hook in hand as Alan skillfully edged the boat closer to the object. When they neared the object he called to Alan. "We've got a body." He reached out and hooked it with the long boat hook. Alan cut the engines and came back to the deck to lend a hand.

With a short length of small rope in his grasp he managed to get a wrap around the body and vest. "I'm not sure we can get this guy in the boat out here in this debris. Can you hold him while I try to back out of this rip to some slower water?"

"I can try," answered Gant.

Pulis returned to the cabin and put the engines in reverse. The boat moved with the tide and away from the floating tangle in the center of the riptide. Once clear of the tidal mess he cut the engines and returned to the aft deck. Bill was maintaining his grip on the rope. The two men managed to get a second rope around the body. Once it was secure Bill reached to the neck of the body to feel for a pulse. It was an unnecessary act. The body had been in the water for more than 24 hours.

"Let's go back to the anchor and tie up. I'm not sure we can get him into the boat without help. I'll call the troopers on the cell phone and let them know what we have." Old trooper instincts and training were kicking in.

Pulis gently drove the boat back to where they had dropped the anchor line. Bill climbed to the bow to retrieve the rope and secure it to the bow cleat. Once done he reached into his vest pocket for a cell phone to dial 911. When the operator answered he identified himself.

"This is Bill Gant. I am on a fishing vessel in Cook Inlet off Anchor Point. We just retrieved a body from the inlet and need a trooper boat out here."

"You say you have found a body in Cook Inlet?" Came the professional voice.

"That's correct. I'm a retired trooper and know what a body looks like. The tide is running and we're unable to lift the body out of the water without assistance. We need a trooper out here right away. Write this down, it's the GPS coordinates." Gant read the numbers from the screen.

"Please hold while I send a trooper."

After several minutes of questions and pauses a male voice came on the line. "This is Captain Rollin Caswell. Is this you Bill?"

Chapter 2

Pulis and Gant were both stationed in Fairbanks when they first met Rollin Caswell. He was a young trooper like the other two, full of life and willing to get involved in any adventure the others attempted. Over the years the three worked together many times and, though they seldom saw each other, were still friends.

"I've dispatched a NOAA (National Oceanographic and Atmospheric Administration) enforcement boat to your location. Two troopers from Homer will be on the boat with the NOAA officers. They're leaving the Homer harbor now and will be at your location in approximately one hour. Can you stay at your location for that long?" There was concern in Caswell's voice.

"The tide is almost slack now, so we shouldn't have any trouble," replied Bill. "This is going to cost you a lot, you know. We're losing our fishing tide right now."

Caswell laughed, "It costs me every time I associate with you two. What's your cell phone number in case I need to call you back?" He copied down the number and continued, "I'll give this number to one of the troopers on the other boat and have them call you when they get close."

Pulis now stood on the rear deck with Gant, who put the phone on speaker in order for him to hear the conversation. "We'll keep an eye out for the boat. You might pass on to them that we are a 24-footer with a cabin and yellow hull. It will make it easier for them to spot us."

"I really appreciate the help. By the way did you recognize the victim?" inquired Caswell.

Gant looked at Pulis who shook his head. "I think I may know who he is, Cap. He's wearing suit pants and a tie. He looks like one of the officers from the savings and loan on the east end of town. I'm not positive, but he looks like a guy I've seen working there. I don't know his name, but you might call them and ask if anyone failed to come to work today."

"Thanks, Bill. I'll call them. You two come in and make a report when you get back to town. I'm going to give the responding troopers this information. Call me if you need anything."

"Will do, Cap," replied Gant. He closed his phone and turned to Alan. "Wanna try fishing?" he joked.

While waiting the two ex-troopers ate a sandwich and drank more coffee. Out of curiosity Gant turned to his partner and asked, "What do you suppose happened to this guy?"

"I don't know, but I don't think he died by accident. When we were putting the ropes on the body I saw what looked like bullet holes in the back of the life vest. I didn't see any blood, but the water would have taken care of that. I think he went into the water yesterday, probably late in the day."

"I didn't see those holes. Damn, if that's the case then we have a murder on our hands." Gant was now leaning over the side to see if he could spot the holes in the victim.

"Hey, Partner!" Pulis commented, "This isn't our case. We're just bystanders in this one."

Gant nodded agreement. "You're right, Alan. I got carried away. I'm like the old fire-horse, when the bell goes off I just want to go to the fire."

"I've had enough bodies to last me a lifetime," said Pulis. "Let's rig some rods for later."

Just over an hour later a big black boat appeared. Gant's phone rang. It was the Homer trooper verifying the location and saying he could see the yellow hull of the boat. Five minutes later they were alongside. The two troopers on the NOAA boat assessed the situation and decided to take the body aboard their boat immediately. Gant and Pulis untied the ropes and handed them to the troopers on the other boat. Once the body was safely on board, the NOAA skipper moved his huge boat close and the two troopers jumped to the Hewescraft to speak with the witnesses.

"I'm Trooper Stone and this is Trooper Milikowski. Captain Caswell says you two are retired troopers and can be trusted to come into the office to make a report. I just need some details about the time and circumstances of finding the victim. Are you willing to do that for me?"

"With one stipulation." commented Pulis.

"And what would that be?" asked Trooper Stone.

"When you get back on your boat I'd like for you to roll the body to one side so we can see the back of the life vest he's wearing."

"I can do that, but why would you want to see his back?"

"Because I think there are two bullet holes there," answered Pulis.

Stone and Milikowski looked at each other in disbelief. They immediately turned to face the NOAA sailor on the rear deck of the big boat. "Fred," he called to the man, "Roll that body up on his side and show us his back." Fred did as he was instructed.

"Holy Smoke!" commented Stone. "It does look like two bullet holes there. I'll look to make sure, but I'll have to call the captain and let him know. Thanks for the tip." A few more questions and the men jumped back to their own vessel, waved and motored off toward Homer harbor.

Pulis and Gant watched the boat fade into the distance before Alan picked up a rod and put some herring on the hook. The tide had changed and was beginning to pick up speed when Gant pulled in his last fish, a nice 45 pound Pacific Halibut. They pulled the anchor and headed back to Anchor point where they had launched this morning. The tractors backed the trailer into the water and took the boat to dry land. Pulis went for the truck while Gant put gear away and made the boat ready to travel. He was just ready to enter the truck with Alan when his cell phone rang. It was Rollin Caswell.

"I just heard from my men in Homer. They say you two spotted bullet holes in the victim while he was still in the water. Is that true?"

"Yeah, Cap. We mentioned it to the trooper." Gant confirmed the information for Caswell.

"Is it possible for the two of you to stop at the office on your way home? I have something I want to ask of you both."

Gant looked at Pulis who nodded, "We'll be there in a little more than an hour, cap."

"Thanks, guys. See you then."

"I hope he wants to buy us a tank of gas for our trouble," said Alan Pulis.

A little more than an hour later the two men pulled their boat trailer into the parking area of the Soldotna Trooper Post. The girl at the front desk ushered them into the office of the commander who had been expecting them.

"Got any hot coffee, Cap?" asked Pulis.

The captain grinned and used the intercom to order three cups of fresh coffee to be brought to the office. While they waited Caswell broke the question to them.

"The state has cut our budget to the point we're maxed out with the personnel we have available. I'm authorized to hire outside help on a short term contract to qualified people when the need arises. I want to know if the two of you would be interested in investigating this case on contract. You'd be fully commissioned officers in practice, but on a contract basis. You will only be responsible for those duties associated with this case. Are you interested?" The coffee came and the server left the office. Rollin Caswell leaned back in his chair, holding his coffee cup, waiting for an answer.

"How long is this contract good for, Cap," asked Pulis.

"Only until the case gets through the courts," answered the captain. "I'll try to give you all the help you need and pay all expenses associated with the case."

"Can you include a tank of gas for the boat? We lost a lot of fishing time today because of this case." Gant was joking, but in essence, agreeing to a contract.

"I'll see what I can do about that, Bill."

"Have you checked with the bank to see if their employees all showed for work," asked Pulis.

The captain searched through some papers on the top of his desk to retrieve a sheet and handed it to Alan.

Pulis read the sheet with Gant reading over his shoulder. It stated one of the employees of the Savings and Loan office had failed to report to work today. They had sent someone to the employee's home but found no one there. The missing employee was an assistant manager who worked in this office for more than two years. His name is Stanley Phelps.

"If we take the job we would need an office and a computer. We might need a car, too. Can we have until morning to give you an answer?" It was Gant making the inquiry.

"Sure," replied the captain. "Sleep on it and come in and see me tomorrow."

In the cab of the truck Alan turned to Bill and asked, "Well, Partner, what do you think? Should we take this on?"

"I hate to admit this, but it sounds kind of exciting to me. We don't have anything to do but go fishing. I say let's go for it." Bill Gant was ready to go.

"I hate to have you agree with me. It never turns out well. I say let's do it. What's the worst that can happen? They might fire us? We used to be pretty good at this kind of work. We still know what we knew. I think we can do this and have some fun in the process. I'll meet you in the captain's office at eight in the morning to make out the paperwork and write a report on us finding the victim."

Gant was laughing, "Did you see the surprise on that Trooper Stone's face when you told him there were bullet holes in the body?"

"That was kind of funny, wasn't it?" Pulis replied. "A lot of things have changed since you and I were doing this. So, let's try to look like we know what we're doing. I really don't like being laughed at."

Chapter 3

The two men met in the parking lot of the trooper headquarters building at 8 the following morning. Both were dressed in a sport coat and tie and wearing leather shoes, polished. The receptionist led the recruits to an office in the back of the building. There were two desks, two computers, office supplies and filing cabinets.

"Just like home," commented Gant.

"I'm glad you noticed. I thought for a moment I was having a flashback," replied Pulis.

There were two packets on the desks. Alan opened his stack to review the contents. It was the usual entry application data request. The second sheet was a contract application for state workers. The third was health information. The pages went on and would require several hours to complete. Gant was inspecting his packet, a twin to the packet Pulis had looked at, then took off his coat and hung it on the coat tree beside the door.

Both men were through the first page when Captain Caswell came in to say hello. "Good morning," he greeted.

"Mornin', Cap. You can see we're prompt and doing the paperwork as instructed," Gant joked.

"You are such good little boys," quipped the captain.

"We should be done with this application process by noon. I think we need to have a meeting to discuss the direction you want us to take in the investigation." Pulis was being serious for a change.

"Good point, Alan, and that's the reason I came in to see you this morning. The autopsy is scheduled for 10 this morning. I should have the result around noon. It won't be complete but we will have an initial report. I have some other things to pass on to you when you finish here. We need to get you hired and ID badges issued so you can get into the building. See you later." Caswell gave a wave of his hand as he turned to leave the office. He knew these men were far past the paramilitary protocol defining rank in the trooper regime. He also knew they were both highly skilled investigators with the reputation of a "get it done" team. He was pleased they took the task.

It was just before noon when the new hires came into the captain's office wearing new ID badges. When they entered and sat down he reached into the center drawer of his desk for two wallet badges. He gave one to each man. Both opened and read their badge designation declaring them INVESTIGATOR.

Gant smiled and turned to Pulis to say, "Boy, we're Important now!" Pulis only chuckled.

The captain took a file from his desk drawer and opened it. "You were right about the victim being an employee of the Savings and Loan Company. The manager called yesterday to report one of his employees missing. I think the first order of business should be to meet with him and confirm an identity. You two saw the body and will know from the employee picture if it's the same person."

"How tight do you want to supervise us, Cap?" asked Pulis.

Captain Caswell blew out a long breath. "I've known you two for a long time and I know you won't comply with anything I say, so let's just agree on you two keeping me informed about the case every step of the way. I can't set you loose on the world without some kind of restraint. You know the rules, stay within them. I want you to investigate properly and thoroughly, but right now we don't know where this will lead and I want you to track down every possibility. Agreed?"

"Sounds good to me, Cap," agreed Pulis with Gant nodding his compliance.

"OK, get out there and do the job I'm paying you for. Oh, by the way, the front desk has a voucher for one tank of gas for your boat. Spend it wisely. There's a car for you in the lot. Here are the keys. Now, go to work."

The two new-hires returned to their office to retrieve their coats. They found the car the captain had provided, checked it out and climbed inside. They called dispatch to tell them they were on the road. The first stop would be to see the manager of the Savings and Loan Company.

In the bank lobby they were directed to an office where a secretary greeted them and led the investigators to the office of branch manager Gordon Miller.

"How do you do, gentlemen, and what can I do to assist you?"

Bill Gant spoke. "We would like to see the file picture of your missing employee."

"Certainly, I have his file here." He reached into a drawer to find a personnel file. The first page held a picture of the assistant branch manager, Stanley Phelps. He handed the open file to Gant.

Gant took the file and leaned over a little to show the picture to his partner, who nodded recognition.

Gant spoke again, "Mister Miller, we don't have a positive ID, but it is possible he was the one found floating in Cook Inlet yesterday. My partner and I found the body and we agree he is the one in the picture. I'd appreciate it if you would keep this information to yourself for the time being, next of kin notification and all that."

"I understand. This comes as a great shock to me. Stan was a wonderful employee and was in line to take my position when I move on. I'm due to be promoted in a couple of months. This, too, is privileged information." Miller spoke in a sad voice.

"Mr. Miller, can we get a copy of this file to take with us? We would really like the original if possible," asked Alan Pulis.

"I would rather not give the bank copy of the file, but I will have my secretary make you a full color copy of everything in the file." He pressed the intercom button to call his secretary. When she arrived he handed her the file and asked to have a true photo copy made of everything. She accepted the file and left the room.

When she had gone he continued, "What happened to Stan, can you tell me how he died or what happened?"

"I'm sorry, Mr. Miller, but an autopsy has not yet been done and I would rather not speculate at this point." It was Gant avoiding the question.

"I understand. I want to say that both I and my bank wish to help in any way we can. Is it alright to call the home office and inform them of this?"

"I would appreciate it if you would hold off doing that until we call you tomorrow." While Gant was explaining Pulis was frowning at the banker.

"Very well then, I'll wait until I hear from you." At that moment the secretary returned with a high quality copy of the file. "Thank you Arlene," Miller said and dismissed her.

"Thank you for the file," said Gant, picking up the copy. "We will be in touch. By the way, did Stan have any special friends here at the bank?"

"No, not really, he was rather reclusive. There is a waitress in town he dated from time to time.

I don't know her name. She's a good looking one though. I'll ask around and see if anyone knows her name. She works at the diner on the corner up the street."

Pulis did the asking now, "Did Mr. Phelps have any enemies at the bank? Or maybe someone he would confide in or didn't like or a rival for the promotion you mentioned?"

"Oh, no, he was well thought of here and everyone respected him for his knowledge. He was very well educated in this field."

"Did he present any references when he was hired?" asked Gant.

"I'm sure he did, but all that was handled by the main office in Anchorage and there is nothing in his personnel file about his history."

"Would that be a common practice within your bank?" again, Gant was asking.

"Yes, it would be common. The master personnel file for all employees is on file in the home office. Mine is only for reference in case of a disciplinary problem or some other personnel review. But, believe me, there will be nothing in his file. He was one of the best bankers I have ever seen. I learned a lot while working with Stan."

"Do you have any knowledge of where he worked before coming to this office?" Pulis was beginning to see a pattern and becoming suspicious about the past of Stanley Phelps.

Bill Gant handed the banker his card, "If you learn of anything about his past, please give me a call. Alan and I are tasked with writing a picture of this man. An unattended death is a difficult thing to investigate. Thank you for your help with this matter." He put out his hand to shake the hand of Gordon Miller.

The two investigators walked back to their car and sat while making notes. Pulis was the first to speak. "Does it seem strange to you that a man could work here for two years and no one knows anything about his past? This is beginning to smell like a transplant to me."

"I'm beginning to get the same feeling," replied Bill Gant. How about you and I drive to Anchorage and visit the 'home office.'

"Good idea, but before we tell the captain what we want to do let's go to the diner up the street and see who works there. It's lunch time anyway."

"Sounds good to me; are you buying? The autopsy report may be here by the time we finish lunch." Bill thought it was important to learn the identity of the woman Stanley Phelps was dating.

The two men spent an hour at lunch attempting to determine which of the two waitresses would be the friend of the victim, Stanley Phelps. Both men agreed it was the very tall, dark haired and long legged one. The other was too young and not pretty as the banker had described. Luckily the tall one was the one waiting on their table. When she came to offer more coffee Alan took a chance.

As she poured more coffee Pulis asked in a quiet voice, "Excuse me miss, but do you know a man by the name of Stanley Phelps?"

She stopped pouring and stared at him with a shocked and startled look. "Who are you and why is that any of your business?" She stood erect to walk away.

"Take it easy, miss, we only want to know if you know him."

"I don't care what you want, leave me alone." With that she stomped back to put the coffee pot on the burner.

Alan and Bill received no more service and the bill for lunch was delivered by the other waitress.

Back in the car Bill turned to Alan and said, "That went well, don't you think?"

Pulis snickered, "I think we struck a nerve. She knew him alright. We had better not have another conversation with her at work. She seems a little sensitive. We need to find out when she gets off work and have another talk with her. Right now I think we need to go to the office and see if the autopsy report is in."

"Do you think the Captain will want to know how smoothly this interview went?" asked Gant, laughing at his partner.

"Smart aleck," replied Alan Pulis, a little put out with the jab to his ego.

Chapter 4

Pulis and Gant were back in the trooper headquarters reviewing the autopsy report when the captain came to their small office. "Have you finished reading the medical report?" he asked.

"Just finishing now," reported Pulis. "The more I learn about this case the more I don't know. My instincts tell me there's something going on we don't know about. This report confirms that suspicion. It says he was shot twice in the back with a small caliber gun, probably .22. The M.E. will have the bullets tested and identified. The thing about the shooting is—everything. I don't think he was murdered as much as assassinated. The M.E. says there are signs of restraints used on the wrists. He also says the bullets were placed in the lower portion of the lungs which means the victim didn't die immediately. This gets crazier by the minute."

"Let me add to your craziness theory," the captain commented. "The victim didn't exist prior to his coming to Alaska. We can't find anything in a past history for him. We have vital statistics, but none of it checks out. He had no past." Gant and Pulis looked at each other remembering their earlier thoughts along the same line. "I called the Director and asked him to contact the U.S. Marshals and ask for some help. This sounds like a transplant. Could be he was on the witness protection program. This is only speculation, but it is beginning to add up like one."

Gant scratched his head and read the description of the wounds once more. "Alan and I had the same thought, Cap. I think you're on the right track and we would like to go to the home office of the Savings and Loan Company to take a look at the master personnel file on Stanley Phelps. If you're right, the information in the file won't be verifiable. We'd like to call and make an appointment to see the personnel manager tomorrow. Alan and I can drive up and check it out."

The captain rubbed his chin, thinking, "Go ahead, call and make the appointment. Let's try to find out who this victim really is."

Pulis broke into the conversation, "We have another request, Captain. Can you have someone discreetly check out the waitress at the diner? We tried to talk to her, but she clammed up. We need a name and address in order to talk with her away from her job. She's the tall, good-looking, dark haired, curvy waitress down there. She didn't want to talk to us at lunch time."

"Is she connected to the victim?" inquired the captain.

"We think she is. The bank manager said Stanley Phelps was dating a waitress there and she fits the description. We need to find out when she came here and, other than dating, what connection she had with Phelps."

"I'll have someone check it out for you. I'll let you know when the Director gets back to me about the Marshals. Get your reports done and get out of here for today. Make an appointment with the Savings and Loan office in Anchorage for tomorrow. Let me know what you learn."

"Sure thing, Cap." Pulis waved as the captain left the office.

"I'll call Miller and get a phone number for personnel in Anchorage." Gant said, dialing the local number for Gordon Miller.

Gant had just finished making the appointment with the president of the Savings and Loan for the next morning when the receptionist came in with a sheet of paper in her hands. It was the name and number of the waitress from the diner. She also had a sheet containing a background check of Leila Hunter.

"Look at this, Alan," Gant said, handing the sheets to his partner.

Pulis read the sheets before commenting, "She looks to have the same past as our friend Stanley Phelps: non-descript and sketchy. It says here she works until 3 o'clock. Let's go follow her home and see if we can have a private conversation with the lady."

"Good idea. But try to be a little more charming this time, will you Alan? I think you frightened her this morning."

"She should be glad to see me, Bill. I left a tip on the table when we left."

"You are smooth, partner."

The two waited in their car in the parking lot of the restaurant until she came out. She stopped to smoke a cigarette before getting into her older Ford Taurus. She started the car and drove across town to an apartment complex where she parked under the carport. They gave her a minute to get inside before following her. She lived in an upstairs apartment on the right. Pulis knocked on the door and waited.

Leila Hunter was shocked when she opened the door to see who was knocking. She tried to close the door, but Pulis had his foot against it. "Get out of here before I call the police!" she shouted.

Pulis held up his shield, "We are the police. We just want to talk to you. Can we come in a few minutes?"

"I don't want to talk to you," she said.

"I think you should. Do you know a man named Stanley Phelps?" Pulis asked.

"Yes, I know Stan. Why?" She stopped trying to close the door.

"I think we should have this conversation inside and in private. Can we come in?"

"Oh, all right." She stepped back to allow them to enter.

Once inside Bill Gant said, "We have some bad news, Miss Hunter, I think you'd better take a seat and listen."

She backed into the small dining/kitchen area and dropped into a chair. "Have a seat, please. What kind of bad news?"

"First of all, I'm Bill Gant and this is Alan Pulis. We are investigators with the Alaska State Troopers. We understand you're friends with a man by the name of Stanley Phelps. We'd like to ask you about him."

"Why? Has something happened to Stan?"

"I'm afraid so, Miss Hunter. He's dead. His body was found floating in Cook Inlet yesterday morning. His identification has been confirmed by the Medical Examiner and the Alaska State Troopers."

She held both hands tightly against her mouth to stop the scream. Instantly she began to sob. Pulis brought a tissue from the kitchen counter. She dried her eyes. "What happened?" she asked.

"I'm sorry to have to tell you that we think he was murdered" Pulis said in a calm voice.

"Oh no, he said this could happen," again she was sobbing and wiping her eyes.

Pulis sat in a chair across the table from her. "I know this is a bad time, but we're investigating his death and we need to ask you some questions. Do you feel like talking to us?"

"I guess. It's over for him now. I'll help you if I can, but I don't know much."

"Thank you," Gant said as he produced a small recorder to place on the table. "Let's start with your name. Are you Leila Hunter?"

"I wasn't always, but I am now."

"Can you explain that for me?" asked Gant.

"I came from New Jersey. I knew Stan there. We were planning to get married. He was the comptroller for a huge trucking company. They had all kinds of other businesses, too, but Stan never told me what they were. He never talked about his job." She was sobbing again. "Sorry," she said as she wiped her nose. "One day he said he was quitting and moving and that he would send for me when he was settled."

"Let me clear up a couple of points, Miss Hunter."

"OK, what do you want to know?"

"You said you had another name before you came here. What was that name?"

"My name was Lucile Mc Dermot before I came here. We had it changed."

"And what was Stanley Phelps name before moving here?" asked Gant.

"His name was Steven Collier. He graduated from New York City College as a CPA. He was at the top of his class and landed a high paying job with that trucking company. He had been there several years. Something happened there. He never told me what it was, but right after he started making plans to leave there. He came here first and changed his name. He got a good job with the Savings and Loan Company and has been there ever since. He sent for me and I came right away. That was two years ago. I loved him very much and he loved me. Oh, God, how did all this happen?"

"Did he leave any books or things with you in case something happened?"

"Not really. He gave me some keys to his car and his house and a key to a safety deposit box at the bank, but I've never looked inside it." She was crying softly now.

Gant turned to his partner, "Can you think of anything else, Alan?"

"No, I think that's enough for now. I hope you'll let us come back if we think of anything further, Miss Hunter." Pulis thought they had taken her to the limit at this time.

"I would like to ask that you not tell anyone how Stan died. Right now we don't know who's involved and you may also be a target." He gave her one of his cards. "My number is there. If for any reason you feel threatened by anyone, call me day or night. Alan and I will be out of town tomorrow, but we can have someone come to your aid if need be." She noted Gant's compassion. "I'm sorry we had to be the ones to bring you this bad news, but we're also here to help you if you need it. Do you have any questions for either of us before we leave?"

"No, I'll be fine. Stan once told me he was in a lot of trouble and that this could happen. We thought it was over, but I guess it isn't. Thank you for being so kind." She was crying harder now.

In the car Pulis began to shake his head. "You know, partner, I think we're in the middle of a witness protection case. Everyone will be lying to us from now on. We had better go to the office and give the captain a heads up. It'll be interesting to see if any of this story checks with the one in the personnel file in Anchorage."

"This Phelps guy had some powerful enemies. You said yourself that it looked like an execution. I'm beginning to agree with you. Someone wanted him to die slowly and see it coming. They shot him in the lower part of the lung, shoved him into the water and let him gasp for breath, knowing he was about to die. It looks like he was killed for a reason. We need to find out what that reason is and perhaps we'll find the killer. I also think we need to be aware of the kind of people we're dealing with. These folks are professionals without mercy or remorse. Let's talk with the captain and get him to help us with the Marshals."

Minutes later they were in Captain Caswell's office bringing him up to speed on this new information.

Chapter 5

The two investigators arrived in Anchorage early the next morning. Neither had eaten breakfast and both were in dire need of hot coffee. With this in mind they stopped at Judy's, a small local café on the Old Seward Highway. They ordered coffee and pancakes and eggs for Pulis and an omelet and hash browns for Gant. Both sipped coffee without saying anything. Gant retrieved a morning newspaper from an empty table and scanned the headlines. Their order came and the friendly waitress asked if there was anything else. Both said no.

Back in the car, Pulis was at the wheel. He turned to Bill Gant and asked, "What's the name of the Personnel Manager we're to meet?"

Gant opened the file on his lap and looked inside, "Mr. Landau it says here. Do you know where the office is located?"

"Yeah, it's that new office building on Arctic Boulevard," replied Alan. "Do you want to take the lead on this one?"

"Sure, I probably won't make him as angry, at least not for a little while. You do have a tendency to irritate people, you know."

"OK, I won't say anything until you run out of nice things to say. Just give me a nod when you want me to rough him up."

"My, aren't we sensitive this morning?" Both men laughed.

They found the office building and were right on schedule for the appointment. The receptionist was expecting them and showed the two troopers to a corner office. There she introduced them to Mr. Landau's personal secretary, Carol Whiteside. She was in her mid-50s, attractive and all business. She punched a button and notified Mr. Landau his appointment had arrived. She showed them into the office and offered refreshments, which they turned down.

Bill Gant turned to Mr. Landau and introduced himself and Alan Pulis. "We are investigating the death of one of your employees and were referred to you by Gordon Miller. He said you would have all the background information on the employee."

"Yes, he called and notified me you were coming. He didn't, however, say Stanley Phelps was dead. This is distressing. How did he die, if I may ask?"

"We suspect he was murdered. That's why we need more details about his past. May we see the personnel file of Mr. Phelps?" asked Gant.

"Certainly, I have it right here." Landau reached into the lower right desk drawer and retrieved the file. The folder was over an inch thick. "The information in this file is confidential and I insist you view it as such. The Savings and Loan Company values the privacy of our staff and customers. I'm sure you will understand."

"Of course, Mr. Landau, we understand. What you must understand is that we are investigating a crime and state statutes provide that our need is greater than those of your bank." Gant took the file and opened it, then handed it to Pulis. "I don't mean to be demanding, Mr. Landau, but you must also understand we may be looking for a murderer who has killed one of your employees. I would think you would be interested in helping us achieve our mission."

Landau was visibly flustered. "Of course I'm interested in finding the one responsible. I'm sorry if I sounded brash, but I have a responsibility to the company and our customers. I will be happy to assist you in any way possible. You must respect my position here. I am willing to cooperate and I hope you are willing to reciprocate."

"We'll do our best to protect the name of your company and clients. We're conducting an official police investigation and the information we gather is not for public use." Gant turned to Pulis, "Alan, do you see anything in the file we should discuss with Mr. Landau?"

"No, but I think we should have a copy of this file. There is a lot of information we should be checking out," replied Pulis.

Gant again addressed Landau, "We can get a warrant and seize this file, but I think we could do with a full copy of it. Will that be alright with you, Sir?"

"Certainly," he picked up the phone and asked his secretary to come in. When she entered he said, "Carol, will you please take this file and make a complete copy for the men? And please, do it discreetly."

"Yes, Sir," she said, taking the file and leaving the room.

"Tell me Mr. Landau," Gant asked after the secretary had gone, "Did you know Stanley Phelps personally?"

"We've met on many occasions, mostly business meetings. He had been with us for a little over two years. All of that, except the first three months was in our Soldotna branch. He has made quite a name for himself within the company. He had a talent for modernizing and streamlining our procedures which have saved the company a great deal of money and time. He was a very bright and personable young man."

"Did you hire him when he came to this company?" asked Pulis.

"I was on the interview board, but the hiring was done by my predecessor. I've been the head of personnel for a little more than a year. Mr. Lathrop who headed the department before me became ill … cancer. After his death I became head of the department."

"Who would have been in charge of checking his credentials and references? Did you do that?" asked Pulis.

"Yes, I was in charge of that phase of the hiring, and as I recall he had an outstanding resume and references. Understand this was over two years ago and there's been many hires since that time. I did review his file and remembered most of it upon reviewing. I recall him being well educated and having banking experience. I also remember calling and talking with his previous employer who recommended him very highly."

Again Pulis was asking, "I saw in the file that his previous employer was Midwestern States Bank in Bemidji, Minnesota. Do you remember when you called, if you talked with the personnel manager, the bank branch manager or Phelps' supervisor, and do you remember his name?"

"I don't remember his name, but it will be in the file. Like I said there have been a lot of calls since that time. I do remember, however, that whomever I talked with had endorsed Mr. Phelps in glowing terms and his performance here has justified that evaluation." Landau seemed to be defending his reason for hiring Phelps.

"Has anyone ever come to you and asked about Stanley Phelps, you know, how he was doing, his job performance, his financial standing or any other personal questions?" Gant was now asking.

"Not that I recall, but even if they had I would have to get permission from the office upstairs to release that information." Again Landau was being defensive.

"I'm curious, Mr. Landau, does your bank make a practice of hiring people introduced to you by the U.S. Government? I mean, if a G-man came in here and asked you to hire a certain person, would you be inclined to hire them?" Pulis asked.

"We do not work for the U.S. Government. We are regulated by them and their agencies, but we do not work for them. We make our own decisions and hire whom we like." Landau was now sitting erect in his chair. "I think, if you have nothing further, I need to get back to business. Carol will have your file for you at the front desk. Thank you gentlemen," Landau said curtly, dismissing them.

"I think you're right Mr. Landau. However, if we feel the need to ask about anything else we will be back and expect your full cooperation. Thank you for your time, sir." Both troopers stood and moved toward the door. Outside the office they picked up the copy of the file. Pulis scanned it to see if anything was missing. It appeared to be an accurate copy. They thanked Carol for her time and left the building.

Once in the car they called the captain on the cell phone. "Hi, Cap. We have you on speaker phone so we can both hear you. We just came from the Savings and Loan Company offices. They cooperated to a point, but every time we mentioned government the personnel officer became defensive. We have a copy of the personnel file. We haven't read it thoroughly yet, but so far, we haven't seen anything suspicious."

"OK, get back here. We need to make a plan. The autopsy report should be done by the time you get here." Captain Caswell was a busy man and had better things to do than chit chat with two investigators.

"See you in three hours, Cap." Gant hung up the phone and turned to his partner. "Drive slow, Alan. I don't think the captain is in a good mood."

"You have that effect on me most of the time," replied Pulis while navigating the downtown Anchorage traffic. "Leila Hunter says she and Phelps were friends and lovers in New Jersey before he came here. The bank confirmed he was from Minnesota. I smell a manufactured past. I'll bet we find his social security card is only a couple of years old and there isn't anyone in Bemidji who ever went Walleye fishing with Stanley Phelps."

"I think you're right, Alan. I wonder if the Captain is having any luck with the Marshalls. Somehow I doubt we will ever get an official response from them, but Rollin has a lot of friends in high places and might be able to learn something from one of those old friends." Gant paused to think a moment, "If this was a gang hit, and it looks like it, we'll never find out who pulled the trigger. I think these wiseguys were probably after something specific. If they got it they are long gone. If not they may still be in the area and if Leila was part of his past she may be next on the list to be hit. I don't like it when we have no evidence and have to operate on guesses. I think we need to keep an eye on Leila Hunter."

"I hadn't thought of that, but you're right. How are we going to accomplish that little trick? We can't watch her 24 hours a day and we have no evidence to justify assigning someone to watch her. I think the best we can do at this time is to warn her and have her keep an eye out for suspicious people. She works in a public place and is vulnerable almost all the time. Look at Phelps, he was dressed in his work clothes and was probably picked up after getting off work at the bank. He knew the dangers and was still snatched and killed."

"This is one time we should talk it over with our supervisor." Gant went back to reading the personnel file. "When you get to Girdwood stop and I'll get us some water to drink on the way home."

Captain Rollin Caswell was waiting for them when they arrived back in Soldotna. They were instructed to meet with him in his office. The two contract troopers entered the office with the personnel file in hand and were met by the captain who was reading the autopsy report he had just received.

"The autopsy report just came in. You were right about his being shot in the lower lung. I suspect you were also right about why. He has a small amount of sea water in his lungs, but not much. I think this suggests he was shot like that to allow him to live a while and not be able to help himself. It appears he was tortured for some time before he died. He was missing two fingers on his right hand. Three fingers of his left hand had been broken. Whoever killed him definitely wanted something from him."

Captain Caswell handed a copy of the report to Pulis, but it was Gant who asked, "Do you think the killers got the answers they were asking for?"

"I don't suppose there is any way of knowing for sure, but if it had been me they would have gotten anything they wanted."

"Where does that leave us, Cap?" asked Alan Pulis.

"I have been thinking since you called. Locally we're out of options. We have to verify his pasts, both of them. I want you to go to Bemidji and check him out. Then I want you to locate the home offices of that trucking company he supposedly worked for in New Jersey. I want you to check out that company. Be discreet. I don't want you two ending up like Phelps. I'll have airfares arranged for the two of you. Stay together and watch each other's backs."

"When do you want us to leave, Cap?" asked Pulis.

"As soon as we can arrange it, and I have one other thing. When you get to New Jersey I want to know where you are staying. I am going to have a friend of mine contact you. He's with the Marshalls office in New York. He will get you any help you need and I am hoping he will be able to find out if this Phelps is one of their transplants. Anything he tells you will be strictly off the record. Don't jeopardize him in any way. Got that?"

"Sure thing Captain." Both men nodded in agreement.

It was Gant who asked for the help providing safety for Leila Hunter. "It would be better if she would go away and hide, but she has refused to do that."

"I can't give her full-time coverage, but I will do what I can," agreed Caswell.

Chapter 6

There were only two occupied tables when Bill and Alan entered the diner. Leila Hunter was in the far corner filling salt and pepper shakers. The two men found an isolated table and sat. Leila had seen the men enter and proceeded to serve their table.

"How are you fellas today?" she asked.

"We're just fine Leila, thanks for asking. How about you? Are you doing OK?"

"Yeah, I'm OK. I can't help looking over my shoulder though."

"We need to talk to you for a few minutes. Is there a way to do that?" asked Bill Gant.

"Sure, we aren't busy. I'll take a smoke break out back. Come out there with me." They nodded as she went behind the counter to retrieve her cigarettes. The two men followed her to a door in the rear of the dining room and to the outside. She lit up, blew out a big cloud of smoke and asked, "What can I do for you now?"

Gant answered. "We're concerned for your safety. We don't know who killed Stanley or if they might try to come after you for some reason. We'll keep an eye out for you while we're here, but we're going to be out of town for a few days. We're asking you to be vigilant. Watch your back. If you think you see anything suspicious we want you to call our captain. His name is Captain Rollin Caswell." Gant pulled a business card from his shirt pocket. "Take this card. It has Captain Caswell's numbers on it. Don't let the title of Captain fool you. He's a good guy. Don't hesitate to call him if you feel threatened or intimidated in any way. We want you to stay safe."

Leila took the card and read it. "I don't think I'm in any danger, but I thank you for the thoughts. Now you do have me worried. Is there something you aren't telling me?"

"Miss Hunter, we are truly worried about you. We got the autopsy report and it indicates your friend was the victim of a professional hit man. Those people leave nothing undone. We think that if they suspect you're involved in any way they will come after you in an attempt to get information."

"But, I don't have any information. Stan never discussed his business with me, NEVER!"

"Our problem is that the hit men may want to know if you do have any information they're after. You have to realize these are ruthless men. We don't want you to take any chances. If you see a strange car following you; call the captain. If someone follows you in the grocery store; call the captain. If you just get an uneasy feeling; call the captain." Bill reached out and squeezed her shoulder, "We want to keep you safe."

She looked again at the card in her hand, "Alright, I'll be careful. Thank you for worrying about me." She tucked the card into her shirt pocket. I'll keep my eyes open."

Alan spoke up, "Leila, I hope you fully understand that this is not a game. It's real and you are in real danger. Take it seriously, please."

They said goodbye and walked to their car. Suddenly, Leila Hunter felt very alone and vulnerable knowing her protectors had walked away leaving her on her own.

Their flight was the last one of the day from Kenai Airport. The captain drove them there reviewing his cautions on the way. "Stay near the phone and keep me in the loop all the way. I really don't want to read some headline about you in the newspaper."

They had a two hour lay-over in Anchorage. "I'll buy the first beer," volunteered Pulis. Two layovers and twelve hours later they were checking in at the Airport Motel in Bemidji, Minnesota. They had rented a car at the airport, put their bags in the room and eaten breakfast. Pulis held the personnel file in his hand while Gant drove following the dashboard GPS to the Midwestern States Bank. Once inside they asked one of the tellers for directions to the Personnel Office.

They were directed to a small cubical style office in the corner of the lobby area where a pleasant looking lady, Bill guessed to be in her mid-sixties, was seated behind the desk. The brass sign in her desk read Clara Svenson, Personnel Manager.

"How do you do, gentlemen? I'm Clara."

"How do you do, Clara? I'm Alan Pulis and this is my partner Bill Gant. We are investigators with the Alaska State Troopers. We're investigating the death of a person in Alaska and have been directed to you by a Mr. Landau, personnel manager for Savings and Loan Company of Anchorage, Alaska. Do you have a few minutes to speak with us regarding this matter?"

"Of course, can I offer you something, coffee or a soft drink?"

"Oh, no thank you Ms. Svenson. We're fine."

"Please call me Clara. We're pretty informal around here. So, what is it you want to speak with me about?"

"May I ask how long you've been in this position in this bank?" asked Pulis, still carrying the file from Anchorage.

"I have worked at this bank for more than 40 years and have been personnel manager for the past eleven." Smiling, she said this proudly, "I will retire next spring."

"Then you are just the person we wish to speak with," said Gant.

"And what would this be about?"

"As my partner Alan told you, we are investigating the death of a man in Alaska. He worked for Savings and Loan Company in the Soldotna branch. We were able to get his personnel file from the main office in Anchorage and came here to try to verify his background. He had been with the bank in Soldotna just over two years. His resume states he worked here for a period of time before moving to Alaska. Would you still have a file on him?"

"We should have. What is the name?"

"Stanley Phelps," Gant gave her the dates he reported working at this bank.

"I don't remember him right off." She spun her chair around to dig into a file cabinet behind the desk. She went through the drawer twice before asking again, "What was the name again?"

"Stanley Phelps, he claimed to be an assistant manager here until he left to take a position in Alaska," Said Gant.

"That is strange. I can't seem to find a file with that name. Give me a moment to ask our branch manager." She stood and walked to the office next to here where the branch manager was located. Several minutes passed before she returned. She had a puzzled look about her when she returned.

"I'm sorry gentlemen, but our branch manager Mr. Brooks says that file was sent to Minneapolis quite some time ago. For the life of me I can't remember him. I must be getting old."

"Is there a reason the file was sent to Minneapolis?" asked Pulis.

"Mr. Brooks said it had been requested by the home office. He couldn't remember anyone by that name either. Funny thing, too, he would have been Mr. Brooks' assistant during that time. If you will give me an address I will contact the home office and have them send you a copy of the file, if that will help you." Clara was being pleasant and helpful, but they were learning nothing.

"Tell me Clara, does this bank have any contact or do business with government enforcement agencies?" a good question by Pulis.

"We have contact with regulatory agencies on a daily basis, but I don't know of any other business we do with the government. Is there a specific agency?"

"I'd rather not say at this time," said Pulis. "We're just checking out the past of the deceased which led us here. Thank you for being so helpful." He gave her a business card. "If you can locate this file I would appreciate it if you would send me a copy. We'll only be down here for a few days and we're leaving Bemidji tomorrow."

"I'll do my best. Is there anything I can do for you while you're here?"

"No, but we thank you for your time and for being so helpful." The two men stood, "It has been a pleasure meeting you, Clara. If you're ever in Alaska, please feel free to contact us. When you retire we could take you fishing. Come and see us. Thank you again."

Back in the car Bill asked Alan, "Well, what do you make of that?"

"It's just a guess, but I would say Mr. Brooks is up to his bow-tie in this deal. Someone here was involved and I really don't suspect Clara. No, my money is on Mr. Brooks. It wouldn't surprise me to find he is connected to the Marshalls in some way." Pulis grinned, "He may be a transplant himself. In any case I think the cat is out of the bag and we had better start to watch our backs."

"I agree with your assessment. I think we may have learned more from what we didn't learn than what we did learn. It will be interesting to meet with Rollin's friend in New Jersey. How about some lunch?"

"Do you think we can find a restaurant that serves something besides Lutefisk?" asked Pulis.

"I never noticed before, Alan, but you're a snob. What have you got against Lutefisk?"

"Nothing, in fact I've never eaten it, but if that's what you want we can get some."

"I've eaten Lutefisk and I like it, but it has to be cooked correctly and it has to be hot."

"I think your mother must have been frightened by a Norwegian," noted Pulis.'

The compromise was lunch at McDonalds. They ordered two big Macs with fries and a tall drink, the all-American lunch.

"I think it's time to start watching ourselves," commented Gant. "I don't think anyone will get to us before tomorrow, but you can bet, if our suspicions are correct, we will have company by the time we reach Newark. We're assuming the government is behind this, but we have to expect a threat from the bad guys who could be looking for us by now. We've been pretty open about this investigation up until now. I don't think we can continue to be this public. Someone will try to stop us if we're on the right track."

"I guess it wouldn't hurt to be a little cautious." Pulis said this between bites and wiping sauce from his chin. "So far the most dangerous thing I've seen is this burger."

"How about we go back to the motel and get some rest and go to a good restaurant for dinner and have something nice, maybe a steak and wine. We are on Per Diem, remember."

At the motel they called the captain and caught him up on the events of the day. They let him know what they had learned and what they suspected. He had been a cop for a long time and understood what they were experiencing. He told them to keep on doing what they had begun and to be thorough. He also told them he had not heard from Leila Hunter.

In the afternoon they drove around the town and were impressed by the number of schools, hospitals and other public facilities. In the evening they found a restaurant serving some local Walleye and quality wine. Neither of the men were big drinkers, but the California white wine was good and a perfect complement to the local fish. They bought a local newspaper and returned to the motel to watch TV and relax. It would all begin again in the morning when they boarded another airplane for Newark, New Jersey in pursuit of the history of Stanley Phelps.

Chapter 7

The flight from Bemidji to Newark was long with a three hour layover in Chicago. The two troopers wandered the airport mall looking in souvenir shops, but bought nothing. There were thousands of other people in the aisles doing the exact same thing, but neither Alan nor Bill saw anyone they recognized. Time passed slowly before they were called to their boarding gate. The flight was just over an hour, but seemed much longer in the commuter plane. They picked up their bags from the carousel and made their way to the Avis Car Rental counter to check out the car they had reserved. It was a major campaign to find the car and make their way out of the airport area and into downtown Newark. Again the GPS in the dashboard saved them from getting lost in a strange city. Even so it took more than an hour to drive to the hotel and another hour to park and check in. There was a message waiting for them at the front desk. Gant signed the registration forms while Pulis read the message.

"It's from the Captain's friend in the Marshall's Service," Pulis reported as they walked to the elevator. "He wants us to call when we get to the room. He says the captain filled him in on what we were doing here."

"What's his name?"

Pulis looked at the paper in his hand, "David Kinney, U.S. Marshal it says here."

"Okay, let's find our rooms and call him."

David Kinney answered on the first ring. "David Kinney," he said.

"Hello Mr. Kinney, this is Bill Gant with the Alaska State Troopers. My partner Alan and I just checked in and picked up your message. Is it possible to meet with you?"

"That's why I called. I would rather do this outside the office if possible. Would it be okay if I came to your hotel this afternoon?"

"Sure, we're in rooms 621 and 623. What time would be good for you?"

"Depending on traffic, forty five minutes to an hour, will that work?" asked Kinney.

"We'll be waiting for you."

After hanging up he reported to Pulis, "He says he'll be here in about an hour. How about we get some coffee while we wait?"

"Good idea, Partner. I sure hope he has some idea about this trucking company. We're strangers in a strange land; out of our environment, so to speak. We could use some help here." Pulis looked into the mirror and straightened his tie. "Let's go get some pie and coffee."

They had just returned to their room when there was a knock on the door. It was the Captain's friend who introduced himself as David Kinney. Introductions were returned and Kinney entered the room.

"You said the captain had filled you in on the situation. Our problem is that we don't know any of the players in this game. Alan and I are flying blind. We figure we're dealing with professionals and can't afford to make too many mistakes."

"That's why I wanted to get to you when you first arrived. I can help you a little." They sat at a small round table in the hotel room. Pulis took a notebook from his pocket and began to write. "What I'm about to tell you is completely off the record. I would never tell you any of this, but Rollin told me you two were to be trusted. You must be good, because he never says that about anybody."

"Thanks for the vote of confidence, Dave. We can keep a secret. Rollin must have told you that we're retired and this is a contract job. We have no axes to grind with anyone. Your information is safe with us." Alan Pulis was doing the explaining.

"You're about to jump into some very deep water and I want you to know what you're up against." Kinney had cold, gray eyes and wore a concerned expression on his stern face. "First of all, your assumption about Stanley Phelps being a transplant is correct. About two and a half years ago he was working for Ace Trucking Company. He was a comptroller there. I'm told he was very good at his job. The owner of the trucking company is a man by the name of Salvatore Roselli. Have you ever heard of him?"

Both men shook their heads. "Who is he anyway?" asked Pulis.

"Some refer to him as the Don or Boss of the local criminal cartel. In the old days we called them Mafia, but whatever the name, he's the head of the local crime syndicate. He's a big deal. He has omnipotent power in Newark. Be careful, he's dangerous."

"And Stanley Phelps worked for him?" asked Gant.

"Yes, he handled all the money for the entire syndicate. He was an important part of the cartel. Salvatore Roselli is a ruthless individual, a modern day Al Capone. Nothing moves in this city without permission from Roselli. He started years ago with a delivery van working around the warehouse district. He became associated with the Teamsters Union, the Stevedore Union and the Longshoreman's Union. In those days he gained a reputation for eliminating competition and taking over their routes. By the time law enforcement agencies became aware of him he already owned half the delivery trucks in the city and he kept on growing. Anyone who chose to fight him died or disappeared. He's still the head of the largest criminal organization in the city. He's a rich and powerful man and a ruthless enemy."

"How did Phelps get cross-threaded with Roselli?" asked Pulis.

Like I said, he was the comptroller for Ace; in those days his name was Steven Collier. He'd worked for Roselli for several years and was a trusted member of the cartel. At some point, we believe it was because of a woman, Collier began to siphon off profits from the company. This part is guesswork because Collier never admitted to anything. He came to us two and a half years ago and said he would give us names and dates and account numbers and specific crimes, some of which were murders, tied directly to Don Salvatore Roselli. What he wanted in return was to disappear from the face of the earth – forever." Kinney paused a moment.

"Would you like something to drink, Dave?" asked Bill.

"No, I'm OK. It's just that I'm not used to talking this much." Gant nodded and listened again. "Like I said, he came to us. We notified the FBI and they took over the investigation. The information was good, but the proof was weak. The FBI made several cases and took at least four hit-men off the street. All four were convicted, but none of them rolled over on Roselli. The FBI never had enough real evidence to arrest him. That was when we changed his name and moved him to Alaska. There are other details about the move I'd rather not discuss, but you get the idea."

"You haven't given us much encouragement for interviewing this Salvatore Roselli, Dave. That was the entire reason for us to come here. You have done a nice job of giving us an outline of the happenings, but like the FBI, we don't have any proof." Pulis sounded a little sour in his assessment.

"I understand your frustrations, Alan, but what I've just revealed to you is not for publication. It's off the record information. I only passed this much on to you because you won' get any help from my office or the FBI. Rollin wanted me to prepare you for what you 're getting into. I can't tell you enough how dangerous these people can be. You can't trust anyone in this city. Roselli has eyes everywhere. I wish I could come with you, but I have to be back in my office in New York in the morning." Kinney's face mirrored his concern.

"I'm sorry Dave, I didn't mean to dismiss what you've told us, but we still have no idea what to expect when we meet with Roselli. We need some kind of advantage and right now I don't see one." Pulis was being honest with the Marshal and trying to avoid being critical.

Kinney gave a long sigh, "I know you guys need something to go on, but I can't give it to you. There isn't anything to connect Ace Trucking or Salvatore Roselli to any criminal act. We know he's involved in everything, but we have no proof. We're as frustrated as you. Sorry fellas."

Gant entered the conversation, "Can you give us any ideas about approaching Roselli, anything at all?"

"This afternoon I had some outside interests call and make an appointment for the two of you for tomorrow morning at 0900. The reason for the visit is genuine. You're investigating the death of a man who once worked for Roselli. You can play it dumb and get what you can, but make no mistake; this is a very intelligent and ruthless man. Don't underestimate him. He'll be at the main warehouse." Kinney reached inside his jacket pocket and produced a city map. "I've drawn out the route to the warehouse from your hotel. You might want to put the address in your GPS for later. When you get there you'll be met by a well-dressed gorilla by the name of Vito Roma. He is about five-eight, polite and lethal. He'll be the one to take you to Roselli."

"Thanks for arranging the meeting, Dave. The Cap told us you were a good man and I can see why he likes you. You've given us a lot of fresh information, but not much hope. Right now I'd rather walk through a stand of spruce trees in Alaska at night without a gun, than walk down the street in Newark in broad daylight, but we do what we have to do." Gant was summarizing, "Can you think of anything else we need to know?"

"Just be careful and watch your backs. I wish I could be there to back you up, but I can't. All I can do is pray for you." Kinney stared at the floor for a moment, "Tell Rollin hello for me when you see him. And call me if you need anything. My cell number is on the card I gave you. If you need any records checks made I may be able to help you there. I have some friends in that department."

"Can we buy you dinner before you head back?" asked Alan.

"Thanks for the offer, but I have to be getting back to the city. Stay in touch and good luck."

David Kinney said goodbye at the door. Back inside the two men both shook their heads. "This looks like Mission Impossible to me," said Pulis.

"You may be right, Partner," answered Bill. "Let's look at that map, and then go to dinner. The hotel has a steak house and a bar. We can eat here and save driving in this city traffic."

Dinner in the steak house was exceptional. Omaha Steaks, baked potatoes, creamed cauliflower, thick sourdough garlic bread and iced tea. Both men opted for the American Apple Pie for dessert. They finished off with coffee before returning to their rooms. They said good night and agreed to meet in the coffee shop for breakfast at seven in the morning. Inside his room, Gant checked the time and dialed the captain. The four hour time difference made it work for him.

"Hi Captain, Bill Gant."

"Bill, good to hear from you. I wondered if you would call today. How is it going? Have you met with Dave?"

"Yes, he was here and gave us a lot of information. I'm a little concerned. From his assessment, we may be beating a dead horse. We have an appointment with Roselli in the morning. Your pal Dave says this guy is a big Mafia type and very dangerous. I guess what I am trying to say is, don't get your hopes up too high."

"I understand, Bill, just do what you can, be careful. I want the both of you back here in one piece. I feel a little helpless not being able to help you from here."

"Don't worry Cap, Alan and I know what we're up against. We plan to take care of ourselves. I think we'll be OK for the simple reason these guys are used to getting their own way all the time. They may get cocky with the two rubes from the wilds of Alaska. After all how smart can two cops from the frozen north really be?" Gant chuckled, thinking he may be able to put the shoe on the other foot. "We'll call you tomorrow when we finish our meeting with Roselli."

Chapter 8

The route on the map given them by Kinney was identical to the route dictated by the lady's voice on the GPS. It took almost an hour to cross town and find their way through the industrial area to the fenced yard and warehouses of Ace Trucking Company. Most of the loading dock doors were open and five trucks were still loading cargo. The trucks varied in size from small delivery vans to large semi rigs. Men were busy with forklift trucks and hand carts moving products from inside the warehouse to the vans at the loading docks. Gant was driving this morning and found a space near the fence where it was unlikely one of the trucks would hit the rental car. There was a set of steps and a man-door on the left end of the dock. The two troopers made their way in that direction.

They were just reaching for the latch to open the door when a voice from down the dock stopped them. "Hold on there," said the voice. "What do you want here?"

Gant and Pulis saw the man striding across the loading dock. He was short and wore a suit and tie. This seemed a little strange for a warehouseman especially since the morning temperature was already nearing 80 degrees. Both men suspected this was the man Kinney referred to as Vito Roma.

The man approached them and as he neared he asked, "This is a private dock, whaddaya want here?"

"My name is Bill Gant and this is Alan Pulis. We have an appointment with Mr. Salvatore Roselli at 9 AM. Who are you?"

"I'm Vito, Vito Roma. I'm the manager of the warehouse."

"I think Mr. Roselli is expecting us. Would you please check and see if he's in?" asked Gant pleasantly.

"Wait here, I'll check," replied Vito.

He disappeared inside the man-door. Pulis turned to Gant and grinned. "Nice act."

"Wait until you see Act II. I'm also a juggler."

The two men waited a few minutes for Vito to return. They watched the men loading trucks, but saw nothing out of the ordinary. Several minutes passed before Vito came back, held the door open and said, "Come with me."

The inside of the warehouse was a huge expanse. Stacks of goods stood on pallets and several men with clipboards watched the loading process. Vito led them across the floor to the rear of the warehouse where an enclosed area with large windows and a door with a sign reading, OFFICE. Vito led the way into the office, then to another office inside. A gorgeous blond lady in a yellow dress occupied the desk in front of the second office. Vito spoke to the blond while they all waited, "Tell him they're here."

She lifted the office phone, punched a number and announced, "Your appointment is here Mr. Roselli." She paused a moment with the phone to her ear before hanging up and announcing, "He's expecting you, please go right in."

Vito led the way into the office. "Here they are, Boss." With that introduction he stepped back and sat on a large leather couch while Bill and Alan remained standing. The man behind the desk wore a crisp button-down L. L. Bean shirt and tan cotton slacks. He had black hair flecked with gray. He was a well-muscled man who spent a good deal of time in a gym somewhere. His eyes were a very dark brown, almost black.

"I'm Salvatore Roselli, you can call me Sal. I own this business. I'm a very busy man. Exactly what is it you want to see me about?"

"How do you do, Mr. Roselli? I'm Bill Gant and my partner here is Alan Pulis. We're investigators from Alaska. We're investigating the death of a banker. This banker has a very confusing past. By that I mean he'd changed his name somewhere along the line and we traced his other name back to a person who once worked for you. We know him as Stanley Phelps, but we suspect the name he used when he worked for you was Steven Collier. Does that name mean anything to you, Sir?"

"You say he's dead? How?" asked Roselli.

"I'm sorry to have to be the one to tell you this, Mr. Roselli, but we believe he was murdered. It's a tragedy. He was well thought of at the bank where he worked in Alaska. I have a picture of him. Will you tell me if it is the same man?" Gant took the picture from the file he held.

Roselli looked at the picture thoughtfully. "Yes, this is Steven. Who could have possibly killed him? He was such a nice fellow. He was the best accountant I had ever met. He worked for me for many years, right here in this office. He made me a lot of money."

"We have no idea who killed him. That's why we came to see you. We needed to learn if you know of any reason someone would want to harm this man?" Gant tried to keep an innocent face.

"Vito," Roselli asked his bodyguard, "Did you ever know anyone who didn't like Steve?"

"No, Sir, Mr. Roselli. Everyone liked Steve, he was quiet and calm around here. As far as I know he led a rather sedate lifestyle. He never got involved in office politics, never talked about the other employees or any of the stuff most people indulge in."

"You are welcome to talk with any of the office personnel if you like. The men on the dock probably never knew him," said Sal.

"Did he have any special friends here in the office or out of the office, for that matter?" asked Gant.

"He had a girlfriend somewhere in town, but I never met her." Again he called to Vito, "How about you, Vito. Did you ever meet Steve's girlfriend?"

"No, Sir, I never did. I think he went with her for a long time, though."

"Steve's office was the one on the other end of the outer office. The fellow in there now is Lane Mason. He's a good man, not as good as Steve, but he handles the job. Have my executive secretary show you around the office. Her name is Patty Dawson. You saw her when you arrived."

"Thank you for your time, Sir. I hope you will allow us to come back if we have further questions. We would make an appointment, of course." Gant took a card from his pocket and handed it to Roselli. "This is my business card and has my cell phone number on it. You can reach me at that number here in town for the next few days if you think of anything you can tell us."

Roselli took the card and placed it on his desk. "Introduce them to Patty, Vito. Then come back in here for a minute." It seemed like a pleasant dismissal.

Vito stepped out of the office with the two troopers and introduced them to Patty Dawson. "Show them around the office, Patty. I have to go back and talk with the boss." He turned and reentered the office leaving the two investigators standing at the front desk.

Patty smiled at them and introduced herself. "I'll help you any way I can. Can you tell me why you're here?"

"We're investigators from Alaska looking into the background of a man who used to work here. His name was Steven Collier. Did you know him?" Pulis had stepped right up to talk with the pretty young lady.

"Oh, yes. He was really nice. He kept mostly to himself. That was before I was Mr. Roselli's secretary. I used to have one of those desks out here on the floor. I was an inventory clerk. Mr. Collier had the office down there on the end."

"It's none of my business, but how do you get along with Mr. Roselli and his right hand man?" asked Pulis.

"Mr. Roselli treats me really good. He pays me good, too. Sometimes I think he just likes to have me here to greet customers. I don't like Vito, though. I've seen him get mean with drivers and warehousemen. He really scares me. Did you notice he carries a gun under his coat?"

"Yes, we noticed, but didn't mention it."

"I don't want to get into trouble at the office, but I think you should know something about Mr. Collier. Can we talk after I get off work?"

"Sure," said Alan, "we can pick you up after you get off if you like."

"No, I don't think that's a good idea. I don't own a car so Mr. Roselli pays for me to take a cab to work and home every day. I think I had better meet you away from here a little later." Her eyes darted to the office door several times.

"We could buy you dinner if you can suggest a decent restaurant."

"I can call and make a reservation at the Wagon Wheel. It's not far from my apartment and I can meet you there."

"What time would be good for you?" asked Alan.

"I think seven. I have a card from there on my desk. It has the address and I'll meet you there at seven."

"We'll be there. See you then. Be careful, we think these people could be dangerous," Pulis advised.

As the two men walked back to their car they saw Vito standing on the loading dock. "Vigilant cuss isn't he?" remarked Gant.

They put the address of the restaurant into the GPS and followed the track to the place. It looked nice enough. From there they followed the pointer back to the hotel. On the way they chatted about the visit to Ace Trucking Company.

"I haven't seen a snow job like that since last winter in Alaska," said Gant, "Did you hear anything you believed?"

"Not a word. To tell the truth I was a little uncomfortable with Vito sitting behind us. You saw the gun, too, right?"

"Maybe we can firm up some of our suspicions tonight at dinner. Patty sounds to me like she's really frightened and wants to unload some stuff about her boss. I guess we can afford to listen to a cute blond when we're forced to." Gant laughed and Alan just shook his head.

There was valet parking at the restaurant. Bill and Alan handed the attendant the keys and waited inside for Patty to show. Minutes later a cab pulled up out front and she stepped out. She had changed into slacks and a white blouse. Pulis walked outside to meet her and escort her inside.

"Thank you both for meeting me here. I didn't want to talk at the office. You never know who's listening." They were shown to their table and then seated. "Could I have a glass of wine?" she asked.

"Of course," said Bill and ordered a bottle of Riesling for the table.

They were sipping the light wine when Patty began. "I told you I worked there when Steven was the comptroller. Well, not long before he disappeared there was a big uproar. Mr. Roselli was screaming at Steven that he was suffering big losses. Mr. Collier tried to explain he couldn't account for cash he never received. There was a big battle and some of the people working there never came back. I don't know what happened to them. Some of them never came back to get their paychecks. It was a mess. Mr. Collier was really scared and not too much later he vanished. Vito and Mr. Roselli were furious." She sipped the wine. "You should understand the way it is around our office. There are a lot of people who come in and out. You never see them at any other time. I don't know what they do or why they come into the office, but Mr. Roselli seems to know them all. Another thing, they're all afraid of Vito."

Pulis thought a moment, "When they come to the office are they carrying anything? Did they bring a bag or briefcase, anything like that?"

"Yes, usually, how did you know that?"

Alan looked at Bill who nodded. "Did these same people come into the office when Steven Collier worked there?"

"Oh, yes, but back then they just came in to see Mr. Collier. They used to be friendly back then, but not anymore. They come in looking glum and leave the same way. Sometimes Vito follows them and chews them out in the parking area. I know they're all afraid of him."

"Do you have any idea what they're doing each time they come?" asked Gant.

"Not for sure, but I suspect they're delivering money from somewhere. I've never seen it, but it's the only thing that makes sense to me." Her glass was dry and Pulis filled it again.

"Patty, we think you're working for some very dangerous and ruthless people. We can't prove it, but we think it would be best if you found other employment. Can you do that?"

"Yes, but I don't think Mr. Roselli would like for me to leave." She was now becoming a little tipsy.

"I think we had better order dinner," said Bill Gant. He motioned for the waiter who came to take their order. The troopers left the questions alone until they had eaten and Patty's wine wore off a little.

They were all sipping strong dark roast coffee when the conversation went back to her work. Gant was speaking now. "Patty, we think you're in real danger. We have a friend who can make arrangements for you to move away from here without Sal Roselli knowing where or why. There may still be danger involved, but it'll take a while for them to find you. Our friend is with the U.S. Marshal's office. They'll protect you until we can put Roselli out of business. Would you be interested?"

"Oh, yes. I have been so scared this past year, it's unbearable. Please help me." She was sobbing now and it was difficult to know if it was the fright or the wine.

Gant handed Pulis the cell phone to call Dave Kinney.

Chapter 9

Pulis had stepped outside to use the telephone in private. It took several minutes to explain the entire situation to David Kinney. Kinney agreed with Alan that Patty Dawson was in danger and should be moved as quickly as possible. "I don't make the final decision on these moves, but I do have a lot of influence on the outcome. In your best guess, do you think she's in danger tonight?" asked the Marshal.

"I don't believe she's in any more danger tonight than she has been. I'm sure we caused some concerns when we went to the offices of Sal Roselli today, but he's the one who chose her to show us around. She should be safe for another day." Alan hoped he was right. Patty was a valuable witness and he had no desire to harm her or anyone else. "Do you think we need to move her to a hotel tonight?"

There was a long pause. "I don't think so, Alan. Sal and his boys will be worried about the two of you but not her. Let me call you in the morning and let you know about getting her moved."

"OK, Dave. I'll talk with you tomorrow." Pulis turned and walked back inside the restaurant, stopped in the restroom for some relief and returned to the table.

Bill was talking to the young blond and she was giggling. It seemed to Alan that Bill had calmed her fears somewhat. "What did you find out, Alan?"

"We won't have a final answer until tomorrow. We want you to go to work as usual tomorrow, Patty. Try to act normal so no one will get wise to what we're planning. Can you do that?"

"I think so. Thank you so much. I'll never be able to thank you enough."

"Let's get out of here," said Bill. "We can drive you home tonight."

"Thank you." The effects of the wine were now gone and she was steady on her feet. She seemed more confident now. She had hope.

The valet brought the rental car around. Bill drove while Alan sat in the back seat. Patty Dawson sat up front next to Bill Gant. She gave directions to her apartment building. When they arrived she thanked them again and opened the door.

Pulis stepped out of the back door of the car and said, "Good night Patty. We hope that by tomorrow all your worries will be over."

"Oh, I hope so. Good night." With that Patty turned and walked to the apartment building. The door was opened by a security guard. She entered, turned and waved before disappearing inside.

It was nearly ten when the two men returned to their rooms and said good night. Bill wasn't sleepy and turned on the television to watch the news. He was bored and walked to the window to look out onto the city streets. There were still people walking the streets. Cars, mostly taxi cabs, seemed to fill the streets below.

"It must be the money," Bill thought to himself, *"I can't imagine anyone wanting to live in the city except for the money."* He shook his head, turned off the television and found his bed.

Both men arose at 6 AM, showered and shaved. They met in the coffee shop for breakfast. An hour and a half later they sat in the front seat of their car planning their day when Alan's cell phone rang. He answered. Not recognizing the number on the screen. "Alan Pulis."

"Alan, this is Dave. I'm on my way over to Newark. That girl you called about? Patty Dawson?"

"Yeah the one I called and asked you to help, what about her?"

"Newark police just called our office and let us know she either jumped or was pushed from her apartment balcony last night. He said she showed up on a list from our office. It must have been the inquiries I made last night. I'm sorry Alan. I thought she was safe."

"Hold on," Alan turned to Bill, "Patty Dawson is dead. She jumped or was pushed from her balcony last night.'" He put the phone back to his lips, "Where can we meet you, Dave?"

"As soon as I finish with the police I'll meet you downtown in the park. We can talk there"

Pulis put the name of the park in the GPS and Bill Gant followed the pointer to their destination. On the way Pulis asked, "She was happy when she left us last night. I doubt she jumped. She was probably pushed. It's more likely she was thrown off the balcony. What reason could they have for doing that? Do you think they followed her from work?"

Bill screwed his face into a furrowed frown, "Or, perhaps they followed two hick cops from the warehouse yesterday."

"Oh, God! Do you suppose they followed us and saw her meeting us for dinner? Ah, Bill, I hope we didn't cause her death. I couldn't live with myself if I thought that."

Bill and Alan found the park with no trouble and waited in the parking lot until Dave showed. He parked near them and waited at a small gate leading to a walking path. The three men walked down the path to where there was a new park bench. While they walked Alan Pulis scanned the neighborhood for signs of someone following them. He saw none, but kept watch in any case.

"OK, Dave, what happened to Patty Dawson?" asked Pulis.

"The city police and FBI are still on the scene and investigating, but I was in the apartment. It looked like marks of a struggle in the nape of the carpet. For my money I'd say she was helped over the rail on the balcony. I saw the body. Too bad, she was a pretty thing."

"We had dinner with her last night and she was scared out of her wits. She wanted out. We promised to help her and called you. I hate to say this, but I think we're the ones who got her killed. I think Roselli or Vito had someone following us after we left the warehouse. My guess is that he saw us at the restaurant and followed us to her apartment. When they saw her get out of our car they went to her place and tried to get information from her. She probably refused and they threw her off the balcony," Pulis was rubbing the back of his neck. "What floor is her apartment on, Dave?" He asked in a quiet tone.

"She lived on the seventh floor. A long way to fall," said Kinney. "The FBI has had people working this case for a long time. Roselli is clever and keeps himself insulated from the dirty work. Vito manages all the illegal enterprises and the men who enforce them. The problem is proof. Witnesses die off quickly in this town. But the feds are good at their job and if there is anything to find, they'll find it."

"It might pay us to look in on the grieving Mr. Roselli. He might not expect us to come around right now. We really don't know much more now than when we arrived."

"OK Alan, but if you disappear we'll know where to start looking. If you go down there again watch out for that big lummox, Vito." Dave was warning the men unnecessarily. "One other thing."

"Yeah?" asked Pulis, "What's that?"

"Watch your backs. Keep your eye on the rear view mirror. I would bet that if they followed you last night they're still following you. Be careful."

"Thank you, Dave. We'll get back to you if we get to talk with Roselli." The two Alaskans stood and walked back to their car.

Once inside the car Bill Gant opened his phone and dialed Captain Caswell. "Hi, Captain," Gant began. "We have some bad news. We found a possible witness, but she was murdered last night. We're dealing with heavy hitters her, Cap."

"Are the two of you in any danger," asked Caswell.

"Maybe, but we're going back to the trucking company right now. We don't have any other leads and haven't learned much. We thought we'd go back and see if we could shake something out of the woodwork."

"Be careful, Bill. Unless you have something to go on I want the two of you to make plans to come home. You're out of our jurisdiction and without backup or technical help. Let the FBI handle those people." Caswell was being cautious and truly worried about his men.

"That's our plan, Cap. We're headed over there now. If we don't come up with something concrete we'll make reservations to get home. We'll let you know how we make out. Talk to you later." Gant closed his phone and turned to his partner. He shrugged his shoulders.

"I'm beginning to think we're not welcome here," said Bill.

"Me too, Partner, me too." Pulis was trying to think of another approach, but couldn't. "What the heck, let's get it done and go home."

Half an hour later they stepped out of their car inside the parking area of Ace Trucking Company. They climbed the few steps to the man-door at the end of the loading dock. Before they could open the door they were met by four warehousemen. They turned to face the line of muscle when the man-door opened and Vito appeared, gun drawn.

He motioned for the others to back away, but held his gun on the troopers. "You don't have an appointment and you're trespassing. It would be in your best interest to leave now."

"Gee Vito," said Pulis, "Mr. Roselli said we could come back any time. We just came to visit with him a couple of minutes."

Vito pressed a button and spoke into his small radio. He spoke in low tones and faced away so Bill and Alan couldn't hear what was being said. He mumbled a couple of more times and returned to face the visitors. He put his automatic back into its holster and said, "Come with me."

He led them inside and to the office of Salvatore Roselli. There was no one at the desk that had been occupied by Patty Dawson. Inside the inner office Roselli was again seated at his desk and again Vito took a seat behind them. Bill and Alan stood in front of the large, polished desk.

"I thought you two got what you wanted yesterday," stated Roselli.

"Just a couple of things, Mr. Roselli. By the way, where is your cute little secretary?" asked Pulis.

"If it's any concern of yours, she had an accident and won't be in today. What else did you want?"

Pulis thought it was a good thing the boss was unhappy and dug at his disposition again. "I forgot to ask yesterday, when Steven Collier left your employ, did he leave on a good note or was he fired?"

"I told you then and I repeat…he was a good employee. I loved the man. I trusted the man. I was never able to find out why he left. I always assumed he followed some woman. Now if there is nothing else."

"Do all your employees leave unexpectedly, like Steven Collier and Miss Dawson? Or are there some employees who retire and live happily ever after?" asked Pulis.

Roselli spoke to Vito, "Get these two wise guys out of here and don't ever let them inside the warehouse again. If they show up shoot them for trespassing."

"OK, you two, out, now." ordered Vito.

They marched ahead of Vito all the way to their car. "You heard the man. Don't come back."

Vito stood in the parking lot and watched as they drove away.

"Man that felt good," said Alan.

They drove back to the hotel to make arrangements to fly to Alaska. They finished packing and called David Kinney one last time.

<h1 style="text-align:center">Chapter 10</h1>

B ack at the hotel they went to Gant's room to call Kinney. Kinney had been waiting for their call. They exchanged pleasantries and thanked Kinney for his help.

"I've enjoyed working with you two. You certainly have a different style than I'm used to dealing with. It's been fun. How soon will you be leaving Newark?" asked Kinney.

"We plan to call the airport as soon as we finish with you."

"Don't bother calling the airport. I have changed your flights," Kinney informed the troopers.

"You WHAT?" shouted Pulis.

"I didn't realize we were on speaker phone, Alan. Don't get excited," explained Dave. "My boss had me change your flights. When you get to the airport you're to check in at the United Airlines counter. Tell them who you are and give them your tickets. They'll have new tickets for you, first class, and will send you to the VIP Lounge. The ticket agent will check your bags. Do not, I repeat, do not check your weapons. Wear them on your belts. You will be escorted to the lounge and taken to an executive office there. The two of you will be Air Marshals on this flight. You'll be first class and will fly from Newark to Denver, to Anchorage. You'll be leaving two hours later than the other flight, but will arrive in Anchorage an hour ahead of your original flight."

"That was nice of you, Dave," replied Alan. "What's going on?"

"The regional director will be waiting for you in the office of the VIP Lounge. His name is Emilio Perez and he's in charge of the entire East coast for the Marshal's Service. I've convinced him to bring you the file on Salvatore Roselli and his trucking company. He's the one who appointed you Air Marshals on this flight. He'll tell you whatever there is to learn about Steven

Collier, AKA, Stanley Phelps. Collier had been an informant for the FBI. He'd been passing information to them about Roselli and his racketeering and extortion and murder and whatever else he was doing. The Director will fill you in and give you the file."

"I guess I owe you an apology, Dave," said Pulis. Sorry I came down on you."

"I understand, Alan. This trip hasn't exactly been a vacation for the two of you, has it?"

"No, and I'm still feeling guilty about the death of Patty Dawson. She was a nice lady who just wanted out. I can't help but blame myself for what happened to her."

"Forget it Alan. You can't change it. One other thing, you'll be wearing your weapons on this flight. Under no circumstances are you to draw your weapon while on the aircraft. If you fire it could cause catastrophic damage. If you encounter a situation on the ground or in the terminal, fine, just don't draw it while on the plane." Dave Kinney was delivering his dire instructions to the men in lieu of a three week course at Marshal Academy.

"Dave, Bill Gant. We want to thank you for all the help you provided us while we were here. I want to extend an invitation to you to visit Alaska and to go fishing with Alan and me. We appreciated you keeping us pointed in the right direction. I think we learned most of what we came for. There are still some unanswered questions, but that's how it always is. Thanks Dave."

"Thanks, Bill, I would like to go fishing with you." Dave Kinney was sad to see the men go. It had been fun working with them. "Remember, check in at the first class counter and check your bags. They'll take you to the VIP Lounge to meet with Perez. Hey, a word of caution. Perez is fanatical about his name. Whatever you do, use his entire first name. Don't ever call him Emil. He goes ballistic when someone calls him that. Have a good trip home and stay in touch. It's been a pleasure."

"Thanks Dave. It's been good working with you, too. Hope to see you soon." Bill closed the telephone and looked at his partner.

Pulis grinned like a Cheshire Cat. "It looks like we are going to be VIP's, Partner."

"We have a little time, would you like some lunch before we go to the airport?"

"Sure, the coffee shop here has some pretty good food," replied Alan.

They took an hour for lunch, bought a newspaper and relaxed in the lobby. Gant checked out for both men and came back to where Pulis was seated.

"Don't look up, Alan, but our friend Vito is over by the front desk. You were right he is following us."

Alan folded his newspaper and handed it to Bill. He stood and stretched his back, casting a furtive glance toward the front desk. Vito was standing there with his back to the men. He turned back to Gant.

"You know, Partner, I think we should say goodbye to our old friend. He looks lonely standing over there all by himself," said Alan.

"You are such a kind person, Alan." The two troopers walked to the front desk and tapped Vito on the left shoulder. The poor man nearly jumped out of his loafers.

"Hi there, Vito, nice to see you here. Can we buy you some coffee or something?" Pulis began.

"What do you two schmucks think you're doing?" asked the surprised Vito.

"We were just checking out and getting ready to go home. What are you doing in our neighborhood?" Bill inquired.

"None of your business," Vito snapped.

Pulis slapped him on the shoulder, "Come on, Vito, can't we be friends? We're on our way to the airport and I'd hate to leave with hard feelings between us. Let's shake hands and part friends."

Vito shrugged his massive shoulders and stepped back. "We'll never be friends. I'll be glad to see you two nuts leave town. Good riddance to you. Don't bother to come back."

"Sorry you feel that way, Vito. We don't come to Newark often and didn't want to leave without saying goodbye. Come see us in Alaska sometime, old friend." Pulis piled on the charm.

"Don't hold your breath," hissed Vito. "Just get out of town and stay gone."

Bill and Alan watched the big enforcer march across the lobby toward the front door without looking back. They saw him pile into the front seat of a black SUV parked at the curb. He looked back inside the hotel to see the men watching and left them with an obscene gesture.

"We probably shouldn't expect a Christmas card from Ace Trucking Company," remarked Alan.

Bill Chuckled and said, "Let's go to the airport."

They used express check-in for the rental car and walked into the terminal. They found the United Airlines counter and first class check in window. The lady behind the counter seemed to have expected them, giving them each an envelope with first class tickets and boarding passes in exchange for the tickets they presented. They checked their bags with her and were about to ask directions to the VIP Lounge when she said, "Please come with me. I'll show you to the Lounge. Mr. Perez is waiting."

The ticket agent was tall with an athletic, square build. She strode swiftly through the crowds of people milling around the airport lobby. It was difficult to keep up with her pace through the throng. It was quite a long walk to the unmarked door she opened with a magnetic card. Inside she led them to a corner door and opened it with her magic key. Inside was a small, but comfortable office with a man seated behind the desk. She did not follow the men into the office, but said, "Security personnel will come for you when you are to board your flight." With that she closed the door and departed.

As soon as the door was closed the man behind the desk spoke. "Hello, Gentlemen, I'm Emilio Perez. Which of you is Bill Gant and which is Alan Pulis?"

Alan took the statement as a challenge, "I'm Pulis and this is my partner, Bill Gant. What have you got for us?"

"I'm glad to see the two of you leaving. You've been a fly in the ointment since you arrived. The FBI has advised us that you've been sticking your noses into an ongoing investigation. I'm not happy and neither is the FBI."

"Tough! You got one of your witnesses murdered in Alaska. We might have prevented it if you had informed us about what was going on. Everything's a big secret to you people. You think you're more important if you fail to inform other agencies and hold more information than they are allowed to have. Well, congratulations, Emil. Because of that practice you caused us to lose a witness. We could have prevented her death if you'd seen fit to inform us of the full situation. So, keep your 'I'm not happy' speech to yourself. Now, what have you got for us? We have things to do." Pulis stood in front of the desk scowling at the man in the blue blazer and striped tie.

Instant anger showed on the face of the Marshal. "The name is Emilio Perez. You can call me Mr. Perez." His face reddened as he pushed a file toward Alan. "This is a summary of the FBI investigation. I'm authorized to tell you that Collier was talking with the FBI and giving them information about Ace Trucking Company. When it looked as if he had been found out we were asked to place him in the witness protection program. We moved him to Alaska more than two years ago. His girlfriend followed him, something we attempted to discourage. He moved her anyway. She changed her name and joined him. You should know we suspect Collier moved a great deal of Sal Roselli's money somewhere. We don't know where or how, but Roselli is still looking for it. The word is that the amount was more than four million dollars. The money is still missing. Our guess is that Roselli found out where Collier was moved to and went to get the cash. We think Collier wouldn't tell them where it was and they killed him. They would have killed him anyway, but we don't think he told them where it was hidden. The only person who might know where the money is now would be the girlfriend and she's refused to talk with the FBI."

Pulis picked up the file and handed it to Gant. "You're a piece of work, Emil. If what you say is true, you're jeopardizing the life of another person,

Lucile Mc Dermot. Thanks for the file. I think we can do without your help from now on. I don't like doing business with people I can't trust."

"Hopefully we'll never have to associate with each other again. Goodbye gentlemen, and have a nice trip home."

He stepped from behind the desk and marched to the door, shoving it open and storming out. Pulis felt rather proud he had managed to insult the Area Director of the U.S. Marshals Eastern District.

An hour later the Terminal Security Officer came to escort them to the loading gate. With him as escort they bypassed all security and were seated in first class before the other passengers were allowed to board. Bill used his cell phone to call Captain Rollin Caswell to let him know they were on the way home. He also informed his boss it was time to put a full time watch on Leila Hunter, AKA Lucile Mc Dermot.

Pulis spent most of the trip to Denver reading the FBI file. Bill Gant slept.

Chapter 11

The men were met at the passenger gate by two TSA agents who escorted them to another gate in the same terminal. Again they were allowed to enter the aircraft ahead of the other passengers. "Your baggage is being transferred to this airplane right now. Have a nice flight, Sirs."

Both men slept most of the five hour flight from Denver to Anchorage where they retrieved their luggage and caught the first commuter flight of the day to Kenai. The Beechcraft 1900 made the trip in less than 25 minutes. Their car had been moved to the short term parking area by one of Captain Caswell's men and the keys left in safekeeping with the ticket agent on duty. They tossed the two bags into the rear seat of the car and drove to Soldotna, an 11 mile trip.

"Why don't we stop at the diner and have some breakfast. I don't know if Leila is working this morning, but we can have something to eat before we go to the office." Bill Gant was worried about the waitress and Pulis shared his concern.

"Good idea," replied Pulis.

They spotted the tall, shapely waitress through the window as they walked across the parking lot. Inside they found a booth in need of busing and sat. Leila had seen them come in and made her way to the booth to begin clearing the dirty dishes. She returned in a minute with a bar mop and water glasses and menus tucked under her other arm. "I'll be right back with coffee," she said.

When she returned she had two cups of coffee and an order pad in her hands. "Good to see you two again. What do you want to order?"

"Good to see you too, Leila. We need to see you, privately. When can we talk?" asked Gant.

"I get off at noon today. We're really busy and I can't get away before then."

"We'll see you at noon. Let's see, I want sourdough pancakes and two eggs, over easy." Leila wrote Gant's order on her pad and turned to Pulis.

"And you, Sir? What would you like?"

"I'll have hamburger steak and eggs, over medium, hash browns and a large orange juice."

She made the notes. "Comin' right up," she said as she turned toward the order window in the kitchen.

The two sipped their coffee while watching her efficient practice of her trade. She bused tables, poured coffee and took orders never wasting a trip. She had her arms full in both directions. The second waitress on the floor had half the tables to serve and was having trouble keeping up. She was young, blond and inexperienced.

The order came and she poured more coffee. "I'll see you later," she said in a low tone.

The investigators ate their meal and left a tip. Captain Caswell was in his office when they entered. He wasn't in uniform. "I see you two finally decided to come back to work," he greeted as they stepped into his office.

"Good morning, Captain. Good to see you, too." Pulis spoke as the two took seats on the other side of the desk. "We didn't get any real evidence, Cap, but we confirmed our suspicions. We got one witness killed. The Newark Mafia is mad at us, and the Marshal's Service was glad to see us leave. Other than that our trip was uneventful." Pulis gave the thumbnail report.

"Yes, I've heard some of your exploits. I had a nice chat with Emilio Perez of the Marshal's Service. You two made quite an impression on that gentleman."

"Good old Emil," commented Pulis. "I'm sorry, Cap, but he and I didn't see eye to eye, so to speak."

"So I gathered, however, David Kinney of the Marshals gave the two of you a glowing report. He made a special effort to say you two had nothing to do with the death of that secretary. We can talk about all this later. Today I want you to write your report. We can review it tomorrow and try to come up with a plan to solve the murder we're dealing with in our jurisdiction." Captain Caswell gave his instructions and added, "I've also had a call from the FBI about the death of that secretary. They say it's possible the goons from Ace Trucking followed you and saw her with you. When they questioned her about it they got ugly and tossed her off a balcony. They also said one of them grabbed the handrail on the balcony and left a full left hand print. A preliminary identification came back to a man who works for Ace Trucking. The name is Vito Roma. The FBI is trying to locate him, but he seems to have fallen from the face of the earth. Do you know this Roma character?"

"Yes we do, Cap. He's one of Sal Roselli's goons. He threw us out of the warehouse at gunpoint the last time we were there. It will all be in the report." Gant had made the comment, but worried where Vito had gone.

"I'm going home and mow the lawn. Get your report done and I'll see you two on Monday. It's been a long week for you and I appreciate your efforts. Good job, guys. Why don't you finish the report and go fishing tomorrow?"

"That's a great idea, Cap. Are you buying the gas?" asked Pulis.

"I bought the last tank. You're on your own on this one." The captain stood to leave. "Get some rest, you need it."

Gant and Pulis went to their own office and began to work on the details of the report. It was past 11:30 when they closed the file cabinets and left the office. They parked on the frontage street across from the rear of the restaurant and waited, watching for anyone or anything suspicious. There was nothing to be seen and they sat quietly. At 12:15 Leila came out the rear door of the café and lit up a cigarette. She stood in the sunshine smoking and pacing before climbing into her little white Ford. The officers followed her car to the apartment complex and watched as she entered. There were no other cars in the area and felt safe to follow her to the apartment. They knocked on the door and it opened immediately.

"Come in," Leila said nervously, glancing down the stairwell.

"Good to see you, Leila," greeted Gant. "How have you been?"

"Hi there, fellas, I've been fine. I've had the heebie-jeebies since you were here last. I jump at every noise and look at strangers like they were from Mars. Did you find out who killed Stan?"

"We think so, but we still have no proof," Pulis offered.

She stared at the floor, "I've been thinking about Stan lately and trying to think who could have done this to him." She looked back at Gant, "One time Stan said if anything happened to him that he had me taken care of. He never elaborated on that statement, but he said if something happened to him I could live comfortably, anywhere I wanted, for the rest of my life. Do you have any idea what he meant by that?"

"Please, sit down, Leila," said Bill, holding on to her shoulder, feeling her shiver from fear.

She sat at the kitchen table and Bill sat next to her with Alan on the other side of the table. Her shoulders sagged and her head bent forward. She was surrendering to her fear.

"Hey, Lady, things aren't that bad. Cheer up a little. We're here to help you." Gant tried to be cheerful and confident, but inside he felt the same as Leila. "What I'm about to tell you is pure speculation. We have no proof, but everything we've learned points to our conclusion." She lifted her head a little to listen. Alan and I think Stan stole a lot of money from the man he worked for. We think his boss Sal Roselli is the big mafia boss in Newark and is running his extortion money, drug money, prostitution money and all his other illegal cash flow, through the trucking company. We think Stan, or Steven as he was known then as comptroller for Ace Trucking Company, began to siphon off huge sums of cash to put into his own account somewhere. It must have been a lot of money, because Sal got wise. Steve Collier was scared and contacted the FBI offering to give information about Roselli's criminal enterprises in trade for protection. The feds took him up on the offer and moved him to Alaska.

"Yes, now that I think about it he was awfully edgy those past weeks before he left Newark," Leila was listening intently now.

Gant continued, "The U.S. Marshals wrote him a resume and invented a past to match it. They moved him to Alaska where they thought he'd be safe. But Sal Roselli didn't take kindly to having someone out there with knowledge of his criminal empire. He may or may not have been aware of the missing cash at that time, but we suspect he was. The Marshal Service is very good at what they do and Steven, now Stanley, had disappeared without a trace. Now don't take this personally, but we think Vito Roma knew Stan was dating you and thought if he watched you he would find Steven Collier. The tactic worked and they came here to get the cash back and to eliminate a witness. We think Vito or one of his men picked Stanley off the street one night when he finished work and drove to Homer. We think they took him out to the middle of Cook Inlet where there were no eyes watching and tried to get the location of the cash he had stolen from them. We don't know if he told them where it was, but we doubt it. They killed him anyway and dropped him in the inlet. That's where Alan and I became involved. We found his body and reported it to the troopers."

"You mean you and Alan are the ones who found Stan's body?" asked Leila Hunter, her eyes wide with terror.

"Yes, we found him," admitted Bill Gant. "We're both retired from the troopers and Captain Caswell asked us to investigate the case. We're on contract until this case is solved."

"I guess you already know I'm scared to death. I haven't slept since you first contacted me. I keep thinking the same people will come after me and I'll end up like Stan."

"We understand your feeling, Leila. Now, don't take this the wrong way, but Alan and I own a small fishing boat and we go halibut fishing as often as we can. You aren't working tomorrow, so why not go fishing with us. There is no way anyone can find you out there with us. You can relax for a day and have some fun. The weather is supposed to be nice and the sea calm. You don't need anything but a fishing license and to dress warm, How about it?" This was the first time Alan had heard this idea, but he liked it.

"Oh, I couldn't put the two of you out like that. I love to fish, but I would be imposing."

"You won't be imposing, Leila, we have to watch out for you anyway. What better way to do that than to go fishing?" These were the first words Alan had spoken, but they affirmed the sense of the idea.

She hesitated, but finally agreed to go with the two men. "What time shall I meet you?"

"We'll pick you up out front at six. The tide is just after eight and that'll give us two hours to drive to Anchor Point, launch and motor out to the fishing spot. We'll bring coffee, sodas and food. Captain Caswell is buying the gas." Alan Pulis was more cheerful than usual and genuinely looking forward to the trip.

"Don't get careless, though. Stay inside if you can. We don't want something to happen to you tonight." Bill Gant was showing his concern. He was beginning to like this young woman.

At the restaurant two men sat in a booth. One very large man dressed in a cotton shirt and khaki slacks, the other in jeans and a flannel shirt. The Oriental lady waiting tables asked what they wanted to drink.

Chapter 12

The following morning, promptly at six, Bill Gant walked up the stairs to Leila Hunter's apartment. He tapped gently on the door. It opened instantly revealing a tall, stylish, smiling, lady. She had a jacket draped over one arm and a plastic bag in the other.

"Lunch," she said, lifting the bag a little higher for him to see.

"Let me carry that for you," offered Bill. She stepped out of the apartment and Gant pulled the door closed, testing to make sure it was locked. "You can ride in the front seat with Alan and I'll sit in the back and check out the lunch."

Towing the boat through the city streets the trio drove south toward Anchor Point and the morning launch. Alan unhooked his truck from the boat trailer and found a parking spot. Bill had loaded Leila and all the gear into the boat while waiting for Alan to return. The tractor hooked up to the trailer as soon as Pulis was inside. Bill and Leila took seats in the small booth-like seating while Alan sat in the captain's chair. There was no wind and the water was glassy making the launch easier than usual. Once the boat was floating Pulis lowered the motors into the water and started them to idle and warm. He put the motors into reverse to back into deeper water while the engines idled.

"Alan and I agree you should be the hook baiter today," joked Bill.

She giggled, "If I do, I am only giving you ugly bait."

Now both Bill and Alan laughed, "We can see this isn't your first trip." Alan dropped the engines into gear and began the hour-long trip to the fishing spot. It looked like it would be a happy and relaxing day for all three fishermen.

Vito Roma and his partner Dallas Freed awoke early, not being used to the long Alaska days. At half past six in the morning the sun was high in the sky and the temperature rising. The two men drove around the area to become familiar with streets and businesses available in the area. They had spotted the

Savings and Loan Company building the night before. There are two routes to Kenai and Roma took the one closest to where they had stayed in a motel. This was the Spur Highway. A very pleasant drive through a wooded countryside populated with mostly scattered houses. In Kenai they found the local businessman's hangout, Louie's Restaurant. They found a booth and sat. The waitress, a short, thin, no nonsense lady with a very long braid hanging down her back, brought water and menus.

"Coffee?" she asked.

"Yes, black for both of us." Vito had not looked up from the menu.

Both men marveled at the array of animal heads and hides hanging in the dining room. There were two large Bull Moose heads, a muskox, an elk, a salmon shark and several bear hides on the walls.

"I think we should come back here someday and go hunting. From the looks of things it must be pretty good around here." Dallas had never seen this many trophies in one place. "I would sure like to kill a big moose like that one," he said, motioning toward the large head over their booth.

"We haven't got time for that," reminded Vito. "We've got business to take care of."

The waitress was back with coffee. "Have you decided what you want?"

The two men ordered and the waitress marched away. "We have to find that girl. She shouldn't be hard to find in a town this size. I wish we had a picture of her. It's Sunday and where we come from most businesses are closed. Almost everything is open here. She could be almost anywhere. We'll find her."

Dallas reached for the back of his head and scratched. He took a large drink of coffee, looked Vito in the eye and said, "Vito, I know you want to get the job done and get back, but in the past, when we tried to hurry, we screwed up. Personally, I don't want to go to jail in Alaska or anywhere else for that matter. How about we take a day off? Let's find a good guide to take us fishing and relax for the day. The bank will be open tomorrow and someone there will know who this woman is and where she can be found. I think it would make more sense than running around like a couple of tourists."

Vito was silent for a minute. "OK, Dallas, you're probably right."

They finished breakfast and sat for a while. The place was busy and the waitress seemed impatient to clean the table and seat someone else. Vito took the hint and waved her over. He gave her a $50 bill and said, "Keep the change."

She looked at the bill in amazement as the men climbed out of the booth. "You two come back again, now. Have a nice day."

Dallas waved as he made his way through the crowd toward the front door. Outside the sun was warm and the smell of salt water was in the air. They decided to drive around the local area and familiarize themselves with their new locale. They drove to North Kenai and back to Soldotna. They drove to

Sterling and then up Funny River road. The one thing they learned was that not all roads went anywhere, but dead ended at a beach or river somewhere. The countryside was beautiful, but they quickly learned there was only one road onto the Kenai Peninsula and consequently only one way out. It was time to research other methods of escape in the event one was needed. At the Soldotna Airport there were several small companies offering charters to nearly any destination in Alaska. This seemed to be the most sensible way to leave an area with only one road.

"I tried to learn to fly once. That was when I was busted for the bank job in Ohio. They didn't offer flying classes while I was in prison," joked Dallas.

"It doesn't seem like it, but it's getting late. Is there anything you want to do before we go back to the hotel?" asked Vito.

"Stop at the first store you see and I'll get a six-pack to take back to the room. I think I'll just drink a beer and watch some football on TV."

Vito thought about it and decided to do the same.

It was six-thirty in the evening when Pulis and Gant stopped in front of the apartment building. All three fishermen were tired from the back-breaking labor of halibut fishing. Constantly pulling four pounds of weight from 180 feet of water becomes hard work, but the effort is worth the strain. They had caught their limit of six halibut. The largest was about 60 pounds and the smallest was near 45 pounds; a lot of delicious white filets.

Leila gathered her belongings from the rear seat of the truck. She was tired, but relaxed. "I want to thank you both for a wonderful day. This is the first time fishing halibut for me. I loved it. Will you let me go again sometime?"

"When we finish investigating this case we'll be retired again and we fish all the time. I think we can sign you on as a deck-hand. You can cut bait and clean fish. If you're good we'll let you clean the boat." In all honesty Pulis had enjoyed the third member of the crew today.

"Don't let Alan put you off," interjected Gant, "we can always leave him home and you can drive the boat."

"Thanks again fellas. I had a lot of fun and it's the first day in a while I've been relaxed." She smiled a weak smile, "I'm off tomorrow and I'll probably sleep all day, but perhaps I'll see you Tuesday morning for breakfast?"

"Sure thing, Leila, glad you enjoyed it. We'll filet the fish and vacuum seal them for you. I'll put them in the freezer and deliver them to you in a couple of days. It was fun for us too. Remember, if you need us for anything just call, we'll come a runnin'" said Bill.

The two watched her walk into the building before starting the truck.

The following morning, Monday, the two investigators were in their office working on the reports order by Captain Caswell. It was mid-morning when their phone rang.

After an informal greeting Marshal Kinney asked that the two of them get on the line. "This way I don't have to say it twice. How have you two been?"

"You know us, Dave, keeping a low profile," said Pulis.

"Yeah, right, the two of you just came down here, made my life miserable and went home to rest up, is that it?"

"Pretty much, how have you been?" again it was Pulis speaking.

"I have some up-dates for you. I just finished talking with the FBI down here. They're telling me the hand print they got from the railing in Patty Dawson's apartment is definitely from Vito Roma. They've been looking for the guy and say he's disappeared. The Bureau thinks the person with Roma the night he tossed Dawson off the balcony was an ex-con by the name of Dallas Freed. I'm told he's somewhat of a nutcase and to watch out for him. They both work for Sal Roselli doing wet work and heavy lifting. Both of them are missing. We all think Sal sent them to find Stan Phelps' girlfriend and they could be in your area."

"Are there any pictures of these two hoods available?" asked Gant.

"Yes, and I'll send them to you right away." Kinney softened his tone, "Be careful up there. These two are bad guys. That's why Roselli keeps them around. If they are in Alaska you need to be aware. They have a bad habit of showing up without notice, killing a victim and leaving the same way. In fact they may be the ones responsible for your case; the ones who killed Phelps."

"Send us the pictures. Alan and I have met Roma, but we don't know Freed."

"One other thing, that girl, Lucile Mc Dermot, you know her as Leila something, we think she's in real danger. If those two thugs find her she'll probably die an unspeakable death. She should be protected. I mean closely protected. She may not know anything at all about what Phelps did, but Roma and Freed will go to any length to find out what she knows."

"We're keeping her under watch, Dave. She seems to be a really nice person. I'd hate to see anything happen to her." Bill Gant was surprised at himself for taking it so personally.

"That's all I have, but I thought you should know. I'll send you the photos right away. Good talking with you. You can go back to sleep now." Kinney laughed and hung up the phone.

Alan was the first to speak, "Let's see the Captain and fill him in. I think we need to watch Leila full time, what do you think?"

"We need another car. Do you want the first shift or the second?" asked Gant.

"Take our car and I'll get another. There's another apartment complex up the street and I think the parking area there has a view of her building. I'll bring you a Coke and some lunch in three hours. Let's go see the Cap."

Gant and Pulis informed the captain of their conversation with Kinney. They explained their strategy and received a go-ahead from the captain. Gant went to the bathroom and out to the car to drive to his post. Pulis went to the office and waited for the photos to arrive.

Three hours later Pulis came to relieve his partner. He had the photos in hand and gave a copy to Gant. "Anything going on here," he asked.

"I haven't seen Leila come out. Other tenants have come and gone, but not her. I haven't seen any strange vehicles or people hanging around. I didn't see anyone doing a drive-by, but since we don't know what they may be driving it'll be difficult to recognize them," said Gant, grateful for his relief.

Pulis opened the door to go back to his car, poked his head back inside and said, "Go home and get some rest. I'm good for four hours. I brought coffee and a crossword puzzle." He waved and returned to his vehicle.

"You should have brought a bucket," thought Gant.

Inside the apartment Leila was unaware of the eyes guarding her. She spent the day cleaning her apartment and relaxing. She ironed her uniform for the next day and watched television. Her body ached from the strenuous activity the day before. She hadn't realized fishing took so much effort.

Chapter 13

Leila Hunter was an early riser. Gant was now on watch and noticed the curtain pulled open in her apartment window. He was stiff and needed to stretch. Stepping out of his car into the cool morning air, raising his arms above his head and yawning he noted the morning sun was in the North East quadrant headed in a circle toward the South West quadrant, a trip that would take 18 ½ hours. He walked around his car a couple of times and was about to climb inside again when Pulis drove up to hand him a steaming hot cup of fresh coffee.

"Are you just getting up or just getting home," asked Gant.

"I won't tell you anymore because you tell everyone." Pulis looked rested and ready for the day. "The restaurant opens at six. She'll most likely be going to work any minute now. I'll take over now and you can go home for a shower and change clothes. I'll meet you at the café when you get back."

"Thanks, Alan, I need to clean up. Nothing happened last night. There was no sign of life from her apartment after you left last night. Not much traffic on the street. There were a few late-night drunks feeling their way home, but no activity around this neighborhood. I haven't seen any river guides this morning, but then I remembered this is Monday and they don't work today."

Gant was about to leave when his cell phone rang. It was Leila.

"This is Gant," he answered.

"Hi, Bill, I just wanted to let you know I've been called in to work this morning. I'll be leaving here in about twenty minutes. Will you and Alan be coming in for breakfast?"

"We just talked about that. I'm going home to clean up and I'll be back to meet him at the restaurant. How do you feel this morning? Did you get rested?"

"I have a few sore muscles, but I rested well." She paused a moment then continued, "I want to thank you two for being so caring and watchful. I enjoyed the fishing trip, but I could never have rested last night without you keeping an eye out for me. I hadn't realized how nervous I had been feeling. Thank you, both of you, for being there."

"Our pleasure Leila. Now you just go about your business and pretend we aren't there. We'll be around. Give me a call if you notice anyone or anything suspicious."

Gant gave Pulis a short rendition of the phone call before driving toward home. An hour later he was back in the restaurant ordering breakfast with Alan sitting across the booth from him. Leila had brought the cops menus and coffee before moving to another table to take the order for that table. She collected the money for a meal from a party leaving the café and returned to take their order.

"You guys look pretty good for someone not getting much sleep last night. What can I get you for breakfast?"

"We never sleep. We survive on black coffee and crossword puzzles." All three laughed at his joke. "I'm having a waffle and patty sausage," ordered Bill.

"That sounds good, I'll have the same." Pulis handed her the menus. "The fish will be frozen by this afternoon. Do you have a freezer in your apartment?"

"Yes, but it's a little one. I don't have room for much in there. Just bring me about six packages of halibut and you two keep the rest." She gave them a small wave of her hand and spun around to deliver the order to the kitchen window.

When she was gone the two discussed the plan for the day. "If you want to sit on her for a while this morning, I'll go to the office and check in with the captain. Is there anything you want me to do for you while I'm there?" asked Gant.

"You might try to find out where Roma has gone. I'm worried he may show up here. When Leila gets off today we can try to find out what she knows in regard to the missing cash. It seems to me the money is the key to all this."

"I think you're right, Alan, it's the only thing that makes any sense. Stay on your toes, Buddy. We're playing with professionals this time."

Their order came and conversation ceased. When they had finished breakfast and settled the tab with Leila the two men parted. Gant drove to the office and Pulis parked at a vantage point across the street. He could see traffic coming and going from the parking lot. Through the window he could observe Leila working inside.

About the same time at Louie's in Kenai, Vito and Dallas found a booth and were being served by the same short, slim, all-business waitress who served yesterday. "I see you two found your way back," she commented. "Do you want coffee this morning?"

"Sure," said Vito as he picked up a menu.

She returned with two cups of hot coffee, "Have you made up your minds?" she asked.

"Biscuits and gravy for me," ordered Vito.

"That sounds good, the same for me," said Dallas.

The mini-waitress marched off toward the kitchen window to place the order.

"We need to go to the bank and see if anyone knows where we can find Steven's girlfriend. This is a small town and someone will know. We'll have to be careful, though. In a small town like this, and us being strangers, we could make someone wonder what we want. We've been lucky so far and no one is paying us any attention." Dallas had experienced small towns in the past and knew how easily suspicions could be raised.

"Let's go to the airport and talk with that charter operator again. We need an escape route in the event of an emergency and I think an airplane may be the best bet. We just need to find someone who will fly us out without getting too curious." Vito liked the atmosphere in the area thinking it would be a good place to spend time and to relax.

"Which stop first, Vito, the bank or the airport?"

"The bank," replied Vito, "We have to find that girl."

Breakfast came and the two men ate and enjoyed every morsel. They sat, relaxing and drinking coffee. The waitress kept their cups full. When they had drunk their fill they asked for the ticket, paid the amount with a healthy tip for her.

On the drive back to Soldotna Dallas commented, "I can't get over how laid back everyone is here. It's sure a far cry from Newark."

"Don't get too comfortable, Dallas. We're here to do a job," Vito cautioned.

The bank lobby was open when they returned to Soldotna. Dallas took a hundred dollar bill from his wallet and waited in line for a teller. When his turn came he stepped to the window where he was greeted by a smiling young lady with a cheerful attitude. "I just need to break this bill down, ten fives and five tens, please." She took the bill and opened a drawer to make the change. "I have an old friend who once worked here, Stan Phelps. I heard he died."

She turned back to face him, counting his change, "Thank you, sir"

"Did you know Stan?" he asked.

"Yes, we all liked him. He was going to be our next branch manager. What a nice man. It was tragic about him."

"He had a girlfriend, I don't recall her name. Is she still in town?" he asked casually.

"Yes, her name is Leila -- something. I've forgotten her last name. She still works at the diner up the street, nice lady. You can't miss her she is the very tall one."

"Thank you, I'll look her up."

"You have a nice day, now," she said smiling a perfect smile.

Dallas met Vito at the front door, nodding. Outside he passed on the location of their quarry. They drove to the restaurant and parked. Through the large windows they could see the tall, busy waitress working.

Across the street Alan Pulis was sitting, watching. A car had parked at the diner, but no one stepped out. "They must be talking on the cell phone," thought Alan, making a note in his notebook.

The two men were devising a plan to pick her up after she finished her shift, but they didn't know when that would be. They were working on the problem when their cell phone rang. It was Gino Rinaldi. Vito had left him in charge while he was gone.

"Vito, I got some bad news for you. The feds found out where you went. I don't know how, but they found out. Someone must have dropped a dime on you. You need to get out of there right now. Sal says you can go back later to finish the job. But, right now you have to leave. Sal says the fishing is good in Costa Rica this time of year. He wants you to take a couple of weeks off starting now, got that?"

"I got it, Gino. I understand the situation," said Vito, "we'll be out of here in an hour. Tell Sal I'll call him later." He closed the telephone and blew out a long sigh.

"Something wrong, Vito?" asked his partner.

"Yeah, we have to pack up and get out of town. The feds tracked us down and are on the way here. We'll have to come back later to finish this job. Let's go to the motel and pack up. I'll make some reservations."

"Right when we had her, too," commented Dallas.

Pulis saw the car leave the parking lot but had not seen the occupants. It seemed strange to him that they never got out of the car, but people do strange things all the time. He made another note in his notebook and resumed his crossword puzzle.

Fifteen minutes after leaving the restaurant parking area the two were leaving Soldotna. Dallas drove while Vito called the airline ticket counter to change their reservations. The task was finished by the time they reached the airport terminal in Kenai. Vito had to explain it was an emergency in order to get an immediate flight out of Kenai. Flights to and from the Kenai Peninsula are full; every flight, every day, all summer long. Dallas returned the rental car while Vito checked them in at the ticket counter. Their flight would board in ten minutes.

"I am very sorry to hear of your mother's passing. Please let our agents know if there is anything we can do to assist you or make you flight more comfortable," said the ticket agent in a consoling tone.

Alan was cooking in the hot car when Bill drove up and motioned for him to come across the street to the restaurant for lunch. Alan needed the restroom more than he needed lunch and followed willingly.

When they met in the parking lot Bill delivered the message he had received from Captain Caswell. "Vito's here. He has some other guy with him. The FBI called the captain to let him know. They're sending two men from Anchorage to meet with us. They will be here in a couple of hours. One of us will have to meet them at the office. That had better be you while I stay here and keep an eye out for Vito."

"A little while ago a car pulled in here and no one got out. They sat in the car for about ten minutes and left. I couldn't see who was in the car, but it looked like it may be a rental. I have the numbers in my notebook. We can run them when we finish lunch. Right now I have to go inside and use the facilities." Alan didn't wait for an answer he just marched straight inside to the restroom while Bill found them a booth where Leila would wait on them."

Chapter 14

The restaurant was crowded. Bill waited while Alan finished his business in the restroom. He returned just as Leila came to serve them. She had a relaxed smile and greeted the men cheerfully.

"Hi, guys, having a good day?" she asked while wiping crumbs from the table.

"Actually it just got better. The men sent to find you are here, but the FBI is coming to help. They should be here in a couple of hours. Don't get careless, though. We don't have any idea where they are and we're going to keep an eye on you. Come to think of it, looking at you isn't such a bad job." Bill meant it as a joke, but he really did like the lady.

Alan was next to ask, "Have you seen any strange characters in here this morning?"

"To tell the truth I haven't had time to look. It has been really busy. Summertime, you know, full of fishermen and tourists. Do you want coffee?"

"Yes, and a club sandwich and potato salad," ordered Bill Gant.

"Make mine a BLT with fries and coffee, I've been working hard all morning."

"I don't have much time to chit-chat today, but if you need anything else I'll be happy to get it for you." She started to walk away, but turned back and said quietly, "Thank you for everything, you have no idea what your help means to me."

Bill gave a small wave of his hand as she turned to walk away.

Both men watched her walk away. When she was gone Alan asked, "You say there are two of them? Who is the second one?"

"The captain says he's some goon by the name of Dallas Freed. I don't know how they know who he is or how they know they're here. You can find all that out when you go to the meeting after lunch. I'll take the stakeout this afternoon."

"You know, I wonder if that car in the parking lot earlier was Vito and his partner, and if it was them, why didn't they come inside and check things out? Do you think they spotted me across the street?"

"It's hard to tell, but I can't imagine they saw you. There could be a hundred reasons for them wanting to come back later." Bill really didn't have an answer to Alan's question.

Leila returned with the coffee. Several minutes later she came back with their order. "Is there anything else I can get you boys?" she asked.

"No, we're fine." As she started to walk away Bill asked, "Do you still get off at noon today?"

"No, I won't get off until around three." She replied as she walked to the next table.

After finishing lunch Bill took up the post across the street from the restaurant while Alan drove to Trooper Headquarters for a meeting with the captain and the FBI agents. The captain led the way to a small conference room where the feds were waiting. Captain Caswell made the introductions, "Agents Greer and Coleman, this is Trooper Investigator Alan Pulis. He and his partner, Bill Gant, have just returned from Newark where they had met Vito Roma and his boss Salvatore Roselli. Alan is one of the men who discovered the body of Stanley Phelps. The two are now investigating the case. They're both retired troopers and know their business, so you can discuss the case with them."

"There really isn't much to discuss," began Greer. "You two probably know more about the case than we do. We got a call from the Marshal's office in New York, a marshal by the name of Kinney. He let us know about the murdered banker and about your trip to Newark. He said this Vito Roma and someone else, probably Dallas Freed, followed you two when you met with Roselli's secretary. When you dropped her off they went to her apartment, beat her, questioned her and threw her off a seventh story balcony. Is that the way the story went?"

"That's pretty much it," acknowledged Pulis.

"Our office in New York and officers in Newark have been investigating Roselli and his trucking company for several years. Your dead banker came to us a couple of years ago and asked to be relocated in exchange for information about his boss, Salvatore Roselli and his illegal activities. My report says he gave us extraordinarily accurate information. He wanted out of the business and came to us. He had a girlfriend and wanted to get married, but didn't want to involve her in the criminal aspect of his life. He said he was quitting for love. We took the information and had the Marshal's Service move him here to Soldotna, Alaska. We thought he would be safe here. I guess we all underestimated the depth of the Roselli organization. We've yet to arrest or convict Roselli or any of his enforcers, even with the information provided by our witness Steven Collier. Roselli is a very powerful man in New Jersey. He has a lot of political clout and has managed to short-circuit all our investigations. He even managed to get a warrant quashed. I've never heard of that being done before." Greer was showing frustration in his voice. He stopped and took a swallow of water from the bottle in front of him.

"Do you think Vito Roma is here in Soldotna?" asked Pulis.

"We tracked him this far. He and Freed are travelling under assumed names. It's possible they have forged passports. You and your partner have seen him and can identify him. We have pictures and tracked him to Kenai where he rented a car, but we don't know where he is right now. You made a wise move when you decided to watch the girl. I think she is the reason Roma is here." Greer was still doing the talking. "Information from Newark suggests that when Steven Collier left there he had taken a large sum of cash from Ace Trucking Company. We think Roselli sent his hit men to get the money back. It is possible Collier didn't tell them where the money is now and they want to know if his girlfriend has that information. All this is supposition, but our information points in that direction."

"Bill and I sort of had the same idea. We asked Leila Hunter about it and she said she knew nothing about it." Pulis spelled out his theory, "We think she has the key to the location of the cash, but doesn't realize it. We think it may be hidden in some coded data Stanley Phelps had given her."

Agent Coleman finally spoke, "Right now you have her under surveillance, which is good. We are going to Kenai and try to find the rental car. Stay in touch with us and we will keep you informed of anything we learn. Until we locate those two the girl is vulnerable. It'll be up to you to keep her safe until we locate and capture those two. We have a warrant for the arrest of Vito Roma on the charge of first degree murder. The other one, Freed, we'll arrest on suspicion of murder in the same case. Once we have them in custody the two of you can take a day off."

"Thanks for the information, anyway." Pulis didn't like the way he and Gant were being dismissed, but kept his thought to himself. He stood and walked to his little office leaving Captain Caswell with the two agents.

After finalizing some reports Pulis drove back to the stakeout behind the restaurant. He sat next to Gant in Bill's car informing him of the meeting with the two FBI agents. "This sort of validates our thinking about this case, Partner."

"Yup, you're right, Alan, and I have an idea. Tell me what you think of this; we invite Leila to your place this afternoon for a barbecue. We can cook up some of our halibut, have a couple of beers and try to figure out what happened to the money, or if there really is any money."

"You know, Partner, sometimes you amaze me when you have one of these good ideas. You catch her when she gets off work and follow her home. She can follow you out to my place or she can ride with you, but I'll go home and get some fish out of the freezer and put a six pack on ice. I'll have to tidy up the place a little before she comes out." Pulis drove away toward his house, six miles east of town on a small lake.

At ten past three Leila came out the back door to smoke a cigarette before entering her car. She drove directly home with Bill following close behind. When she parked in the carport he stopped behind her and motioned for her to come to his vehicle. They discussed the plan with her agreeing to ride with him. She went inside to shower and change clothes. When she reappeared she seemed like a different person. Her hair was down and styled, her clothing was colorful and neat and her smile was radiant. She climbed into Bill's car and smiled again.

"I'm going to enjoy this," she said. "I haven't felt this relaxed since Stan's death."

"We'll talk about all that when we get to Alan's place, but we want to pick your brain. We think there's something Stan left with you or told you that's the key to where your future security is hidden. You said that's what he told you and we think he had a plan. We just have to figure out what the plan is."

Gant led Leila through the house to the back yard where Alan was busy lighting the grill. The picnic table was set and had green salad, cheese rolls, potatoes ready to put on the grill for baking and corn on the cob wrapped in foil to be placed on the grill with the potatoes. The halibut was seasoned and in a covered dish awaiting the proper time to be cooked. A cooler sat at the end of the table.

"You've been a busy man, Alan."

"There's cold beer and sodas in the cooler. I have to get the potatoes on to cook then I'll be right with you."

Leila took a cold soda from the ice chest. Bill took a bottle of beer. Alan already had one open and sitting on the end of the table. The sun was warm and surprisingly few mosquitoes were buzzing around. Several baby ducks swam near the shore while mama duck stepped out onto the grass to look for a hand-out. Alan saw her coming and walked to the deck to get some cracked corn from a metal container there. He tossed it on the grass near the water causing the baby ducks to follow their mother ashore. He closed the lid on the grill after placing the potatoes inside and came to the table to sit.

"OK, now I have time to talk," he said, taking a long drink of the cold beer.

"I asked Leila if she could think of anything Stan had left her that could be a clue to the hiding place for the money. She said she didn't know of anything."

"That's right," said Leila. I can't think of anything that could be a clue."

"Did he ever give you an unusual gift, something you would have kept?" asked Pulis.

"I can't think of anything," she said. "Although there was one time he gave me a beautiful silver bracelet. He had my name engraved on the inside. It was my old name, so I seldom wear it."

"Is there anything special about the engraving?" asked Pulis.

"No, in fact it's rather plain. Just block letters. It's the only thing I don't like about the bracelet." Leila looked up at the two men, "Do you think that could be the clue?"

"Stan was a banker. Is it possible he put some kind of safe combination or account number in the inscription?" asked Gant.

"I don't know. Remind me when I get home tonight and I'll show it to you."

Pulis soon became busy with cooking again. Bill went into the house and made a pot of coffee. They enjoyed the dinner and Bill noticed how much he liked Leila's company. They all ate more than they needed, but it all tasted so delicious they had kept on eating.

Pulis had found a large paper bag and filled it with frozen packages of halibut. Bill drove her back to her apartment and said good night as she climbed out of the car and walked inside.

Chapter 15

The following morning Bill Gant was in the office finishing his daily reports when the two FBI men came in to see the captain. Caswell called him to his office for the conference. He filled his coffee cup on the way.

Once again Greer did the talking. "We've learned Roma and Freed turned in their rental car and boarded a flight to Anchorage. I had men take pictures to the ticket counter and show them around. We came up with two phony names on a flight terminating in Calgary, Alberta, Canada. The Mounties are checking on them there. I suspect they boarded another flight there under other names. These guys have connections if they can get passports and identification using this many names."

"I understand their boss, Salvatore Roselli, is a big deal in the east coast mafia. Passports and ID's would be business as usual for them," commented Captain Caswell.

"You're right there, Captain. The point of this is that your witness is probably safe for the time being. Something or someone put them wise to us looking for them. I can't give you any guarantee, but I think you can relax a little."

"How sure are you that replacements aren't already in place, Agent Greer?" asked Bill. "After all, Alan and I have already lost one witness and we have no intention of losing another."

"Like I said, we can't give you any guarantees," said Greer.

"What you're telling me is you're leaving town and we're on our own. You're telling me that you won't accept any of the responsibility for her safety." Gant had anger in his voice and on his face. "That seems to be your M.O. You put Phelps here and left him to his own fate. You people don't take very good care of the people who helped you. Personally I wouldn't give you a plug nickel for the safety of our witness and I don't trust you or your agency to give us any information that would help us. I think you have a callous disregard for the life of anyone who isn't a card-carrying member of the FBI. Now if you'll excuse me I have police work to do. Go back to your Anchorage office and wait for your promotion. My partner and I will handle it from here."

With that he stood and marched out of the office, leaving the captain as well as the two agents sitting there with their mouths open. He went to his own office and closed the door. Ten minutes later the captain called him to his office.

"What made you unload on those feds like that? We have to work with them."

"Sorry, Cap, but I've had it with their attitude. They don't treat witnesses like people, only tools to get what they need to make a case. They proved it with Stanley Phelps and confirmed it with the "I wash my hands of it" they are showing with Leila Hunter. I'm sorry, but I'm retired and you can fire me if you want. I'm not cow-towing to them. They're jerks." Gant was still angry.

"I'm not going to fire you, mostly because I agree with you, but when you finish this case you'll go back to being retired and go fishing. I have to stay here and investigate every new case that comes across my desk. Some of those cases will require that I work with the FBI. You just made that a lot more difficult for me." The captain was always a fair and honest supervisor, but felt handicapped by the part-time attitude of his employee. "Like it or not you just cost yourself a friend at the FBI, one who may have helped you in the future. I realize you're still feeling some guilt after the girl was killed in Newark, but we both know these things happen sometimes. None of us is perfect. You have to forget it for now and concentrate on what's important, keeping this witness safe. We will do that with or without the help of the FBI."

"I'm sorry if I embarrassed you, Cap. I guess if I'm not fired I'd better go tell Alan what's happening. Maybe we can both get a night's sleep now."

"Go cool off and come back when you feel better."

Gant left the office and drove to where Alan was sitting in his now sweltering car. He piled into the car with his partner, leaving the door open for fresh air. "I've got some news, Partner. I just ticked off the FBI and the Captain. The feds say Vito and Freed have gone. They turned in their rental car and caught a flight out of Kenai. They flew out of Anchorage to Calgary and have disappeared. Everyone seems to think Leila is safe now. I sort of told the FBI guys I didn't like their assessment or them. That kind of ticked off the captain. I thought he'd fire me, but he didn't. At any rate, Leila should be safe for a little while and we can get a little rest. Want to go fishing?"

"The ever irascible Bill Gant," Alan couldn't help laughing. "I wish I could have been there for that one," he laughed again. "Let's go inside and give her the good news and have a glass of iced tea." Alan was still chuckling as he exited the vehicle.

The two men sat on stools at the counter. All the booths and tables were filled. Leila waited on them, bringing them their tea.

"Can you take a smoke break when we finish our tea?" asked Gant.

"I think so, what's happening?" she asked.

"We'll tell you out there," replied Gant.

She reached into her apron pocket and produced something in a small box. "This is the bracelet Stan gave me. I don't know what you can find, but when you finish I would like to have it back."

Alan and Bill sat on the stools, watching the foot traffic coming and going while they sipped the sweet iced tea. Several minutes later she walked past them and nodded for them to follow. She went out the back door while they exited the front and walked to the back of the café.

"I haven't got much time, we're really busy," she said.

"We won't take a lot of time, Leila, we just wanted to tell you the men looking for you have left town. The FBI is on their tail and they ran. We think you're safe for the time being, but the man behind this will surely send someone else. Please keep your guard up," reported Bill.

"I guess that's good news, thanks." She took another drag from the cigarette and dropped it into a coffee can beside the door.

"Thanks for the bracelet. I'll see to it that you get it back. Remember, if you see anyone or anything you think is suspicious call us right away. We won't be far away."

She stepped up and kissed his cheek. "You have both been wonderful, thank you." With that she stepped back inside to return to work.

Alan was smiling when Bill turned back to him. "I think she's sweet on you, Partner."

Bill grinned back at him, "Worse things could happen," he said.

"Let's go to the office and take a look at that bracelet."

Back in their office they found a large magnifying glass to use while inspecting every mark, crack and cranny on the bracelet. It was silver with Alaska native designs inlaid in polished copper. It was a beautiful piece of jewelry. The outside was truly a work of art, but they found nothing to indicate anything else. The inside had been engraved with Leila's original name 'Lucile Mc Dermot' in block lettering. Again, nothing seemed unusual. The only other mark was a number engraved inside the bracelet. Alan and Bill discussed the number and concluded it was a pattern number or something similar. The two investigators studied the object for more than an hour before admitting defeat.

Finally Pulis looked at his partner and asked, "Say, Bill, do you remember that old guy we met over at Kasilof? The one who claimed he had been in the OSS during the Second World War."

"Do you mean Ole Olafson of the CIA?" asked Bill.

"Yeah, that's him. He told us he'd been breaking codes during the war and did a lot of work for the CIA. Why not take this out to him and see if he can tell us what's on it?"

Both men boarded Bill Gant's car for the twenty mile drive to Kasilof, a small fishing village south of Soldotna on the Kasilof River. Evidence of homes in the village is hidden in the trees and off the main road. Ole lived in a small cabin near the mouth of the river and close to the beach and the salt water. The smell of Alder smoke greeted them when they arrived. Ole was smoking fish. He said he didn't eat it himself, but gave it to friends and relatives, of which both lists were getting short. Now approaching the age of ninety, he led an active lifestyle. He was lean and tanned. His muscles showed he continued to use them for hard work. He sat on the front porch when the troopers arrived.

"Howdy, boys, what brings you all the way out here?" he asked in a cheerful tone.

"Hello there, Ole, did you think we'd forgotten you?" asked Pulis.

"Nah, I knew the both of you were retired now and too busy for old fogeys like me. Come in out of the mosquitos." He stood and walked into the cabin with Bill and Alan following.

He took a seat at the kitchen table and motioned for them to do the same. "What is it you boys have on your mind?" he asked.

"We need the help of an expert code man, Ole, and you were the first one we thought of," Bill was holding the box with the bracelet and handed it to the old man.

"What kind of code," he asked, furrowing his brow and donning his spectacles.

"We don't know, that's why we need you. It has to do with a case we're working," Pulis explained.

Ole looked surprised, "You guys went back to work?"

"Only for this one case, Ole, we found a body in the inlet and the trooper Gods asked us to investigate the death. The victim gave this bracelet to his girlfriend and we need to know if it's a clue to a treasure."

"Hmmpf," said Ole as he turned his gaze to the silver bauble. He reached behind him and took a tablet from the kitchen counter. He began to write, saying nothing, alternating his attention from the tablet to the bracelet. Within minutes he looked up. "Well, there it is," he said, leaning back in his chair and giving the bracelet back to Gant.

"There WHAT is?" asked Alan.

"The code you wanted. It's a bank account number for a bank in the Bahamas."

"How can you tell all that? We didn't see anything except her name and a pattern number or something."

"C'mon, Bill, give me some credit for knowing my business. That's not a pattern number. It's a bank. Offshore banks are numbered and the number, 641, is the number of the bank where this account is held. I don't know exactly which bank, but the 6 means the Bahamas. The other two numbers, 41, is the individual bank the account is in."

"How the devil did you figure that out so quickly?" asked Pulis.

"Actually, Alan, the bank number gave me the key to the code. It's a simple code really."

"How did you know this was a bank number?" asked Alan.

"I have an account in the Bahamas. Not in this particular bank, but in that country."

Bill laughed, "We won't ask you about your account, Ole. What about the rest of the code?"

"Like I said, it's a simple code. He just took the name and substituted numbers for letters. He didn't even offset or confuse the numbers. He just listed them as they are; A is 1, B is 2, and so on. A bank will let you use any number that suits you if you want your own number. In this case it looks like that's what he did. I wrote the number on the pad. You can have that."

"Ole, you're a whiz. This really helps us. We owe you a big one. How about we take you fishing with us when we finish this investigation?" Gant spoke and Pulis nodded agreement.

"That would be great, thanks, boys." Ole was pleased with the offer, "Say, would you guys like some fresh smoked red salmon to take with you?"

"Maybe a little bit, Ole, thanks."

The small paper bag of fish made the inside of Bill's car smell fishy, smoky and wonderful. Both men chewed the freshly smoked sticks on the drive back to the office. Now came the task of deciding what to do with the information they had uncovered.

Chapter 16

I t is difficult to talk while chewing fresh, warm squaw candy. Because of the oil in the fish the flavor of the smoked fish is much richer when made from freshly caught Sockeye Salmon, also known as Red Salmon. The mouth-watering treat, especially when fresh from the smoker, is chewy, salty and delicious. Speaking while eating it will cause a person to drool down his chin. For this reason there was little said during most of the 20 mile ride back to the office. With less than three miles to go Alan wiped his chin and commented, "Man, that's good stuff," he wiped his hands and chin again. Bill had his mouth full and only nodded. "I've been thinking, Bill, it might be a good idea to keep news of breaking the code quiet for now. Vito and his partner are gone for now, but Sal is sure to send someone else before long. Those guys seem to have a way to find out what we know. I think we should keep this to ourselves for now. Leila will be in enough danger without giving the bad guys another reason to attack her. I'd hate to be responsible for the death of another witness."

Bill Gant was wiping his hands and face with a piece of paper towel from the bag of fish. "I hadn't thought that far ahead, but I have to agree with you. We need to talk about it. Hang on, I'm going to stop and get a 7UP, do you want something?"

"Sure, a Diet Coke," said Alan. Bill stopped the car and went inside the Quick Stop, returning a minute later with the sodas, handing one to his partner.

"The more I think about it the more I agree with you," commented Gant. "I think you're right about Sal Roselli sending someone else. My guess is he's already on the way here. We need to do something else with Leila to keep her safe."

"I've been thinking about that, too, Partner. How would you feel about an all-expense-paid vacation? Someplace warm where the fishing is good and dinner dress is informal. Somewhere far away and no one knows nor cares who you are. And to make it better for you, how about you take a gorgeous, dark-haired, long-legged beauty with you?" asked Alan.

"What the heck are you talking about, Alan?"

"There are a couple of things. First we need to go to the bank in the Bahamas and get whatever is to be found in that bank account. You can't do it and I can't do it, but the account will be in the name of Lucile Mc Dermot. She can go to the bank without any questions being asked. Taking her there would keep her under surveillance and safe as well as gather a crucial piece of evidence against the mafia and Sal Roselli. I can stay here and keep an eye out for the hit-man we know is coming."

"Do you think we can convince the captain this is a good idea?" asked a skeptical Gant.

"Of course, he can't possibly turn down one of his ace investigators and refuse to ensure the safety of a key witness in a murder case."

"I didn't know you were such a convincing liar, Alan. This is a side of you I've never seen before. I like the way you think, but will he pay for the junket?"

Alan chuckled a little, "I'll bet he can talk those nice people at the FBI into paying for the whole thing since it'll help close their case in New Jersey. You know how nice and helpful they are. Why, I'll bet they'll pay you per diem and authorize a five-star hotel for the two of you."

"OK, Ok, you convinced me, but for the safety of our witness I think we'd better keep all of this quiet until after we return. I'll pay the expenses in the hopes I'll get it back someday. I don't have the unbridled faith in the FBI that you seem to have." Bill wasn't entirely convinced they could pull this off, but it was worth a try.

Alan reached into the paper bag for another piece of fish, "Now all we have to do is convince the Captain," said Alan.

"You won't have any trouble with that part, Alan. You convinced me."

When they returned to the office they went directly to Captain Caswell's office and closed the door behind them. Caswell listened as the two investigators spelled out the entire scenario. They told him about the bracelet and the inscription inside. They told him about the bank number engraved inside. They explained why it was necessary to take the bracelet to Ole Olafson and the use of his skills as a cryptographer. With detail after detail they laid out the case and their fears of another hit-man being sent to get Leila Hunter. They took turns telling the story, item by item, but in the end it was Alan who delivered the punch line. Before hitting him with the request Alan held out a paper bag and offered the captain a piece of tasty smoked red salmon. He accepted and leaned back in his office chair to chew and listen to the trooper/conmen, using a handkerchief to dab at the saliva dribbling over his chin.

He wanted to urge them to speed up, but the chewy morsel in his mouth prevented it. He just nodded.

Alan continued, "What we're proposing, Captain, is for Bill to take Leila and make the trip to the Bahamas. Let her claim the bank account. We don't know what's going to be in there, but it may contain documentation about Sal Roselli's operation in New Jersey. There may be money in the account, too, but since it was taken outside our jurisdiction and is located outside our jurisdiction, as long as she doesn't bring it into our jurisdiction she can have it. The FBI may see it differently, but as I see it, no one has reported it stolen. Since it is probably money gained by illegal means, extortion, drugs, protection, and who-knows-what else, it is not germane to our murder case." He paused a moment, giving Caswell a chance to wipe his chin and break into the conversation.

"What did the two of you do prior to becoming troopers, sell snake oil or vacuum cleaners?" the captain wiped his mouth again. "I don't have the money to send you and a girlfriend on an all-expense paid vacation to the Bahamas. I'm not the FBI. They may pay for the trip if you bring back evidence to convict Roselli, but we can't afford it." The captain laughed, "Nice sales pitch, though."

"We're not done yet, Cap," continued Alan, "We'll pay for the trip. What we need from you is permission to keep Bill, not me, just Bill, on the payroll while he's gone. That way if he meets any opposition from Immigrations, FBI, Bahamian Police, or Bahamian Banking officials, he can say he is representing the Alaska State Troopers. It really won't cost that much in the end, because we're going to have to watch Leila on a 24 hour basis anyway. There's no telling what Bill will run into and he needs to be able to flash his trooper shield if necessary."

"What does the witness have to say about this?" asked the captain.

"We haven't talked with her about it, but since she is in danger if she stays here, I think she'll be agreeable. After all she stands to come out of it with some cash."

Captain Caswell turned to Gant, "What have you got to say about all this, Bill? I haven't heard one word from you."

"He gave me the same argument, Cap. I couldn't think of a way to say no. It's a good idea, even if it did come from Alan. I know this is a gamble, but it's the logical step in the investigation. This is a murder case and we need to follow up on all leads. This is just an unusual case. Look at the trip to the east coast, for instance. It was a long-shot, but it told us who our victim really was and gave us a probable reason for his death. It was useful. I think this is the same thing. We should do it."

"OK, you two get out of my office. I'll call the Colonel and run it by him. If he says it's OK I'll arrange it. But, don't get your hopes up." The captain dismissed them while wondering if he could be as convincing with his boss as these two had been with theirs.

In their office the two investigators were writing their findings in the logs. They had worked for more than an hour when Alan stood to stretch his back. "We are going to have to log the bracelet into evidence, you know. Leila will be unhappy with that, but the way it stands, it is evidence."

"Yeah, I know. I'll let you explain that to her," Bill said, grinning at his partner.

"Oh, no, you're the lady's man not me. You'll have to do the dirty work this time." Alan sat again, then asked Bill, "There is one piece of fish left, do you want it?"

"No, you go ahead." His desk phone rang. It was the Captain asking them to come to his office.

"You two must have pictures of the Colonel shoplifting or something. He thought your idea was worth a try. There will be some ground rules, though," the captain spent a half hour explaining the terms under which he would allow Bill and Leila to travel under official sanction of the department. "If you try to color outside the lines in any way, shape or manner, you'll lose your official status. Do you understand and agree to the terms?"

The reality of the situation was beginning to set in. He was going to be a long way from a backup. He knew his official status would only help him if he ran into an incident with another agency. The long reach of Sal Roselli was another problem. It wouldn't help him there. Bill Gant agreed and the captain continued to lay out the travel schedule. Finally Bill, with a pad full of notes said, "I think before we go any further I should ask Leila if she is willing to go along with this. She may not want any part of it."

Gant called the restaurant and waited for her to come to the phone. "Leila Hunter," she answered.

"It's Bill Gant. We have to talk with you right away, it's important. Is there any way to get away from work early?"

"I can call the afternoon girl and have her come in early, if it's that important."

"It is. Do it, please. We'll be out back waiting and follow you home."

"It'll take her about a half hour to get here and I can leave then."

It took a little longer, but the relief girl finally showed and Leila came out of the restaurant, stopping for a short smoke on the way to her car. Bill and Alan followed her home, entering the apartment building behind her. Inside she closed her door and asked, "What in the world is this all about?"

Bill Gant was the one to explain. "We want you to take a leave of absence or vacation from your work. I want you to come to the Bahamas with me. We were able to find a coded account number on the bracelet you gave us. We have it in the evidence locker now. What we need from you is to go with me and claim the bank account. In all likelihood there'll also be a safety deposit box listed. We think there's evidence in the box that will put Salvatore Roselli away for life. If that happens, you'll never be threatened by him again. We think there's another attempt to be made on you in the very near future. We're trying to prevent that from happening. If you don't go Alan will be here to protect you while I'm gone. If you do go you stand to be the owner of a large sum of money that you'll never be able to bring into the United States."

"You want me to quit my job and run off to the Bahamas on the premise there may something in a bank account there that may be in my name and a safety deposit box that may be there with my name on it. That seems to be a pretty large leap of faith on my part. I've already lost my fiancé and now you want me to stick my neck back into the same noose? I'm going to have to think that one over."

"Leila, I understand your hesitation, but we think it's the best way to keep you safe. We can't make you come with me, but we need your help. If we get what we're looking for it'll convict Sal Roselli, Vito Roma, who probably killed Stan, and a lot of others. I have no idea how much money is in the numbered account, but it's sure to be substantial. Like I said, it's not likely anyone will challenge your ownership of the cash as long as you don't bring it into the U.S. You could be a very rich lady."

"Can you come back in an hour or so?" Leila asked. "I need to take a shower and think about it."

"Unfortunately we need an answer right away. Take your shower and think about it. We'll come back in a little while."

"Do you think she'll go along with it?" asked Alan.

"It's hard to tell, but I hope she does." Bill had his notebook in his hand making notes while Alan drove. "I need to find my passport."

An hour later the two troopers were back at the apartment. They knocked on the door and waited. At first they thought Leila had left, but finally she opened the door and allowed them inside.

"I've been thinking about what you said and I'm having a difficult time making up my mind. I've thought about it and realized that it may be the only way to catch the people who killed Stan. I've tried to put him out of my mind, but he'll always be with me. I don't care about the money, I can always find a job, but if there's a chance this could lead to Stan's killer I'll do it. How much time do I have to get ready?"

"I'm going back to the office now to find out," said Bill. "As soon as I know I'll call you."

"Will I be going to work tomorrow?" she asked.

"I don't think so, Leila," said Bill. "I'm only guessing, but I think we'll be leaving tomorrow or the next day. I'll call as soon as I know."

"I'll be waiting," she said.

Gant and Pulis returned to the office and began to finalize the travel plans.

Chapter 17

Captain Caswell was waiting for them when they returned. "Come into my office, I have some news for you." They followed him hoping for some good news. The captain asked Bill to close the door behind him and for the two of them to be seated. There was an open folder on his desk.

"I don't know how you two do it. The Colonel has authorized your trip. You can pick up your tickets at the Alaska Airlines desk in Anchorage. There will be two tickets, one for you, Bill, and one for Leila Hunter. There will be an envelope there with a state credit card to be used for your expenses. Keep all your receipts. If you buy any sunglasses and flip-flops they will be billed back to you. Leila Hunter will have all her expenses paid while she is with you, however she will not receive any reimbursement for wages. "

Alan looked at Bill and shook his head. The two had not counted on this kind of cooperation by the head trooper.

"You're booked on Alaska Airlines flight 231 to Denver. There, you'll change to American Airlines to Atlanta and on to Miami. You'll have to buy a ticket on the commuter flight from Miami to Nassau, but they fly every hour or so. There are reservations for the two of you at a hotel in Nassau. It's supposed to be somewhere in the vicinity of the bank you are going to visit. You'll fly out of Kenai on the first flight tomorrow morning. This folder has all your schedules and directions. The rest is up to you."

"All this is a lot more than I expected, Cap. Thanks for all the help. I guess I should go home and pack, but first I have to see Leila and let her know we're leaving in the morning. Alan can drive us to the airport."

"One other thing, Bill," Captain Caswell opened a desk drawer and removed a manila envelope. "I've fronted some cash for incidental expenses, taxi fares and the like. Don't spend any of it in the casino. I want an accounting of the monies spent out of the envelope." His tone became somber, "I want you to be careful, Bill. You won't know who'll be watching you, you won't know who you can trust and you won't know who may be trying to get whatever information you find away from you. I guess what I'm saying is don't take any chances."

"Thanks, Cap, I know the risks. I'll call you when I can to let you know what's happening. Since I won't have a weapon I'll be a lot more cautious." They shook hands. Bill picked up the folder and envelope on the desk, saluted and left the office.

"I'm going by Leila's place and tell her we'll pick her up early in the morning," he told Alan. I'll buy breakfast at Louie's. I'll have a lot of the captain's money in my pocket."

"I'll finish my daily reports before leaving today. I'll see you in the morning. Good luck, Partner."

On his way to see Leila he tried to make a mental list of the things he needed for the trip. He stopped at the apartment building and climbed to the second floor. She answered his knock and let him inside.

"What did you find out?" asked Leila.

"Pack your bag. We leave early in the morning. Alan will drive us to the airport and I'm buying breakfast in Kenai. Be sure to have your passport handy. We have reservations at a hotel in Nassau for three nights. That should give us at least one day to enjoy the sights."

"I hate to say this, but I'm scared." She was staring at the floor.

"We'll be just fine, Leila," Bill said in a calm voice, "no one knows when or where we're going, including the FBI. So, unless someone recognizes us along the way there should be no trouble. Relax. How often do you get to go all-expenses-paid for three days in the Bahamas?" He patted her hand to reassure her.

"OK, Bill, I'll be ready in the morning."

When Alan came to get him in the early morning he had a small suitcase and a carry-on similar to a laptop computer case. The carry-on contained all the papers and files he was taking with him. He checked his shirt pocket to confirm he carried his passport. He locked the door and stopped to review his actions. Had he forgotten anything? 'I guess not,' he thought. He put his bags in the trunk of the car, closed the lid and climbed into the passenger seat.

"Good morning, Alan, don't you wish you were going instead of me"

"Not on your life. I like being home. Bring me a souvenir. Remember, you're buying breakfast."

"How come you sound so grumpy this morning?"

"I hate getting up early, I hate eating breakfast at five in the morning and most of all I'm worried about you being out there without me or any other backup." said Pulis.

"That's so sweet of you, Alan, I didn't know you cared that much."

"Seriously, Bill, I'm worried about you going on this trip. I just have a bad feeling about it."

"I'm the one who should be worried. You'll have to worry about who Sal Roselli is sending next. The truth is I think they're probably on the way right now. You're the one in danger. Keep your eyes open, Pard."

Alan looked at Bill and nodded, "Just stay in touch."

Leila was watching out the window and waved when they pulled up out front. Like Bill she had a carryon and checked bag. Unlike Bill, her luggage matched. The apartment light went out and a moment later she appeared at the door. Bill stepped out of the vehicle and opened the trunk where he added her bags. He held the front passenger door open for her, said good morning and closed it behind her. He piled into the back seat and they set off for Kenai.

There was little conversation while they ate. It seemed all the diners were suffering some apprehension. Bill picked up the tab and left a tip for the girl. It was only a few blocks to the air terminal where Leila and Bill took their luggage from the trunk.

"We'll see you the first of next week," said Bill, shaking the hand of his partner.

"Bye, Alan," called Leila.

"Don't let him get arrested outside of the United States," Alan replied.

Turning back to Bill Gant he whispered, "Watch your back, Partner."

Gant nodded, "See you in a few days. I'll be talking to you."

Bill and Leila went inside and checked in at the ticket counter. It was only minutes until they boarded.

In Anchorage it was necessary for them to carry their own luggage to the Alaska Airline counter. As promised there was a packet waiting for them. They checked one bag each, found the tickets in the envelope and asked for their seat number. Bill was surprised when they were booked in first class.

"Someone by the name of Pulis called and upgraded you to first class seating," reported the ticket agent. "Your tickets authorize you to by-pass security and go directly to the boarding area. Have a nice flight to Denver."

"Thank you," Bill said to the agent. He turned to Leila, "That was really nice of the old dog."

"What was?" asked Leila.

"Alan upgraded us to first class."

"Oh, wow, that was nice. I have a problem with my long legs in coach. I assume you have the same problem."

"Yep, I do, too." The two passengers stepped to the TSA officer at the gate and were escorted through the security screening area. They found their designated gate and waited. Leila saw a small kiosk selling books and went in to browse. She bought a book, a John Grisham novel, and opened it to the first page.

Gant engrossed himself in the case summary included in the packet he carried. The outline was furnished by the FBI and summarized the operation run by Salvatore Roselli. The list was extensive reaching into every state on the east coast with exception to New York. That state has its own powerful operation headed by an even more powerful commander. According to the report Roselli had operated the trucking company as a legitimate enterprise until he was approached by a mafia goon who burned his warehouse and killed two of his men. Roselli went to war with the New Jersey mafia. He became more vicious than those he was opposing. It is said he murdered more than 50 people in his climb to the top of the mafia hierarchy in New Jersey. A high percentage of the men working for him are ex-cons with long rap sheets. Vito Roma headed the list. He had been arrested several times in connection with murders, but never convicted. He was convicted of arson of a warehouse owned by a rival, but was released after winning his appeal.

Roselli's organization was involved in the drug trade; meth, heroin, cocaine, marijuana, synthetic drugs and date-rape drugs. They were involved in extortion and shakedown scams which they enforced with physical harm to resistors. Roselli conspired with the local longshoreman's union as well as the Stevedores and Teamsters Unions to control the movement of all freight and goods in New Jersey. He is a very powerful and ruthless man.

An announcement was made by the flight attendant to stow all items for landing in Denver. Once on the ground they received the same escort they had been given in Anchorage. Leila and Bill were escorted to the VIP lounge where they waited for almost an hour for the TSA officer to return and take them to the boarding gate. An airline employee immediately showed them to a seat on the airplane, again first class. The flight to Atlanta was half as long as the one from Alaska, but Bill was becoming stiff and tired by the time they landed.

Another TSA agent met them at the gate and escorted them to another VIP lounge, informing them he would return when their plane was at the loading gate. This time the wait was short, only a few minutes. The plane from Atlanta to Miami was much smaller than the ones on previous flights, but the air was smooth and except for the lack of leg room, it was comfortable.

In Miami they were met at the gate by a man in a pilot's uniform. He asked them to follow him to another boarding gate. He led them to a downstairs area and informed them their luggage was being brought from the American Airline Terminal.

The three of them waited in the small area in front of a door marked GATE 41 A. Minutes later a twin engine turboprop commuter plane was taxied to the loading area. A small tug pulled a trailer to the plane and Gant could see them loading their luggage on the plane. When that chore was completed the man in the pilot uniform led them to the plane. The pilot who taxied to the gate left the plane and the one who had led them from the other terminal removed his coat and climbed into the cockpit. The young, tanned and beautiful, flight attendant closed the cabin door. She walked to where they were seated and said, "I'll bring refreshments as soon as we are over the water. If you need anything, just press this button. Please fasten your seatbelts." She smiled and walked to the rear of the plane and took a seat.

Bill turned to Leila and asked, "How do you like traveling in a private plane?"

Leila only smiled and looked out the window. An hour later they landed in Nassau and taxied to a private hangar. No one had checked their passports. They were led through the hangar to an office and the front door where a limo was waiting to take them to their hotel.

Gant signed the register for two rooms and a bellman led them to fourth floor rooms, collected a tip and went back to the lobby. Bill was arranging his papers from the briefcase when Leila knocked on the door. "Come in, it's open," he said.

"Well, we made it this far," commented Leila.

"I was just looking through my paperwork and making a mental list of things to do tomorrow. Be sure to bring your passport in the morning. You'll need it to verify you identification at the bank. From now on we're flying blind. I don't have any names and have no idea what the process will be. Dress as a business person tomorrow and we'll make our pitch at the bank in the morning."

"I'll be ready, Bill. I can't help thinking about Stan coming here and setting all this up. It just seems so out of character for him. He was a bookkeeper, not a criminal. I don't understand any of it."

"For what it's worth, I don't think he was a criminal either. I think he learned what he had been ignoring all the time he worked for Roselli. When it looked like he might get involved so deeply Roselli wouldn't let him out, he planned his own exit. He contacted the FBI and began to give them information in exchange for safety. What he apparently didn't tell the FBI or Roselli was that he was setting up his own retirement account. He set it up in your name which makes me think he did all this for love, for you and him to live happily ever-after. I don't know how Roselli found him. He probably has an informant working for the FBI. I think he had an insurance policy in a safety deposit box; evidence against Roselli and his organization. I believe he thought having this information would keep him safe from Roselli. In reality it was probably the thing that made Sal keep looking for him."

"I just want to get this over with and go home." Leila looked at him with sad eyes, "Don't get me wrong, Bill, I'm enjoying the trip with you. I like you a lot and when all this is over perhaps we can see each other sometime."

"I'd like that, Leila, but it can't happen while the case is still open. It would jeopardize the outcome and neither of us wants that."

"You're right, Bill, but would you mind taking me to dinner? I'm hungry."

Chapter 18

The following morning, under a bright blue sky, Bill Gant wearing a white shirt, gray slacks and a light weight blue blazer met Leila in the lobby. She was wearing a white silk blouse, white slacks and white sandals. Her hair was long and pulled back at the sides. The two walked into the sunshine, waiting for a cab the concierge had called for them. There was a smell of tropical flowers and salt sea air. Bill was forced to squint into the morning sun, but Leila had a pair of Foster Grants in her hand.

Gant was carrying the briefcase he had brought from Alaska. An older Mercedes with a Taxi sign in the door stopped in front. Bill opened the door for Leila and they both sat in the rear seat. The young, pleasant, driver asked their destination.

"Central Bank of Bahamas, on Market Street," he replied.

"Do you think there'll be any trouble getting what we want?" asked Leila.

"I think they'll want to verify our identity, but, if our decoding is correct, it should be OK."

The drive was pleasant. The streets were busy, but clean. The people they saw were a happy looking group of mixed races in bright color dress. As they passed the waterfront there were several large yachts seen anchored off shore. Driving through one neighborhood they saw well-manicured lawns, palm trees and neatly trimmed houses.

"Is this your first trip to Nassau?" asked the driver.

"Yes, we just arrived last evening. It's beautiful" replied Leila.

"We are a happy nation. I hope you enjoy your stay."

Minutes later they arrived in front of an impressive bank building. The large bronze signage in front declared the name. Bill paid the driver with U.S. money, opened the door and assisted Leila as she climbed out. The two walked up the walk and into the lobby of the large bank. Bill looked around to see where he needed to go, but had no clue. To his right was a row of glass cubicles with a clerk in each one. He stepped into the first and asked for some help. The young man behind the desk said he would be happy to assist them.

"We're here to locate a numbered account in the name of my client, Miss Lucile Mc Dermot. Can you tell me how we should go about doing that?"

"Of course, I may be able to help you. Please come in and have a seat, both of you." Once they were seated he turned to his computer. "Please spell the name for me."

Leila obliged. The clerk tapped the letters into the machine and instantly grew a frown. "I'm sorry, but I will not be able to help you after all." He stood and said, "Please come with me. I'll show you to the office of Mr. Jarreau, our bank manager." He led them across the lobby to an office where a secretary sat behind a large teak desk. "These nice folks have an account here that can only be accessed by Mr. Jarreau. Will you please tell him they are here?"

"Of course, please have a seat and I will tell him you are here." She stepped from behind her desk and went to the door at the rear of the room. Gant noticed the only reading material on the coffee table was the Wall Street Journal. A moment later she came back and said, "Mr. Jarreau will see you now, please come with me."

The office was the nicest office with the most expensive fixtures Gant had ever seen. The secretary ushered them to large upholstered chairs in front of a giant, hand-carved desk. The man behind it was in his mid to late 50s. He was slightly rotund and well dressed. "How do you do?" he greeted them. "My name is Carlton Jarreau and I am the manager of the bank's numbered accounts. My receptionist didn't take your names because you are here in regard to a numbered account and some of our clients prefer to keep their identities private."

"That is not our case," stated Gant. "I am Bill Gant and this is the owner of record on the account, Lucile Mc Dermot. As identification, she will show you two passports. The reason for this is that she has recently changed her name. I am sure you are familiar with such things."

"Of course, may I see the passports, Miss Mc Dermot? And I will need the number on the account."

She gave him both her new and old passport along with a card taken from the hotel with the number written on the back. The banker studied the pictures and information and gave her passports back to her. "Thank you, Miss Hunter." He turned to the computer and typed the number 12 21 3 9 12 5 13 3 4 5 18 13 15 20. The entry prompted some other entries, but once done a list of items came on the screen. "Ah," said the banker as he picked up the telephone to call his receptionist, "Bring me file number 11,296." He hung up the phone and continued to read the screen. "My information says you have $9,631,511.89 in U.S. Dollars in your account. Is that amount correct?"

Gant looked at Leila and back at the banker. "I'm sure it is, Mr. Jarreau. We have no plans to move the money at this time."

"We appreciate your confidence in our bank, Mr. Gant. I am waiting for my receptionist to bring me a file folder from the vault. My computer says you also have a safety deposit box listed under your name. Since the transactions have all been done by wire we still hold the client key. It is filed in the vault for safety reasons."

"Thank you for your caution," replied Gant.

"Can I get you some refreshments, iced tea perhaps?"

"Oh, no thank you."

"Since you are leaving the account with the bank, I will be giving you several booklets you can use to guide you through future transactions with the bank. It will be very simple. I will be giving you an identification code number which you can use to verify your identity when doing business with the bank. I urge you to keep this code number secret. You will be able to move money into or out of the account by identifying yourself with this number. You will be able to make these transactions by telephone, fax, bank draft, wire transfer or any other legal means. I must warn you that the U.S. Government will be contacting you if any money is transferred into the United State. Tax considerations, you know."

The receptionist tapped on the door and entered. "The file, Mr. Jarreau," she said as she laid the file on his desk.

"Thank you Alice," he said without looking up. She left the office without stopping.

Jarreau opened the file folder, which was sealed. Inside there was a large manila envelope which contained another envelope. This one he handed to Leila. She opened it and found a letter and a key to a safety deposit box.

"If you wish to open the safety deposit box at this time I will have someone assist you."

"Thank you Mr. Jarreau, you have been very helpful. We may want to open the box if you can give Leila a few minutes to read her letter and make up her mind. Can we have a few minutes?" asked Gant.

"Certainly, you may use my office. I'll go do a couple of things in the bank and return. If you need anything, just open the door and tell Alice."

Jarreau left the office. Leila was reading the letter she had been given. There were tears running down her sweet face. Several minutes later she wiped her tears and turned to Gant. "You were right, Bill. He was scared. He said he thought Sal Roselli was about to make some changes in his organization and he was to be one of them. Stan gathered ten million dollars from several bank accounts. The accounts were mostly outside the U.S. and no one seemed to notice. He wire transferred the cash here to this bank under my name. He says the safety deposit box contains enough evidence to send Sal Roselli away for life. He wanted to keep me away from Roselli and his gang. You were right about something else, too. He did love me." She was sobbing now.

"We have to make a couple of decisions right now, Leila. Are you going to allow me to have the evidence in the box?" asked Gant.

"Yes, if it will put Stan's killers away." She spoke through the tears, doing her best to stop them.

"OK, another thing. How much cash do you want to take out of the account right now?" he asked.

"I don't think I'll need any of it. I'll decide later what to do."

"Alright, let's open the box and see where we stand."

"OK, Bill, call Alice." Leila was wiping the tears with a handkerchief when Jarreau walked in.

"Are you all right, Miss Hunter?" he asked.

"Oh, yes, just a little emotional at the moment." She dabbed her eyes once more. "Is it possible to see the safety deposit box now?"

"Of course, you will have to come to the vault with your key, but you can bring the box back to this office if you wish. Come with me."

The trio marched toward the rear of the bank, around a stairwell and behind the teller booths. At the rear of the building there was a very large vault with a gigantic steel door. A guard was posted outside the vault door and another inside. Jarreau escorted them inside. The guard followed them to the number Jarreau had requested at which point the guard produced the bank key to the box and asked Leila to insert her key in the other lock. Together they opened the door. The guard lifted the heavy box out of the vault wall and placed it on a table in the center of the room. Gant had brought his briefcase with him and placed it on the table with the box. Jarreau and the guard stepped back toward the door and waited while Leila inserted her key in the single lock on the box. It opened. Inside there were two large ledgers, a file filled with documents and letters. It also contained a large stack of U.S. currency. Gant counted the bundles and estimated the hoard at $10,000. Without reading the documents, he began to place the papers inside his briefcase. He stacked the bundles of $100 bills on top of the documents and closed it with the strong zipper.

He was about to put the box back in its place when Leila stopped him. She reached inside her purse and took out her old passport and placed it in the box. Gant saw her actions and nodded his approval.

Leila called to Jarreau, "Mr. Jarreau, I think I will be keeping this safety deposit box for the time being. Is that permissible?"

"Of course, Miss Hunter, I'll have Alice make out the forms for you to sign."

The guard led them out of the vault and Jarreau led them back to his office where she signed all the papers for the bank and picked up the packet telling her how to handle her numbered account with Central Bank of Bahamas. Alice called them a cab for their return to the hotel. Neither of them spoke the entire trip. Back in Gant's room Leila sank into a large chair and gave a huge sigh.

"I can't believe we did it," she gasped.

"You are a very rich woman, Leila, but you can't take it back to the U.S. or someone in the government will be asking a lot of questions and once they learn how much money you have they will want to claim it. The money in the safety deposit box isn't enough to get anyone's attention but don't get too crazy or there will be someone wanting to take it away." Gant knew she had no real claim to the money in the account, but neither did Roselli.

"I'm going to read this stuff from the box and then call Alan. We have most of the day left and two more nights paid for in the hotel, why not enjoy it?" Bill said, feeling guilty, but enjoying the thoughts of a couple of days to relax.

"Will it be all right?" said Leila. "Can we stay two more days with nothing to do but enjoy it?"

"When I call Alan I'll tell him we are going to be on the flights as originally scheduled. Yeah, we can take a couple of days."

Chapter 19

"It's about time you called me," greeted Alan when Bill Called. "I was beginning to think you'd forgotten me and decided to stay in the sunny south. How are you doing, Partner?"

"Better than expected, Alan. We went to the bank this morning and were treated like royalty. There was a safety deposit box with a lot of ledgers, documents and minutes of a lot of Roselli's meetings. I haven't read them all, but from what I can see there's enough to get him and some of his henchmen the death penalty. We're safe here and I think we both deserve a day off, so I plan to come back on the original flight schedule. I'm going to be carrying some very dramatic evidence with me, so I don't want a lot of people knowing my schedule. There has to be a leak somewhere that got Stanley Phelps killed. I don't want either Leila or me added to the list."

"Good thinking, Bill, I won't tell anyone, except the captain. He keeps asking if I heard from you. By the way, how are the accommodations?"

"Five Star, Alan, in more than 20 years with the troopers this is the nicest I was ever treated."

"How did you like the private flight from Miami to Bahamas? The pilot is one of Dave Kinney's transplants."

"It made me feel like Jacob Got-Bucks; I may never be the same again."

"One of the reasons we made that arrangement was to hide your final destination, in case there was a leak in some office somewhere. We did it for your safety, Partner."

"I want you to know I appreciate it and I do feel safe. We're going to take the rest of the day off and go snorkeling. We may go fishing tomorrow if I can arrange it. I think I could get to like this life. My new partner is a lot easier to look at than the one I have back in Alaska."

"Enjoy yourself, Bill, and remember 'all good things must end', I'll be glad to see you home. By the way, Agent Greer called to say there's no news about the replacement goons. They're watching the office in New Jersey as well as the airport in Anchorage."

"Is there any news about Vito Roma and Dallas Freed," asked Gant.

"Not a word. Kinney said he thinks they may be holed up in some country in South America, cooling off. Give Leila a kiss for me."

"Ain't happening, Alan. You remember my rule?"

"You never get your honey where you make your money," the two men sang out in unison.

"Stay in touch, Bill. I'll see you when you get home."

"See ya, Alan."

Gant called the concierge desk to schedule a snorkeling trip for this afternoon and a saltwater fishing trip on a charter for tomorrow. He also asked her to make reservations for dinner at the hotel.

"There's a very fine international casino not far from the hotel, if you're interested in some gambling. They have a wonderful floor show there as well."

"I had better see how tired I am when I finish the day," said Gant.

Leila looked spectacular in her two piece swim suit and beach towel as they boarded the boat for a small tour and some swimming among the reefs and fishes. "She'll be able to do this for the rest of her life if she chooses," thought Bill.

The day was all a dream for Leila. It was one fantasy after another. The snorkeling was a new experience for both of them. She enjoyed it immensely. Upon returning they took a long walk on the beach, gazing at the sea, admiring palm trees, oohing and aahing over the beauty of the homes above them on the green hills overlooking the sea.

Back in the hotel they both took a much needed nap before taking a shower and dressing for dinner. They drank Champaign, ate lobster hors d' oeuvres, the main course was exquisite Swordfish with seasoned rice. All were enjoyed along with the live chamber music played in the dining room. It was after nine when they finished dinner. They decided to forego the casino and retire for the night.

Bill tried to read some of the information in the file he had taken from the bank, but was too tired and too preoccupied with thoughts of Leila and how much he had enjoyed his day with her.

At ten the following morning a local picked them up to drive them to a pier where a small motor launch waited to take them to the charter boat moored off-shore. The boat called the Sprite was clean and well-kept. The skipper introduced himself to the new fishermen as Claude, originally from Boston. He pointed out the safety features and explained his methods of fishing. He asked if they had a preference as to the kinds of fish they were after. Both said no, just going fishing. The deckhand was a young local boy with very dark skin from working bare-chested in the burning sun.

The boat motored west for more than an hour when the skipper came down from the upper deck to set up the fishing rods and teasers he towed from the rear corners of the boat. "There's been some Blue Marlin working in this area in the past few days and I'm going to tow a wooden plug in case a Yellowfin Tuna is in the vicinity. There are a lot of Barracuda working in here also and could take the wooden plug. If it does, the deckhand will set the hook and give you the rod. If we hook up a Marlin, one of you will have to get into the fighting chair and we'll strap you in and hook the rod to the chair. I can always get another fisherman, but rods and reels are expensive," he joked.

Fishing was slow and the sun was hot. Leila spread sunscreen on her bare body parts. Two hours into the fishing the rod with the wooden plug began to strip line. Both Leila and Bill ran to the back of the boat to see what they had.

"Barracuda, Barracuda," cried the deckhand. He let it run a minute then stopped the line and gave the rod several great pumps.

Bill stepped back and ushered Leila to the rod. The deckhand handed her the rod, instructing her to pull up on the rod and to crank on the way down. Keep the line tight, he instructed.

She fought the large fish like a pro. When it came alongside the boat the deckhand donned a cotton glove with which to grab the line and bring the fish inside the boat. Everyone was excited and cheering the catch. The skipper took a picture of her and her catch while the deckhand reset the rods. The rest of the day saw several fish of different species caught. No billfish were sighted, but it had been a good day of fishing.

The sun was low when they returned to the beach and the hotel. Bill and Leila gave the fish to the skipper as a tip along with a sizable cash reward for him and his deckhand. Again they pair ate dinner at the hotel. Tonight the main course was to be Barracuda.

On the way back to the room, Bill stopped at the front desk to tell the clerk they would be checking out in the morning. "I will have everything ready, Sir. I will have the concierge order your transportation. I hope you have enjoyed your stay."

"We certainly have," said Bill as he turned to join Leila at the elevator.

The following morning Bill called the bellman to take their luggage to the front desk. He paid for both rooms and collected the receipts. The friendly desk clerk directed him to the concierge desk where the young lady said she had ordered their limo. Soon the limo driver entered and he and the bellman carried the two bags to the car. Bill tipped and thanked the bellman before getting into the backseat of the limo with Leila. The driver never asked their destination, but drove directly to the airport and dropped them at the private hangar where they had arrived days before. The driver carried the bags inside where they were met by the pilot who had brought them to Nassau. He led them to the same twin engine plane where they were greeted by the same flight attendant.

The short flight to Miami was pleasant with Leila staring at Bill most of the way. When the plane landed they were once again escorted by a TSA agent through security to another terminal and escorted to the boarding gate. Again they were pre-boarded. This treatment continued the entire trip back to Kenai.

Alan was waiting in the terminal when they arrived. They shook hands and waited for the luggage to appear on the belt. It was early evening here. They had gained four hours on the trip home. Outside the terminal, parked in the handicap zone, was Alan's trooper car. "Welcome home," he finally acknowledged.

"Glad to be back," said Gant. "Any word from the invading army?"

"None. Greer says they're keeping an eye on the airport, but they haven't seen anyone they recognized."

"Do you think we'll have to keep watch on her apartment tonight?" asked Bill.

"I'll cover it tonight. You get some rest. We'll start again tomorrow." Alan had been speaking into the rearview mirror to Bill. He turned in the seat to address Leila. "And how did 'Mr. I'm all business' treat you, Leila?"

"He treated me wonderfully. He is a perfect gentleman. I'm going to try to steal him away from you. We're going to move to exotic places and never see snow again."

"Have the two of you been smoking Bahamian Weed? I don't recognize either of you."

Both Leila and Bill laughed.

"We need to drop Leila at her apartment and I want to go to the office to put this briefcase in the evidence locker. Leila, I want you to take the bank bag out of the briefcase and keep it. We won't be needing that as evidence."

She turned in the seat to look into his eyes. "Are you sure? Is it OK?" she asked.

"It's yours, Leila, I only held it for safekeeping."

"Thank you for a wonderful trip, Bill. Will I see you tomorrow?"

"Sure," he said, smiling at her. It was becoming more difficult to be professional about this relationship.

Bill carried her bags up the stairs to her apartment and set them inside the door, but didn't go inside. "I'll see you tomorrow," he said.

Back inside the car Alan was assessing what he had seen. "Are you sure you can keep this to yourself. She's falling for you and from what I can tell the feeling is mutual."

"I never could fool you, Alan. You're right, I hope this case ends soon and I can see if she's serious. I haven't felt this way about a woman since my divorce and it's killing me to stay away from her. I feel like a school kid."

Alan was grinning and about to burst with laughter. "Believe me, Bill, you don't hide it well." He chuckled and poked a finger at Bill as he drove to the office. "Now, the important stuff. What did you learn? Is there really good evidence in here?" he asked, pointing at the briefcase between them.

"I may come in late in the morning, but you should call Agents Greer and Coleman to come down and take a look. There are minutes of meetings where Sal ordered a hit on someone. It documents burning a business in Newark because the owner wouldn't pay and it goes on and on. The ledgers document payments, both in and out, for extortion, murders, political favors and a whole list of crimes. No wonder Sal wanted Phelps dead. Some of the crimes I read about in the FBI outline are mentioned in this ledger. I think the FBI will be grateful to us forever, or until next weekend, whichever comes first. When the dust settles the goons will be gone and Leila will be safe. I don't know if any of it will prove Vito and Dallas killed Stan, but it will convict them of some other crimes and murders. In any case we'll be out of the investigating business."

"Wow, you have been a busy little cop." Alan could see his partner was exhausted, "Let's log this into evidence and I'll take you home. Get a good night's sleep and I'll see you sometime tomorrow."

"What about Leila?"asked Bill.

"Don't worry, Partner, I'll cover it tonight. Get some rest."

Chapter 20

It was nine the next morning when his phone began to jingle. Gant had just stepped out of the shower when he heard the musical tone. He checked the time and answered.

"Gant," he said gruffly.

"Do you always wake up in a bad mood?" asked FBI agent Greer.

"Oh, hi there, Greer, sorry, I had a long day yesterday. What can I do for you?"

"That's OK, Gant, I understand. I've had some of those days myself. I just called to let you know a hood by the name of Rinaldi arrived in Anchorage this morning. There's another goon with him by the name of Tony Dressler. They're both enforcers for Salvatore Roselli. We don't know for sure where they're heading, but it seems likely they're headed your way. I am sending pictures to your computer at the office."

"Thanks for the heads-up, Greer. Have you talked to Alan this morning?"

"Not yet," replied the agent.

"Well, I just returned from a very long trip and came back with a lot of interesting documentation concerning Roselli's entire operation. It was stashed by Stanley Phelps before he died. I haven't read all of it, but I know it contains names, dates, amounts and an overview of his entire operation. Did you know he grosses more than $300 million dollars a year? I know of Fortune 500 companies that don't do that much business."

"That's unbelievable. And you say you have documentation for all this?" said an amazed Greer.

"I'll be down there to meet with you this afternoon, Bill. I can't believe you've done what our office in New York has been trying to do for years."

"I'm going into the office in a few minutes and I'll run off copies of everything for you."

"At some point we are going to need the originals," explained Greer.

"I'll check with the captain and the DA. If they don't have any objections I'll keep the copies and give you the originals. That's not my decision to make."

"I didn't expect you to be so agreeable."

"I've been on vacation and I'm in a good mood. See you later." Gant hung up the phone and went back to dressing for the day.

On his way to the office he called Alan Pulis.

"Where are you Alan?" Gant asked.

"Still in the parking lot across from Leila's apartment, what's up?"

"Roselli's men are on the way. Do you want some breakfast before they get here?"

"Do you think we have time?" asked Alan.

"Greer said they had just arrived in Anchorage when he called a few minutes ago."

"I'll meet you at the diner."

They arrived at the diner at the same time. Both officers backed their cars into a parking space and walked into the restaurant together. They found a booth and ordered coffee.

"When did Greer call?" asked Alan.

"I was just as getting out of the shower when he called; he said he was sending us photos of the two hoods that came to town this morning. I have to go to the office and copy those ledgers and other papers before Greer gets here today. Will you be OK until then?"

"I'm in good shape, Bill, one of the road troopers spelled me off during the night and I got a couple of hours sleep. Do you need help with the copy work?"

"No, but I have to talk with the captain and the DA. Greer wants the originals of all the paperwork. I don't have a problem with that. There's nothing in it that I could see pertaining to our case. It does, however, nail the lid on Roselli's coffin. It contains all the facts and documentation to convict him of everything but the Lindberg kidnapping." Gant was trying to be funny, but Pulis was too tired to enjoy it.

The two finished breakfast and Pulis drove back to his post. Gant went to the office to meet with the captain. It took him and one of the receptionists almost two hours to copy all the documents. The District Attorney had given permission to send the originals of the evidence to the FBI.

Gant called Leila and asked if she would agree to go to his home and stay. He explained the new killers were on the way and he wanted her out of the apartment. She agreed and packed a bag to get her by for a few days. Gant picked her up and took her to his house while Pulis watched the empty apartment. When Gant came to get Leila he had given Pulis copies of the photos sent by Greer.

Pulis sat half asleep shortly after noon when a red rental car drove by. He compared the photos with the faces in he had seen in the car as it cruised past. He immediately notified Gant, who was on his way back to the office when he got the call. Bill spun the car around and sped to Alan's location.

"They drove past the school and on down the street. There's no outlet on the other end, so they'll have to come back this way. I've been trying to figure out how they knew where Leila lived." Alan looked puzzled.

"Maybe they don't, it's possible they're just driving around getting the lay of the land."

"Let's wait and see if they stop on the way back," commented Pulis.

"We'd better check and see if there any warrants for these Bozo's. Unless they break a law here we don't have probable cause to arrest them," said Gant.

"I wonder if Greer has anything on them?" asked Pulis.

"He's a prominent player in all those documents I brought back. Greer may have something on him." Bill dialed the federal agent's number.

"Agent Greer," he answered.

"Greer, Bill Gant, we just spotted the two guys from out of town. They're cruising on West Redoubt Avenue. They haven't broken any laws here, but we were thinking you may have outstanding warrants for them."

"As a matter of fact, Rinaldi has two federal warrants for him. I'll have to check about Dressler. If it comes down to it, I can always jail him on suspicion of suspicion. We Feds can do that, you know."

"I'm beginning to like you, Greer. Where are you now?"

"About a mile from Soldotna, I was going to your office."

"Do you know where the school is on West Redoubt?" asked Gant.

"I think so. I turn at the "Y" and left at the first street, right?"

"We're parked at the apartment building on the left just before the school. If they come back before you arrive, just follow the sound of gunfire," Gant quipped.

"Give me five minutes." Greer had flashing lights hidden inside his front grille. He flipped the switch and sped toward town. He was a half block away, his flashing lights off. When the red rental car came slowly back toward the waiting troopers Pulis pulled his car into the lane blocking their progress. Immediately Gant pulled his car to a stop behind them. Greer watched the action and sped to the location.

Pulis was first out of his vehicle, weapon drawn. "Take the keys out of the ignition and toss them onto the street and put your hands outside the vehicle," he ordered.

Gant was now out of his car with his weapon pointed at the passenger side window. "You too, Buddy, hands out the window."

There was a tense moment of pause before the car keys came flying out the driver's window. Both men complied by holding their hands out the side windows of the car. "Driver, step out of the vehicle and place your hands on the top of the car."

The driver opened the door from the outside and stepped out. He was a bulky man and struggled to stand up from the low seat.

Greer was now at Pulis' side, "Cover him and I'll do the search," he said, holstering his weapon and stepping close behind Rinaldi. Greer searched him, finding one handgun, pulled his hands behind him and handcuffed the prisoner. Once done he went to the other side of the car and repeated the exercise. Dressler possessed a revolver and a large belt knife. He, too, was handcuffed.

"What are you boys doing here?" asked Pulis.

"None of your business, Cop. We're here on vacation." The words came as if fired from a machine gun.

"You realize carrying a firearm in a school zone is a felony, of course." Pulis stated as if that were the reason they were stopped.

Dressler said nothing.

"Bill, call the impound company and have a wrecker come pick up the car. These boys are going to jail."

"I'll ride over to the jail with you and I'll have the federal warrant numbers by the time we get there." The two prisoners were loaded into the backseat of the state trooper car while Gant ordered the wrecker.

Inside the patrol car Greer turned to Pulis, "You handled that well, Trooper."

Pulis wanted to say something smart, but kept his mouth shut.

Gant followed them to the jail when the rental car had been impounded, arriving while the booking process was still in progress. Neither prisoner had spoken except to answer questions about the booking. Both men were wiping fingerprint ink from their fingers when Rinaldi told the correctional officer, "I want my phone call."

The jail officer led him to a small attorney visiting room where he could use a phone in private. He spent considerable time on the phone in animated conversation.

Dressler was searched and led to a cell in the pretrial dorm while the three policemen waited for Rinaldi to finish his call. "I'll bet you an ice cream bar he's talking with Sal," said Gant.

"No bet," said Pulis.

"It looks like my house guest will be able to go home tonight," Gant said quietly.

Pulis looked him in the eye and said, "You and I have a full night's work ahead of us getting the case ready for the DA in the morning."

"While you two are doing the legal chores, I'd like to see those documents you brought home. By the way, you never did say where you got them," Greer commented.

"You're right, I never did," said Gant.

The speculation about where Rinaldi had called was correct. In Newark, New Jersey Salvatore Roselli was having a tantrum. "Can't these bums get anything right? I pay them good money to take care of business and look what happens. I got two men is South America and two more in jail in Alaska." Marco Cidella was standing in a corner, trying to be invisible as Sal ranted. Tony had inherited the job Vito once had. "Marco! Get hold of Vito and Dallas and tell them to get home right away. The law is going to be looking for them, so tell them I'm sending a private jet to pick them up. I don't want anyone to know they are back, understand me?" Sal said, glaring at his newest right hand man.

"Yessir, Mr. Roselli, right away." Marco welcomed the chance to get out of the office and away from his irate boss.

As Cidella turned to walk away the boss continued, "If that bookkeeper wasn't dead already, I'd have him killed. Maybe I'll have him killed again." Cidella closed the door behind him, shaking his head and walking to his new office. He and Sal were the only ones who knew where Vito and Dallas were "Vacationing."

Chapter 21

Twelve hours after the call from Newark Vito Roma and Dallas Freed stepped out of a large silver color sedan in the yard of Ace Trucking Company. The driver deposited their bags on the loading dock and departed. Marco Cidella met them on the dock and took them to the office of Sal Roselli. It was 4 AM when the group met in Sal's office. Roselli was still angry and close to irrational. He was on the verge of losing a lifetime of hard work and the stress was beginning to show dramatically.

"Vito, I'm glad to see you. Things are going bad and I need you." He hugged his hit-man.

"It's good to be here, Mr. Roselli. Dallas and I are ready to go to work. Tell me what's going on."

Roselli turned to Cidella, "Marco, leave us alone for a while. I'll call you when I need you."

Without saying a word Cidella left the office and returned to his own, or had been his own until now when it would obviously be taken back by Vito Roma.

Once Cidella was out of the office Roselli began to explain. "The FBI has been here asking about you and Dallas. They've had a look-out in the top floor of that abandoned building on 113th street. I seen 'em when they were setting up over there. They come here every couple of days and ask about you two. For that reason I want the two of you to take that jet and fly to Alaska. I want you to finish what you started there. That girl up there has been talking with the police. We have to silence her before she can do us any harm."

"We'll take care of it, Mr. Roselli," said Roma.

"One more thing Vito, Rinaldi and Dressler have to disappear. Gino called to tell me he and Tony had been arrested for carrying a firearm in a school zone. While the Troopers were having them booked a fed showed up with the federal warrants from down here. I'm sending a lawyer up there. You two can ride up to Alaska on the same plane. Have Marco furnish some new ID for the two of you. I'll have the lawyer bail them out of jail, but it will be your job to see they never get back there to court for a trial. The other thing I want taken care of is that girl. She seems to be the connection with the troopers and I want her eliminated, and while you're there I want you to get rid of those two cops that came here to the warehouse. I want them gone!" Roselli issued his orders with an evil sneer on his face. His anger was now making his decisions for him.

"Hey, Boss," said Vito, "that's going to leave a lot of bodies lying around up there. Are you sure you want to do that?"

The evil sneer intensified, "Just do what I told you, Vito," he spat out. "Get this taken care of NOW."

"You're the boss," said Vito. He turned to Dressler, "Tony, are you ready to leave?"

Tony Dressler nodded, not wanting to get into this volatile conversation.

"OK, Sal, have the limo come back and take us to the airport. We'll wait at the plane for the lawyer to show. Tony and I will stop on the way to the airport for some breakfast. By the way, Boss, Tony and I will need some walking around cash for this trip."

"Tony, go get Marco," Sal ordered.

When Dressler had gone Sal opened the safe behind his desk and retrieved a stack of cash. "Vito, I know you don't agree with any of this, but this thing is going to bring down the entire operation if we don't put an end to it now. If we don't get it stopped you can bet we'll all be eating jailhouse food."

"I understand, Sal, you know you can count on me, like always," said Vito, taking the cash and a firm handshake from his boss.

Dallas and Cidella came back to the office where Sal Roselli gave him a list of chores. First was to order the limo driver to return. Next came a more detailed item. Sal wanted one of his trusted lawyers on the plane to Alaska within two hours.

"I want you two to stay in touch with me and to keep me informed about your progress. There can't be any slip-ups this time," explained Salvatore Roselli.

In moments Marco Cidella returned to the office, "the limo is here, Boss."

"Good luck, Boys," said Sal as the two travelers left the office.

As they left the warehouse they kept their heads down to make it more difficult for the observers in the abandoned building a block away to recognize them. Near the airport there was an IHOP. They stopped for breakfast, enjoying the first truly American food in weeks.

The limo driver stopped next to a private jet parked outside a hangar privately owned by the same friend of Sal's that owned the airplane. He had instructed the pilot to follow whatever instructions Vito issued. Their luggage, two carry-on bags were stowed in the belly of the craft. Vito was speaking with the pilot when another car parked on the ramp. The other car, too, had a driver who stepped out to open the trunk and remove a fairly large suitcase. The lawyer stepped out of the car carrying his briefcase and a frown. The large suitcase was stowed inside the aircraft with the others and Vito watched the rather rotund lawyer climb with some effort, into the passenger seating area.

"How much fuel do we have on board?" asked Vito Roma.

"Do you mean gallons or hours," asked the young pilot.

"Miles," said Vito. "Can we fly non-stop to Soldotna, Alaska or will we have to stop somewhere for fuel?"

"We don't have enough fuel to fly to Alaska, but the plan is to stop in Seattle and top off before making the final leg of the flight. We have two pilots on board and the entire flight should be without any bad weather. We'll have a long flight, seven hours flying time, plus the stop for fuel in Seattle. Will you want us to wait while you conduct your business?"

"How long can you wait? It may take two or three days for us to do what we came to do."

"Our boss said to ask you what you wanted and to give it to you, no matter how long it takes," explained the pilot. "We're at your disposal. If you're going to be that long we will get a hotel room and you can call us on our cell phone when you need us." The pilot was young, no more than 25 years old. He was well groomed and dressed in a uniform with a white shirt and tie. He was polite to the passengers, but all business. "There will be a flight attendant serving you. Her name is Susan. She will provide you with anything you need on the flight. We will be in the air all night, so I would suggest you try to get some sleep."

"Thank you, I'll try to do that. We had a long flight to Newark yesterday and I can use the rest."

"We'll be ready as soon as I complete my pre-flight checks. Have a nice flight." With that the pilot whirled around to walk under the wing and begin inspecting the plane.

Vito walked up the stairs to where the flight attendant was waiting. "Can I bring you something to drink, Sir?" she asked.

"Not right now, thank you," he said.

"We'll be departing in a few minutes, Sir, please take a seat and fasten your seatbelt."

Vito nodded his compliance and found a seat. The interior of the plane was plush and well lighted. Two minutes later the pilot entered and the door was closed. The flight attendant took one of the seats and strapped the belt tight. The engines started and the plane began to taxi to the runway. It was amazingly quiet inside the Gulfstream.

"A man could get used to traveling this way," thought Vito.

He was awakened when they started the descent into Seattle airspace. The pilot was the only one to exit the plane while it re-fueled. Within minutes they were airborne again and Vito resumed his sleeping.

When attendant awakened him it was a bright sunny day. "Would you like some rolls and coffee before we land?" she asked.

"That would be nice," he said.

The lawyer found a seat next to Vito and introduce himself, "Good morning, Mr. Roma, I'm Lawrence Woodbury. I work for Mr. Roselli. He said I was to handle the legal processes and I was to do whatever you instructed. What would you like me to do once we land?"

"We need two rental cars brought to the Soldotna airport. I don't want to be seen on the street, so I want you to get three rooms on the ground floor at a good motel. There's a Best Western on the road going toward Kenai. It will be full, but see if you can bribe a clerk or something and get us in there. Once that's done you can go to the jail and confer with your new clients. Don't tell them we're here. It'll be up to you to get them out of jail. I need them. Get them to set bail for Dressler and Rinaldi. There's a nice hotel in Kenai. Get them rooms there and let me know what rooms they're in. Dallas and I have other things to attend, but I'll see you later. Give me your cell phone number and I'll call you."

They exchanged cell phone numbers. Woodbury asked for directions to the jail before gathering his briefcase and driving to the Wildwood Pretrial Facility where he identified himself and was admitted. Both Dallas and Tony were escorted to the tiny attorney visiting room. The guard locked the three men in the private room to do their confidential business. Minutes later Woodbury was knocking on the door to be let out.

There was an arraignment held this morning where both men pleaded not guilty and bail was set at $500,000 dollars each. Woodbury drove to the courthouse to confer with the judge and the District Attorney. The judge had called a Federal Judge in Anchorage to inquire about bail on the federal arrest warrants. The local Superior Court Judge in Kenai was told their half million dollar bail amount on each man would be enough.

Woodbury went to a local bank and obtained a cashier's check in the amount of one million dollars which he delivered to the clerk of the court. The court clerk was very impressed with the number of zeros on the check and filled out the papers authorizing the jail to release the prisoners. He went to the Quality Inn and rented two rooms before going to the pretrial building to get his clients released.

It took nearly an hour for the two prisoners to be changed into their street clothes and to be released into the custody of Lawrence Woodbury.

Woodbury checked the two men into the Quality Inn. Since there was no longer a restaurant in the hotel he gave them some cash for meals. Woodbury drove Rinaldi to the airport terminal where he rented a white Ford Taurus which Rinaldi drove back to the hotel. The lawyer had given them orders to stay in their rooms until morning when he would have further instructions for them.

It was past midnight, but still quite light outside when Vito parked his rental car in the small lot near the head of a local hiking trail and walked up the sidewalk to the hotel parking lot on the corner. There was little traffic in the area making him appear to be just another tourist out for a midnight sun walk. When he found the car rented by Woodbury he checked around for anyone looking. There was no one in the area. He dropped to the ground and slid partially under the Ford. He had built a simple detonating device from two wire connectors and a short length of duct tape. He'd brought an electric blasting cap with him in his suitcase for the job. He attached one wire to the brake light wire. The other he bared the end and wrapped it around the head of a bolt on the frame. He taped the detonator to the fuel tank, rubbed the tape to be sure it had stuck to the tank. Once he was certain everything was right he slid out from under the car and walked back to his own vehicle a half block away.

At six the following morning he called Woodbury and instructed him to call Rinaldi and tell him that he and Dressler were to meet him at a local restaurant. Woodbury was still in bed, but agreed to make the call.

At 6:45 AM Gino and Tony came out of the hotel and climbed into the rental car. Out of habit Rinaldi inserted the ignition key and put his foot on the brake pedal. The device Roma had attached to the gas tank worked perfectly. The full tank of gasoline went off like a huge bomb instantly incinerating the occupants of the Ford. 90 seconds later the fire department was on the scene, but it was too late. They extinguished the flames and found the bodies. The local fire marshal was called to investigate, but there was nothing left to find. The explosion and fire had melted what was left of the car. It was ruled an accident of unknown cause.

Vito Roma heard the news on a local radio station and smiled.

Chapter 22

The hotel clerk was the one to identify the two men killed in the explosion outside the lobby. The two rooms had been rented the previous day in the names of Gino Rinaldi and Tony Dressler. Once the names appeared in the state computer flashing lights began to show up everywhere. Bill Gant and Alan Pulis were notified immediately. Gant had some experience with fire investigation and went to the scene. Pulis drove to the Kenai Fire Department to talk with the Fire Marshal and Police Chief. They shared their initial investigation information, and concurred it would be best if the city provided support for this State and Federal case.

The parking lot around the burned and broken automobile was wet from the fire retardant used to extinguish the gasoline fire. There was a pair of coveralls in the trunk of his car which he put on in an attempt to keep clean. He walked around the scene taking pictures from every angle. A wrecker from the impound yard was standing by to load the car to be taken to the trooper office until the investigation was complete. He walked to the cab of the wrecker to speak to the driver.

"Hi there, Logan," said Gant. "Can I get you to do me a favor?"

"Sure, if I can," replied the driver.

"With the tires burned off and all the plastic trim melted I can't see under the vehicle. Could you hook onto the rear of the car and lift it up so I can see under it?"

"Heck yeah," said Logan. He started the big wrecker and turned around to back up to the rear of the scorched Ford. He jumped out of the truck and managed to reach under the back to hook two chains. Once done he manipulated the levers on the side of the truck and rear of the Ford began to rise. When the car was about three feet off the ground Bill waved for him to stop.

"Just hold it there while I take a look."

Logan nodded and watched as Bill knelt at the rear of the car. It was a bright summer day in Kenai, but the shadow made a contrast of light which necessitated the use of a strong light. He was about to crawl in the mud under the car when Logan tapped him on the shoulder. He was holding a heavy blanket like the ones furniture movers use.

"Here Bill, lay on this. You should wait until I can put a couple of safety stands under the axles."

Logan lowered the cables until the car was resting on the stands.

Bill tossed the blanket on the ground under the car and lay on his back. He slid under the car inch by inch. Using his light he immediately saw the demolished gas tank. Somehow the hole didn't appear to have been made by pressure from the inside but rather a smaller hole with edges forced toward the inside. He took more pictures. Shining his light around he saw what appeared to be a piece of copper wire wrapped around the head of a bolt on the rear of the frame. He removed the wire and the bolt and placed them in an evidence bag. He was about to crawl out from under the car when something strange caught his eye. Another piece of the same type of copper wire had been attached to a wire under the car. The wire connector had melted, but some of the molten plastic had held the small copper wire to the wiring leading to the left taillight. He took more pictures and cut the wire connector from the taillight wire to be placed in another evidence bag.

Other than the evidence of a gigantic explosion erupting from the fuel tank, which was laid completely open by the blast, there wasn't much left of the underside of the car.

He slid out from under the Ford, stood up and brushed off the dirt as best he could.

"Did you get what you needed?" asked Logan.

"For now," replied Gant. "You're taking it to the trooper impound yard. If I could get you to put the frame on some kind of blocks so I can get under it if need be, I sure would appreciate it, Logan. And thanks for the use of the blanket; that helped a lot."

For several minutes Gant sat in his car making notes and studying the wires he had found. Finally he drove to the Kenai Fire Station to meet with the Fire Marshal and Pulis. In the office of the Fire Marshal he laid the two plastic bags, containing the copper wires he had found, on the desk.

"Have you ever seen wire like that on a car before?" asked Gant.

Rudy Lynch, Kenai Fire Marshal, picked up the bags to inspect them more closely. He took a magnifying glass from a drawer to get a better look. "Nope, not on an automobile, but I used a lot of it when I was gold mining. It looks like lead wire from an electrical blasting cap. On this one you can still see some of the colored insulation." He pointed to the wire taken from the bolt head on the frame of the Ford.

"Are you sure, Rudy?" asked Pulis.

"Not 100%, no, but the crime lab will be able to tell you for sure."

Pulis turned to Gant, "Why is it the people we get close to get killed under strange circumstances?"

"And possibly by the same killers for the same boss, I'm beginning to think we should be watching our backs. If Sal bailed these guys out of jail to have them killed, we could be on the list as well." Gant was silent for a second, "Rudy, what kind of damage would a blasting cap attached to a gas tank do to a passenger car? Could it cause that kind of explosion?"

"I'd say yes. You know, dynamite is a slow burning combustible; however the rate of burn can be accelerated if the igniter is faster. If you put a match to some gunpowder on a flat surface it'll burn slowly. If you use an explosive igniter it'll burn very fast to the point of exploding. The intensity is increased by confining the combustible. Like putting gunpowder in a brass casing and directing the explosive force. What I can't tell you is whether or not gasoline will react the same way. You'll have to take that up with the crime lab also."

A short time later the two investigators left the fire station. Pulis suggested they call Greer and meet him for lunch and to inform him of the events of the day.

"Here it is, not even noon and I've already had a full day. I must be getting old," Pulis chuckled; Gant was grinning and continued, "I'll call Greer. Where do you want to eat lunch?"

Bill called Greer and told him to meet them at Louie's Restaurant in Kenai. A few minutes later the three were seated in a booth near the lobby entrance. Bill explained what he had found in the burned car while Alan explained their theories on what had happened.

Greer looked at the evidence bags containing the small pieces of wire. "I think you two have a pretty good handle on this case. I do wonder though, who did Roselli send up here to do his dirty work? A lawyer by the name of Woodbury from Newark bailed these two out of jail. I think Roselli planned this whole thing and sent the lawyer to set it into motion. We could question Woodbury, but he'd claim client confidentiality. The word I get from New York is that Woodbury has worked for Roselli for a very long time. He isn't going to say anything."

"I worry about your first question, who did Roselli send here to do the job? I'm not familiar with Roselli's network, but he seems to favor Vito Roma for this kind of work. If he is the one he sent here, we have to worry about the safety of Leila Hunter. Roma knows who she is and I think he'll do his best to find her and eliminate her." Gant had genuine concerns for Leila's safety.

"I don't know if you've considered this, Bill, but I think you and Alan will also be on the list. If it's Roma who's here he also knows you two."

Gant looked at Greer, "What the heck is your first name, anyway? It probably isn't Agent."

Greer laughed, "Edwin, call me Ed. First names aren't part of FBI protocol."

"OK," continued Gant, "Did you get anything out of the documents I brought back? Anything you can use to nail Roselli?"

"You'll be getting a letter from the New York office. They went crazy over the stuff. They knew about everything mentioned in the file, but they had no proof. The stuff you provided will be the basis for a lot of warrants in New York and New Jersey. It'll take a couple of weeks to put it all together and form an arrest team, but Roselli is going to jail, thanks to the two of you."

"That brings us back to the original problem, Ed. What are we going to do about Roma and his partner, Freed? They must be in town somewhere. I think we need to send some uniform troopers to canvas the hotels and bars to see if anyone has seen them. We have to do it quietly. If Roma knows we're looking for him he may skip again." It was Alan asking the questions now.

"I think there's a more likely possibility, Alan. I think if he knows you're looking for him, he'll become even bolder in his efforts to find and eliminate you and Bill. I think he's our biggest threat right now. I can call a couple of agents from Anchorage to come down and help, if you'd like."

"It seems to me Leila will be in more danger than Alan and me. We're capable of looking out for ourselves. She's a smart girl and is cautious, but doesn't have the ability to defend herself from an attack. She's still at my place and safe for now. Let's just concentrate on finding Vito and Dallas."

"OK, Bill, you two are in charge of the case here, but if you need help call me. I'll be going back to Anchorage this afternoon, if you don't need me. Can you let me take those samples from the bombing up to the crime lab for you?" asked Greer.

"That would speed things up for us Ed, thanks," replied Gant.

Alan was scratching his head, "I've been wondering Ed, you have a lot of surveillance at the Anchorage Airport, how did they get here without you spotting them?"

The question startled Greer, "That's a good question Alan. Could they have come directly here?"

"It's not likely they'd get a charter from any major air link except Anchorage. You don't suppose they came here directly from the lower 48?"

"I suppose they could have. I'll try to find out from the FAA," Said Greer.

"I'll drive by both the Kenai Airport and the Soldotna Airport to take a look for any strange planes," said Gant.

After lunch Greer took charge of the bags of evidence to be delivered to the crime lab. Alan drove back to the office to begin his reports and Bill drove to the Kenai Airport to see if there were any strange planes on the apron. Finding none he went back to Soldotna to check the transit parking there.

The obvious transit parking resident was a beautiful Gulfstream IV. A check of city records indicated the pilots were staying at the Aspen Motel in Soldotna. Bill called Alan and asked him to meet with him at the motel. After explaining his find they went to the front desk and asked for the pilot's room number. The two men walked up the stairs to the second floor, found the room and knocked on the door.

A very young man opened the door to greet them. "Can I help you," he asked.

"Perhaps," said Alan, "We're looking for the pilots of the passenger jet parked at the Soldotna Airport."

"I'm the pilot," said the youngster, "my copilot is in the next room. Is something wrong? Is the airplane OK?"

"Oh, yes, your plane is fine. We were just curious about when you arrived?" asked Alan.

"Early yesterday," said the pilot.

"Are you allowed to tell me who you brought here?"

The young pilot frowned, "I suppose so, but it seems like a strange question."

"We're just checking on the whereabouts of any strangers in town. It's in connection with an incident this morning in Kenai."

"Can you excuse me a minute? I need to call my boss and ask him about this."

"Sure, take all the time you need. We'll wait here in the hall until you finish," Alan was trying to be friendly.

The troopers stepped back into the hall and waited. About two minutes later the door opened and the pilot invited them inside. Pulis and Gant followed him in.

"My boss lives in Georgia and has loaned his plane out for a few days. He said it was alright if I named my passenger. He's a lawyer from Newark, New Jersey. His name is Woodbury, Lawrence Woodbury. I have no idea what his business is here, but I'm told to wait until he calls me to return to Newark."

"I thank you for the information, Sir. Do you have some identification on you?"

"Sure, in my coat, I'll get it for you." As he walked across the room to a coat hung on the back of a chair, Bill reached under his own coat to hold the butt of his weapon. When the pilot opened a pocket on the coat to lift out his wallet Bill relaxed. He fished inside for his identification and handed it to Pulis who wrote down the information on his pad before handing it back to the pilot. "Is there anything more I can do for you?"

"Only one more thing, do you know where Mr. Woodbury is staying?"

"Not for sure, we haven't seen him since we landed. He may be in this hotel, but I really don't know."

"Thank you for your cooperation. Sorry to have bothered you." With that bit of niceness Bill and Alan left the pilot alone in his room.

Chapter 23

After searching all afternoon the two investigators called it a day. Gant felt he needed to go home and check on the welfare of his new boarder, Leila. They had agreed to meet at the office the next morning to finish the paperwork for the District Attorney. Pulis suggested they meet at 5 before the morning shift change made the headquarters building buzz with activity.

Pulis entered the building at 4:45 with Gant following at 4:55. They met in the small kitchen while pouring coffee to start their day. They made a list of what each man needed to accomplish this morning before the court house opened its doors. By the time the day shift began to assemble in the offices they had completed their chores. Officers had begun to stop by their small office to say good morning, each with a cup of hot coffee in his hand. By 8:30 the two had assembled the files, ready for the court.

"I'll buy breakfast," said Pulis.

"I hope so, it's your turn," replied his partner.

They agreed to take Pulis' patrol car to the restaurant almost next door to the headquarters building. They parked with the nose of the patrol car aimed at the log building. Inside they were met by a tall, thin, blond woman who had waited on customers in the area for more than 30 years. Her name was Flo. She was known for her caustic wit. Every local customer knew her and exchanged sarcasm with her.

"Good morning, Cowboys, you're up early this morning," she said, recognizing the two men.

"Good morning Flo. Have you poisoned anyone yet today?" asked Pulis.

"Not yet, you could be the first today. Come with me and I'll find you a booth." She showed them to a booth near a window, "How about it, do you want coffee this morning?"

Both men nodded. She returned in a minute with two cups of coffee and a pair of menus then disappeared to wait on another customer in the crowded restaurant. When she returned she asked, "Have you made up your minds?"

"I'm having the hamburger steak and eggs, over easy, hash browns and whole wheat toast. I think I'll have a small orange juice, too," ordered Bill.

She wrote it all on her pad, "What about you Alan?"

"I think a short stack of sourdough pancakes and two eggs, over easy."

"Got it," she said as she whirled around to place the order with the kitchen.

While they were eating, a dark green car motored by in the traffic. It had been going toward the trooper building next door when the driver, Dallas Freed saw the two troopers through the window. At the next turn-out near the rodeo grounds, he pulled off the road.

"That's them in the window of the restaurant, Vito."

"Are you sure?"

"Yeah, I'm sure. How do you want to handle it?" asked Freed.

Vito studied the area quickly. "Drive over to the parking lot by the café. We'll park in the back and wait for them to come out. I'll get the shotgun out of the trunk and when they open their doors to get in, you pull up behind them and stop. I'll take care of the rest.

The two men had gone to several garage sales and found a fairly new Browning shotgun for a good price. The owner said he had used it for bear protection. He also included two boxes of 00 Buckshot cartridges in the deal. Vito paid cash and took possession. He had gone to a wooded area outside of town to test fire the weapon and found it to be more than adequate for his purposes.

Dallas found a gap in the traffic and crossed the road, turned right into the parking area and drove to the back of the lot, turning around behind the restaurant building. The two assassins sat in the car after Vito took the shotgun from the trunk. He loaded the magazine full of Buckshot loads and put three more in his pocket, just in case.

Summertime is tourist season on the Kenai Peninsula and the restaurant was full, with more customers coming and going in a constant flow. They waited almost a half hour before the trooper investigators emerged from the log building and returned to their patrol car.

Alan Pulis took his keys from his belt and opened the door. He pressed the button to allow Gant to enter the passenger side. As they entered the vehicle and closed the doors the dark green car pulled from behind the building and moved behind the patrol car. Pulis saw the car stop behind him and waited to start the engine. He said something to Gant and failed to see Vito get out of the car. Vito walked down the off-side of the car next to the patrol car until he was in front of the windshield of the car. He could see Pulis sitting in the driver seat, making sure he had the right person. Suddenly he raised the shotgun and fired into the driver's side window, blowing into a million shards of safety glass. He took two small steps forward and fired two shots into the windshield of the trooper car.

A large, black Dodge Ram 2500 pickup truck was parked directly behind the trooper car. Inside Paul Duffy, a local man, was petting his large golden retriever. When he heard the gunfire he looked up to see the action. Duffy reached under the seat and found his Colt Combat Commander .45 Caliber hand gun. He pulled the slide and loaded a round into the chamber as he stepped out of his truck. Vito had finished his job and turned back to the green rental car, carrying the gun in his left hand.

"Stop and drop your weapon!" ordered Duffy while pointing the automatic at Vito.

Vito said nothing, but raised his shotgun and fired. Duffy had been standing behind the open door of his truck which took the full load of buckshot. Duffy ducked instinctively and peered out around the door. Vito opened his car door, tossed the shotgun into the back seat and jumped inside. Dallas gunned the engine and sped away. Duffy aimed at the moving car and was able to put two shots into the driver side window and three shots in the front door. The shots had hit Dallas once in the neck. His wound was spurting arterial blood as he drove. He also had two slugs in his abdomen, but he wasn't feeling the pain. He pulled from the parking lot, turning right, dodging cars as he went. He ran the red light on the corner, speeding through traffic toward the Soldotna Airport.

Inside the restaurant Flo had been startled by the sounds of gunfire and saw Vito outside the side window. She began to shout, "Down, everybody get down, get down." An instant later the gunfire stopped, then suddenly it began again. The patrons were all huddled in their booths waiting for it to stop.

Lying on the floor near the salad bar Flo found the cell phone in her apron and punched 911.

"911 Operator, do you have an emergency?" she asked.

"Yes," she shouted, "This is Flo at the Caribou Restaurant. There are people shooting each other in the parking lot. We need police, NOW."

"Please hold while I send troopers and city police" said the dispatcher. A moment later she came back on the line. "Can you see the shooter?"

"I did to start with, but not now. I'm hiding on the floor and so are all my customers."

"Stay inside and keep down until the officers tell you to move. They're on the way."

Flo could now hear the police sirens as they came closer. The first car in the area was a trooper who had only a half block to travel.

"Is anyone inside the restaurant injured?" asked the voice on the phone.

"No, not yet. The cops are outside now." Flo was still hidden behind the metal salad bar.

"I'll be in touch with the officers. Please follow their instructions." With that the line went dead.

Three police cars, two troopers and one city police car were now in the lot. Paul Duffy had placed his Colt on the front seat of his pickup and raised his hands. The first officer held a weapon on him while the second officer ordered him to put his hands behind him. Duffy was handcuffed while a city officer made his way to Pulis' shot-up vehicle. Immediately he was on the radio to dispatch, "officer down, officer down, we need an ambulance at this location right now."

The other city officer and one trooper went inside the restaurant to check on Flo and the patrons who gave a collective sigh of relief when the uniformed officers entered.

Paul Duffy shouted to the officers, "They went toward the Sterling Highway in a green Taurus. I think I hit one of them."

"Who are you?" asked the officer who had handcuffed him.

"I'm Paul Duffy. I was coming for breakfast when the guys in the green car started shooting at the guys in the other car. They used a shotgun and blew out all the front windows. I haven't had a chance to check and see if they are OK. I shot at the car as they left the parking lot and I think I hit the driver. My gun is on the seat of my truck."

Another siren was approaching now. Two officers had both front doors open on the trooper car attending the wounded officers. The ambulance arrived and took over. They held a compress to the neck of Pulis while loading him into the ambulance. The ambulance drove away at once, headed toward the hospital. Another ambulance came within a minute and the paramedics busied themselves treating Gant. One of the medics approached the trooper interviewing Duffy.

"Both the officers are alive, but critical. The other one is now going into the emergency room with severe wounds. The other medics said they weren't sure he was going to make it. I know this one over here, his name is Bill Gant. He has wounds to the left side of his head and neck and arm. It looks like his vest protected him from the main force of the shot. As soon as he's stabilized we'll be transporting him to the emergency room at the hospital."

"We'll be sending an officer to follow as soon as we can free someone from here. Take good care of those two troopers."

As the medic walked back to his medical crew the trooper returned his attention to Duffy. "Turn around and I'll take the cuffs off. When we arrived we didn't know who was the good guy and who was the bad guy. Thanks for assisting. You may have saved their lives. I'd appreciate it if you'd wait in your truck until we finish."

Just then his radio came to life. "We have injuries and traffic accidents at the light on the Sterling at K-Beach Road. The suspect's car was seen proceeding up Funny River Road toward the airport. I'm in pursuit now and requesting backup."

Two more trooper units were passing the restaurant with their lights and sirens on.

Meanwhile, Vito was fighting for control of the car he was a passenger in. His driver, Dallas Freed was now unconscious. Roma managed to get the car stopped and put the shifter in park. He jumped out, walked around the car and opened the driver's door. Freed was still pumping blood from his neck, but it had slowed to a trickle. Vito pulled his dying partner out of the seat, leaving him on the ground by the side of the road. Stepping over the body he climbed into the driver's seat, put the car in gear and drove toward the airport. He saw a wooded side street on his right and turned. Out of sight of the main road he stopped and jumped from the car. He made his way to the fence at the end of the airport property. There he sat, regaining his composure and attempting to create a plan. He still had to get the girl. Roselli would never accept his coming back without finishing the job. He surmised the troopers had tracking dogs he would not be able to avoid while on foot. He considered climbing the airport fence, but he would be exposed once inside. As he walked by a residence he saw a bicycle in the front yard. No one was around and it seemed a good alternative. He took off his windbreaker and shirt, climbed aboard the bicycle and pedaled toward the main road.

A city police car and two trooper vehicles passed him, red lights flashing. He pedaled toward the airport gate where he turned in to a local charter operator office. He put his shirt and windbreaker back on in order to look more respectable and went inside. He asked the lady at the counter if it was possible to take a flight seeing trip to look at the wildlife. She informed him their pilot was on the way to the office and would be able to take him on a two hour flight. Vito took a roll of bills from his pants pocket and paid cash. Twenty minutes later he was in a small, single engine plane heading west toward Cook Inlet and a bear viewing experience.

On the road the pursuers had lost the car they were chasing. One trooper was sent to continue up Funny River Road while the city police and the other trooper car reversed course to begin searching side roads and streets. It was on the reverse trip they found the body of Dallas Freed.

Captain Caswell took the call and bolted from his office to drive to the hospital where his two investigators were being treated.

Chapter 24

When Captain Caswell arrived at the emergency room doctors and nurses and technicians were scurrying from one room to another, all with serious scowls on their faces. None had time to stop and talk with Caswell. He stood in the hallway and watched the activity for a few minutes before returning to the front desk. He told the receptionist he would wait in the lobby and asked her to let him know if there was any news. She said she would.

He sat in the lobby reading an old Outdoor Life and had worked a two day old crossword puzzle in a discarded newspaper. The outdoor channel was playing on the wide screen TV in the lobby, but Caswell couldn't get interested. He found a soda machine and purchased a Mountain Dew, sipping on it while working his crossword puzzle. His office had stopped referring calls to his phone. The single distraction was a reporter from the local newspaper who came into the lobby and was pressuring the receptionist for information about the two wounded officers. She refused to give him any information, but he pressed her even harder. Finally Caswell walked over to the desk and politely told the reporter he would have to leave. He insisted he was with the press and had a right to be there and would not leave. He had come to get information and was not leaving without what he came for.

The captain was in uniform and found it difficult to believe the young man could be that stubborn. "I'm Captain Caswell of the Alaska State Troopers and I'm advising you to leave right now. You've been told by this lady to leave the emergency room area. You're now trespassing and interfering with the hospital staff and their duties. I've now told you where you stand. If you refuse to leave I'll have a security officer and a city police officer take you into custody. You'll be taken to jail and booked on the charge of trespassing.

Are you beginning to get the picture? Now, either sit down and shut up or leave the building."

"I'm a reporter with the newspaper gathering information on the shooting. You can't stop me from doing that."

"Perhaps not, but I can stop you from doing it here. Make your choice. I'm out of patience with you."

The young reporter started to say something, but changed his mind. His face was beet red as he walked to the exit door where he turned to Caswell, "I'm having my paper contact a lawyer."

"You do that Sonny," remarked the captain.

He waited another hour before a nurse came out to take him into a small office where a doctor was waiting.

"Sorry Captain, we didn't mean to keep you waiting for so long, but we've been pretty busy. First of all I am happy to report to you that both men are alive. The first officer, Pulis, is in critical condition. Everyone involved did an excellent job of slowing the blood loss from the injured artery in his neck. We were able to make a temporary patch to the artery and to close most of the cuts he suffered. Both men were wearing body armor which probably saved both of them. Pulis will be going to surgery in a few minutes to further repair his artery and to try to save his left shoulder which took the brunt of the shotgun blast. I think he'll pull through, but I doubt he'll ever be able to go back to being a trooper. I don't think he'll ever regain full movement in his left shoulder and arm."

"But he'll live, right, Doc?"

"Unless we encounter something unforeseen, yes," said the physician, "We have specialists coming here now to do the surgery."

"What about my other officer, Bill Gant?" asked Caswell.

"He'll be going to surgery also. We managed to take most of the broken glass out of his wounds, but he still has several shotgun pellets in his face, upper chest and arms. He's conscious and responsive if you'd like to speak with him. You'll only have a few minutes before they come to take him to surgery, but I think he'd like to see you."

"Thanks, Doc, which room is he in?" Caswell was beginning to relax from the stress he had felt for the past several hours.

The doctor showed Caswell to the exam room where Gant was laying with gauze patches taped to his head, face, arms and almost all his visible skin. Gant tried to grin when the captain entered.

"Some guys will do anything to keep from filling out a report," said Caswell.

Gant chuckled, but winced with pain. "How's Alan?" he muttered through the bandages.

"Not good, but he's going to make it. He's hurt pretty bad and will be going to surgery as soon as the specialists get to the hospital. The doctor told me they were going to take you up there, too in order to plug some of your leaks. They're going to take you to surgery in a few minutes, but I want you to know we're all here for you. If there's anything you want or need, just let me know."

"One thing, Cap, Leila Hunter is staying at my place. She has to be protected."

"I'll see to it, Bill. By the way, a citizen took on the two hit men. He got one of them. We found his body on the road. The other one seems to have disappeared. As long as he's on the loose I'm going to put a 24 hour guard here at the hospital."

A nurse appeared at the door, "we're ready for him now, Captain."

"I'll look in on you tomorrow, Bill."

"Thanks for caring, Cap."

The ER Doc was standing in the hall when he left Room 5. Captain Caswell stopped to thank the doctor for his good work. He reached inside his shirt pocket to find a business card for the doctor. "The card has my cell phone number on it. You can reach me any time, day or night, at that number."

"The next couple of days will be crucial for both your officers. This patient's condition is rated as guarded, but stable. Officer Pulis is still critical. Neither of them is out of the woods yet. I'll call you if there's any change, for the good or the bad."

"Thanks Doc, I have a Trooper Detachment to run and have to get back to the office, but these guys are not just troopers, they're my friends." Caswell gave the doctor a short salute as he turned to leave the ER.

Vito had returned from his flight and tipped the pilot nicely. He hadn't decided his next course of action, but was working on a plan. A major step in this plan was to remain invisible for a couple of days. He reached into his pocket and found his phone. He checked the time and determined it was evening time on the east coast. He dialed his boss in Newark.

"What's happening, Vito?" said Roselli, without preamble.

"I've taken care of the jailbirds and the cops, but the cops are on to me and I have to keep out of sight. Dallas is dead. He got shot by a bystander when I was doing the two cops. I'm just wandering around the Soldotna Airport right now trying to figure out what to do next."

"I'll tell you what to do next. Find that woman and get rid of her. After that you can get in touch with Woodbury and come home. This whole situation is turning into a kettle of worms. I want it to end and soon. My associates here are beginning to ask questions. They're beginning to wonder if I can handle it. I've assured them it is being handled. Don't make me out a liar, Vito. Do you need more help?"

"No, I can handle it. Right now the problem is that I can't find her. As soon as I do, I'll take care of business. I had to ditch the car, but I see the local flight seeing company has a loaner. I'm going to go over there and borrow it for a couple of days," said Vito.

"Do what ya' gotta do, Vito. I need you back here. We have a business to run." As with the opening conversation it ended with Roselli simply hanging up.

The lady in the charter office was very helpful. She gave him the keys and asked him to fill the tank before he brought it back. "It needs to be run anyway. We keep it for transit pilots, but none have needed it for more than a month."

Since his hotel room had been rented by Woodbury, Vito thought it would be safe to return there and change clothing. He made that his first stop. He needed a shower and some rest.

Back in his own office, Caswell waited for the hospital to call with news of his two investigators. This mess had created a couple of new problems for him. First was who was going to investigate the shootings and second, what was he going to do about Leila Hunter. He thought it was more important to see Leila.

Bill Gant lived in a modest home on the edge of town. His home was secluded and quiet. Five minutes later he was knocking on the door. He saw a curtain move a tiny bit. She was inside and looking to see who was knocking.

The door opened and the pretty waitress invited him inside. "Hello, Captain," she said.

"Hello Leila, how are you making out here?"

"I'm bored to death, but I guess that's better than being shot to death."

"You had better sit down, Leila, I have some bad news."

She sat on the edge of the couch and listened.

"Bill and Alan have both been shot," he began. "They're both in bad shape and both are in surgery as we speak. I talked with Bill and he asked me to take care of you until he gets back on his feet."

"Oh, my God!" she exclaimed, "How did it happen? Are they going to be OK?'

"I don't know, but I'm hoping for the best. I'll let you know as soon as I hear anything."

"Can I go to the hospital and see them?"

"I would advise against that. We've yet to find the shooter and it would be dangerous for you. The other thing is I need to put you somewhere safe. This killer is on a roll and I think you may be on the list of victims. You'll probably be safe here at Bill's place, as long as you stay inside and don't look out the windows. You have my number and I want you to call if you see anyone at all around the house. Don't open the door or look out the window. I'll call you if I intend to come over. That way you will know who to expect. If anyone; and

I mean anyone, comes around I'll move you to another location. Do you need anything? Food, clothing, supplies of any kind?" asked the captain.

"No, Bill stocked the place when he brought me here. I'm so worried about the both of them."

"Me too, Leila, me too; remember what I told you. I have to get back to the office, but you call me anytime. I'll call you as soon as the doctors call me to let me know their condition. I'll have a patrol car drive by now and then."

Caswell was in his office again when his cell phone rang. It was the ER doctor he had spoken with earlier.

"Captain Caswell, I'm calling you to update you on the condition of your men. Bill Gant is out of surgery and doing well, he's been upgraded to Fair condition. His surgery went well. He lost a lot of blood and is weak, but the surgeons removed all the pellets from his body and sewed up his cuts. The plastic surgeon said his face won't show any scarring once he's healed. He's been moved from the recovery room to a room on the second floor. He'll be able to take visitors by tomorrow."

"That's good news, Doc. What about Alan? Is he out of surgery yet?"

"The nurse just handed me a note. He is in the recovery room. He is still in Critical Condition. The vascular surgeon repaired his torn artery. It'll be a couple of days before they know whether or not it is going to hold. They'll be moving him to ICU later tonight, but he won't be able to have visitors for a couple of days. My assessment of the shoulder wound was accurate. It's unlikely he'll be able to use his left arm and shoulder again. It was badly damaged. The bone and muscle tissue was destroyed and they couldn't repair it. They took out a lot of lead pellets from him too. I'm told he'll have a great deal of scarring on the left side of his neck and face. I know the two of you are close, and I hate to be the one to deliver this bad news, I'm sorry."

Caswell blew out a huge sigh, "It's OK, Doc. You aren't the one who shot him. Thanks for everything."

Chapter 25

It was after noon when Caswell went to the hospital to visit his men. He was directed to the room where Bill Gant was lying in a bed watching TV. He seemed to be covered with bandages and Band-Aids. Caswell entered cautiously in the event Bill was sleeping.

Gant saw him at the door, "Come on in, Cap. I'm awake."

Captain Caswell entered and found a chair he pulled close to the bed. "How are you feeling, Bill?"

"Pretty good, I want to go home, but they won't let me. They say I have to stay two more days to prevent infection. I guess I have a lot of holes in me."

"I think you should follow the doctor's advice."

"Have you seen Leila?" asked Gant.

"Yes, I went to your place yesterday and told her what was happening. She was upset, but handling it well. I have officers patrolling the area 24 hours a day. I'll have that continue when you get home."

"Have you seen Alan?" asked Gant.

"No, but I stopped at ICU to talk with the nurse. She said he is still heavily sedated and will be for a couple of more days. The doctor said they were able to fix the artery in his neck, but his shoulder is gone. He'll never be able to use his left shoulder or arm again. It's going to be tough on him," reported Caswell.

"Oh, no, Cap, he won't take it well. Man, I have to get well and take care of him. We've been friends for half our lives. We did everything together. This isn't going to be easy for him."

"Let's get you well first, Bill. I have to put another team on the investigation. We need to get this guy before he kills again. Right now he probably doesn't know you and Alan are still alive. Once he finds out he's surely going to try again. The description given by the bystander who shot Dallas Freed identified Vito Roma as the one with the shotgun. He has to be connected to that lawyer, Woodbury. It'd be too much of a coincidence for Roma and Woodbury to show up independently. They're both working for Roselli. I'll bet the Gulfstream parked at the Soldotna Airport belongs to one of Roselli's associates. I'm going to call Greer when I get back to the office and see what they're doing about him in Newark. It'd be nice if they arrested him and put him out of business."

"That won't stop Roma, Cap. He's like a Snapping Turtle. He'll stay on the job until it's finished, no matter what else happens."

"Roma is here somewhere and it's our job to find him. It's your job to get well. I'll be back tomorrow and visit you. Is there anything I can bring you?" asked the captain.

"Some clean clothes and my walking papers."

"I'll see what I can do about the clothes, but the rest is out of my hands. See you tomorrow.

As Caswell turned to leave the room Gant called him back. "Hey, Cap, there is one thing you can do when you get some time."

"What's that, Bill?"

"Do you think you could find time to bring Leila by to see me?"

"You old dog, I thought you were sick."

"It's nothing like that, Cap, I just feel responsible for her."

Caswell laughed aloud, "OK, Bill, I'll bring her down here this evening. Now, get some rest."

Vito Roma had driven the loaner car through the parking lot of the corner restaurant several times in an attempt to spot Leila Hunter. She hadn't been working where he could spot her. He decided the troopers must have taken her somewhere for safekeeping. He stopped in front of the restaurant and went into the arctic entry to find a newspaper dispenser. Though he should have suspected it he was surprised to find both the Anchorage Dispatch and the Peninsula Clarion were showing headlines of the shooting. He bought both papers and drove back to the hotel.

He carried his papers and stopped at the soda machine near the office to get something to drink before entering his room. He was anxious to read the papers to determine what he should do next. There was a small round table and two chairs in the room where he sat, drinking his soda and reading the Peninsula Clarion. A reporter who had been to the scene wrote an account of the shootout. He'd interviewed a number of people who saw the incident including a waitress by the name of Flo. She had called the troopers to report the shooting and was commended for keeping the patrons safe during the incident. She had seen the action outside the window of the restaurant, but said she had been too busy calling and keeping the patrons safe to get an accurate description of the shooter.

The article went on to say a reporter had gone to the hospital to learn about the wounded police officers, but was turned away. The reporter asked one of the ambulance medics about the condition of the two and was told they were both alive, but in critical condition. The medic wouldn't say anything else about them.

The account in the Anchorage Dispatch was a replay of the one in the Clarion. By the time Roma had finished reading both papers he was angry with himself for not making sure the two cops had died at the scene. He wondered if this was a ruse by the troopers to smoke him out. He thought it impossible the two had survived three shotgun blasts and three loads of 00 buck pellets at a range of eight to ten feet. He had no intention of notifying his boss of this, but decided he would have to remedy the situation at once.

Roma finished his soda and sat at the table working on a plan to finish what he had started. He was sure he would have to go to the hospital to do this. He was angry with himself, but had not finalized a plan, when his phone jingled. It was Woodbury.

"Have you seen the papers," he asked.

"Yeah, I just read it. I can't believe it."

"Mr. Roselli is not going to be happy. What are you going to do about it?"

"I'm not sure, but I'll be doing it today. I don't want these cops talking."

"Do it quickly, I want to leave here as soon as possible, tomorrow morning would be my choice."

"I can't find the girl. She's disappeared. She's the one I need to find. The cops are in the hospital and in bad shape. They won't be moving. I can find them. The girl is my problem. I think the troopers have her hidden some-where. With Dallas dead I have to do it alone, unless you think you want to give me a hand."

"Don't be a wise guy, Roma. You know I can't be involved in anything like that. Just finish the job and be on the plane with me tomorrow."

Roma was about to get tough with the lawyer when the line went dead. "I didn't think so," Roma muttered as he closed his cell phone.

Vito had made up his mind to finish the two men in the hospital and if he couldn't find Hunter he would leave town with the lawyer in the morning. He stopped at a local pawn shop where he found an old World War II fighting knife. It made a good boot knife, easily concealed. He haggled with the man behind the counter and bought the knife for $50. At a local hardware store he purchased a small diamond lap sharpener with the intent of improving the efficiency of the tool. In a donation box behind the local thrift store he found some clothing to fit. They made him look like a local fisherman.

With the knife hidden under his pant leg and inside his boot, wearing a flannel shirt and a floppy fishing hat decorated with Coho Flies he entered the hospital. He found a map of the floor plan and studied it a moment. ICU was on the second floor as were all the patient rooms. That would be convenient for his purposes. At the top of the stairs he saw a nurse in the hallway and called for her to stop a moment.

"Excuse me, miss, I'm a minister from Iowa. I am a friend of the family of one of the troopers injured in the gun battle. Can you tell me where they are? I would like to stop and give them my blessing."

"One in is ICU, but you'll have to check with the floor nurse before you'll be able to see him. The other is in room 236, but there too, you'll have to check with the nurse at the desk in order to visit."

"Thank you, you've been very helpful." She smiled and walked away. Roma walked down the hall to the main patient rooms to find Room 236. He found it with the door closed and a NO VISITOR sign on the door. He was reaching for the knob when a voice behind him startled him.

"You aren't allowed in that room, Sir."

Roma spun around to meet a uniform. It was a hospital security guard. His badge identified him as Vern. "Oh, hello there, I'm Pastor Dean from Iowa. I was asked by the family of one of the officers to look in on them. I'm just here fishing you see."

"I'm sorry, Pastor, but no one is allowed in to see them right now. If you come by tomorrow when the doctor is here you can talk to him. Perhaps he'll give you special permission. Until then, I can't allow you to enter his room."

"I understand, Vern. It is Vern, isn't it?" asked Roma.

"Yes, it is, sir. Now if you'll please come with me I'll show you out." Vern directed.

"Certainly," Roma said, bending down as if to tie his shoe. He lifted his pant leg and pulled out the fighting knife. He whirled around, wielding the blade to strike the guard.

Vern had spent 20 years as a correctional officer in the local prison. The quickness of his reaction stunned Roma. Vern deflected the blade, grabbing the right wrist of the hefty man, stepping behind him and hooking the hand with the knife with the inside of his left elbow wrapping the rest of his lower arm behind Roma's neck and grab his own right arm. This instinctive action made the blade useless and placed the assailant in a choke hold. It was needed for only a half-minute before Roma collapsed, unconscious, on the floor. The security officer put handcuffs on the limp arms of the man before calling for backup. The fighting knife had fallen to the floor. The scuffle had drawn the attention of two nurses who came to help the officer. One of them picked up the knife and took it to the nurse's desk for safe keeping.

Someone had called the local police who were now running up the hallway. Vern was inspecting the cut in his uniform sleeve when they arrived. The first officer on the scene recognized Roma from the pictures Caswell had delivered to the station.

"Good job, Vern, this is the bozo who shot Gant and Pulis. Are you OK?"

"Yes, but the rat cut up my shirt."

"I'll call Captain Caswell and let him know we have the shooter in custody," said the Soldotna police officer.

The captain had been at home eating dinner when the call came. He instantly dispatched two cars to the scene. The captain was in uniform when he arrived at the hospital. Roma had recovered from his choke hold and had been taken to a visitor waiting area away from the patient treatment area.

Caswell recognized Roma the instant he saw him. He approached the mobster, smiling.

"It's a pleasure to finally meet you Vito. I hope you enjoy your stay with us. I'm sure it'll be a lengthy visit." Caswell was feeling a gigantic wave of relief.

The first trooper arrived, "Go to the jail with the city officers and help them book him. Don't take any chances with him. He's a professional."

Caswell ordered the other officer to take statements from everyone in the halls. He saw the Hospital Security Guard standing with his back to the wall, waiting. "Are you alright, Vern?"

"I'm fine, Captain," said Vern, "It's like riding a bicycle, once I needed to do it I remembered how."

"I want to thank you personally, Vern. He was after my men. I'll be sending a letter to your chief. Thank you again."

"Just doing my job, Captain."

"Just the same, thanks. Is it OK if I go in and see Gant now?"

"Sure, I'll bet he is trying to get out of bed to see what all the commotion is about."

Inside the room the light was on, although it wasn't needed. "What's going on out there, Cap?" asked the patient from the bed.

"Not much, but Roma won't be a problem for you now. Hospital Security just caught him trying to get into your room with a big knife. Vern, the security guard, stopped him. I learned he is a very handy guy to have on your side in a fight. He took Roma down without assistance."

"Remind me to never sass him, Cap.

Captain Caswell asked a city policeman to go to Gant's house and bring Leila Hunter down here to visit the wounded trooper. He then sat in a chair beside the bed to visit with Bill Gant.

Chapter 26

On the way to his office the following morning Captain Caswell stopped at the hospital. Trying to be quiet, he opened the door slightly and peered inside. Gant lay sleeping with Leila sitting in a chair pulled close and holding his hand. She, too, was sleeping with her head resting on the blankets. Caswell smiled and backed out of the room.

Rollin Caswell took a chance and walked down the hall to ICU to speak with the nurse. When he asked about Alan Pulis she smiled, "He's awake this morning. Let me check and see if he is up to having a visitor." A moment later she came out of the room, "You can go in now, but please keep it short."

Caswell thanked her and stepped into the room.

"Hi, Cap," said Pulis, barely above a whisper.

"Good to see you awake, Alan, we've been worried about you."

"What happened, Cap? I don't remember anything. Bill and I came out of the restaurant and got into the car. That's the last thing I remember until I woke up this morning. I feel like crap. The nurse said someone shot me and Bill." It was a struggle for Pulis to speak.

"Vito Roma and his partner, Dallas Freed spotted you at lunch. They hid their car behind the building and when you two came out they pulled up behind you. Vito jumped out and began firing. He hit you through the side window and got Bill with two shots through the windshield. I'm glad you were both wearing vests."

"I'm sorry, Captain, I don't remember any of it. How is Bill?" asked Pulis.

"He is still in the other wing of the hospital. Leila is with him."

"What about Roma and Freed?" asked Alan, "Did you get them?"

"A citizen saw the shooting and had a .45 under his seat. He grabbed it and started firing as Freed and Roma drove off. He got Freed, but he managed to drive to Funny River Road. Roma got the car stopped and pulled Freed out onto the shoulder of the road. He took the car and we lost him. He showed up again last night, here at the hospital. He was going into Bill's room carrying a fighting knife. Vern the security guard saw him and choked him out. Roma is in Pre-Trial, going to arraignment this morning. I think we can count him out of the picture for a long time."

"I'll sleep easier knowing he's out of it." Alan's speech was becoming labored.

"I'll leave you alone, Alan. If you need anything at all, have the nurse call me. Good to have you back with us." Caswell stood and Pulis nodded, closing his eyes to rest.

In the hall he spoke with the nurse, "Can you tell me anything about his condition?"

"I can't do that, but regaining consciousness and being alert are very good signs. He is still not aware of the extent of his injuries. Sorry, I don't have more and better news."

Caswell smiled, "Thank you anyway," he said. "If he needs anything at all please call me." He gave the nurse his card which she attached to his chart.

By the time Captain Caswell returned to his office Lawrence Woodbury was on the telephone to Salvatore Roselli to report the arrest of Vito Roma.

"Get him out, I need him," shouted Roselli.

"What do you expect me to do, Sal. Vito was arrested for trying to kill two cops. We don't own the cops here and they take all this very seriously. I don't even know if the judge will allow bail for Vito."

"I want him out. I can't keep sending men up there and having them killed or arrested. Vito is the best. Get him out."

"I'll do what I can, but don't expect too much. It'll be out of my hands."

"Buy the judge, do something," screamed Sal Roselli. "And I need you home as soon as you can. The feds are going to be here soon. My ear in the agency says they have a lot of new evidence and are about to come down on me."

"This whole situation is getting completely out of hand, Sal. I'll do what I can, but there are some things even I can't fix." Woodbury was beginning to fear for his own welfare. He knew Roselli was an irrational man, but even with this kind of money it didn't seem worth the effort and risk.

Woodbury drove to the jail to confer with his client. The officers brought Roma to the attorney visiting room in handcuffs and leg irons. Once in the small room the handcuffs were removed and one leg iron was connected to a steel ring in the wall. It was obvious to Woodbury the officers considered him a true threat.

The officer closed the door to leave the lawyer alone with his client. The instant the door clicked closed Vito demanded, through clenched teeth, "Get me out of here. I have another job to do and then I can get gone from Alaska. I hate this place."

"Sal has been on the phone demanding the same thing. The problem is I don't have any influence in the court system in Alaska. The preliminary report I have states they;re charging you with three counts of attempted murder, one of tampering with evidence, eluding police and my favorite, conspiracy to commit murder. Some of this is to cover their bases, but the heavy charges will never be dismissed. On top of that I expect a warrant from New Jersey for the murder of Patty Dawson. The bottom line is I don't know if I can get you out."

"You're paid to keep me out of jail. Do your job. I can't do mine while I'm in here," Vito would not let on he was afraid this was the time he would go to jail forever.

"You'll be taken to the court house this morning," stated Woodbury, "when you get inside I want you to keep your mouth shut unless the judge asks you something. I don't want you to answer unless I tell you it's OK. When the judge asks if you're ready to enter a plea you'll say 'yes sir.' After that you'll keep quiet unless I tell you otherwise. Is that clear?"

"I hear you, but I don't like it."

"I don't care what you like, Vito. I can't do my job if you are going to sabotage the process with your outbursts. I expect the judge to set another date for a bail hearing. That should occur sometime in the next few days. You have to keep your cool until then." The lawyer had little hope he could get the judge to set bail for Vito Roma, but he was not going to let his client know that. "I'll see you at court."

Woodbury stood and knocked on the door to inform the guard he wanted out. He left the jail facility without saying anything to anyone. Vito was back in irons and led back to the isolation cell from which he had been taken. He didn't resist on the trip back to the cell. The two officers took the leg irons off before he entered the cell and the handcuffs were removed once he was inside and put his hands through the meal slot in the door. The entire process is demeaning and degrading, but Vito had earned the status he now held by attacking law enforcement officers. He would get no slack from the correctional officers.

FBI Agent Greer entered Captain Caswell's office with a grim look on his face. "How are Gant and Pulis?" he asked. "Are they awake yet?"

"Gant is doing pretty well. He should be out of the hospital in a day or so. He's going to need some time to heal before he can get back to work. Pulis woke up this morning. They haven't told him how bad he's hurt. I really don't know how he'll take it. The doctor told me he would never use his left arm again. His recovery time will depend on how quickly the patch in his neck artery heals. I talked with him this morning and he seemed to be doing alright."

"I'm sorry to hear about Alan. I hope he takes it well. Those two men are good cops; a couple of the best I've ever worked with. They're both a little over the center line, but they're both good at what they do." It was a high tribute coming from the federal officer. He held up a file folder, "I have some news to deliver. The State of New Jersey is preparing a Governors Warrant and soliciting extradition for Vito Roma. They want him for the murder of Salvatore Roselli's secretary. The other item is the FBI has a warrant for Vito Roma in connection with gangland activity and organized crime. Sal Roselli is also named in the warrants. The FBI put the case together using information Gant brought to us. It confirms and documents interstate crimes including extortion, arson, murder, racketeering and drug dealing. There are other charges as well, but those will be filed later after Roselli and his mob are in jail."

"Good news, Greer. Does this mean the feds are picking up the tab for medical treatment of my men, hurt while chasing your crooks?" Caswell was grinning.

"Those decisions are above my pay grade, but I wouldn't count on it."

Caswell looked at his watch, "Vito is going to be arraigned this morning. I think I'll sit in the back of the court and listen, want to come along?"

"Sure, Captain, thanks for the invite, I'll buy lunch when we finish."

The court hearing was pretty much as Woodbury had predicted. No bail was set, but a bail hearing would be held on Monday next week. After lunch the two law officers stopped at the hospital to visit Gant and Pulis. Leila Hunter was still sitting in the chair next to Bill Gant's bed. She looked tired, but smiled when the Captain said hello. The doctors had changed the bandages making them all look fresh and clean.

"How are you feeling, Bill," asked Caswell.

"I'm a little sore, but the doctors say my stitches are inside and they don't expect there will be much scarring. The plastic surgeon said if there's no sign of infection by tomorrow he might let me go home, since I have such a good nurse." Leila squeezed his hand.

"That's good news, Bill," said the captain, "By the way I saw Alan this morning. He's awake and seemed to be alert. When I saw him they hadn't told him just how bad his left arm will be. I'm worried about how he'll take it."

"Good to see you doing well, Bill," Greer was being sincere. "I want to thank you for all the evidence you brought to us. The warrants are being written as we speak. There'll be a big raid on Roselli's outfit as soon as the papers are ready. Oh, yeah, I have a report on those wires you found in the bombed car. You were right, DuPont electric primer, first class material. The bureau informs me it fits with the M.O. for a hit man with the name of Vito Roma." Greer laughed, "You done good boy."

"Thank you. Can I be a G-Man now?" Gant was grinning, "I'm retired and this case was a little something to do in my retirement. I think I'll go back to being retired. Forget the G-Man badge."

"I think it's time to let him out of the hospital. He's getting ornery." Caswell turned to Leila, "Take good care of him, Leila."

Pulis was sleeping when the two policemen went into ICU. The nurse said he had taken the news about his arm rather badly. He had been sedated again. Caswell's head hung low and his shoulders drooped as they walked out of the hospital.

"I'm sorry," said Agent Greer. "If there is anything I can do for him, let me know."

The two men discussed several items of importance involving the upcoming warrants before Agent Greer left the office to return to Anchorage.

Chapter 27

Two weeks had passed since Vito Roma had been arraigned and his bail request denied. Woodbury had climbed aboard the private jet and returned to Newark. The legal processes, as encumbered as they are, take a long time to work through the courts and entire legal system. Publicly everything seemed to be on hold.

Bill Gant had been released from the hospital and sent home. Leila had been acting as his nurse, living in his house and tending his medical needs. It was plain to everyone but Leila and Bill the two were becoming emotionally attracted. Bill walked every day for exercise with Leila at his side. He was healing quickly from his wounds.

Fireweed was beginning to bloom everywhere. They begin in early July and are done by August. Locals know when the Fireweed is bloomed out it will be three weeks to the first frost. Most housewives dislike the omen. But like a snowshoe hare turning white it is only an indicator of things to come.

Today is a special day. Leila and Bill are to pick up Alan when he is released from the hospital. He is progressing well, except for the crippled left arm that will never recover; a fact Alan has yet to accept. Leila and Bill had visited every day since he was released from ICU. Bill had asked Alan to stay with him and Leila until he regained his strength, but he refused, saying he needed to be alone and to learn to cope with his new disability. Bill didn't believe him. He thought Alan was selling himself short and feeling sorry for himself, giving in to his depression. He and Leila would have to work on that problem.

Alan was close to his birthday, which is in late July. Bill dragged the Hewescraft to the dealer to have new wiring installed to accommodate the electric reel Gant had installed on Pulis' favorite halibut rod. The electric reel would allow him to fish for halibut using only one arm. He hoped Alan would take it as a gift to help him and not to feel sorry for him. It was going to be a delicate dance when it was presented. To help ease the situation Bill had written a poem for the birthday boy:

> "I always wear my Birthday Suit
> While opening my Birthday Loot,
> My mom always thought it cute
> Her own horn she would toot.
> No one else gave a hoot."

The process of release from the hospital was lengthy, but eventually the nurses finished with final instructions and loaded him into a wheelchair for the ride to the front door where Bill was waiting with a car to drive him home. Alan was unusually quiet during the trip. Leila turned around in the front seat to talk to Alan during the drive to his home. Bill was worried about his partner. The good natured banter and sarcasm was gone. Alan didn't seem bitter, only withdrawn and quiet.

The Hewescraft sat in the front yard. Alan studied it as they drove in. Bill parked close to the front porch to eliminate unnecessary walking for the wounded Pulis. He climbed the steps under his own power and turned again to look at the boat. Gant saw the look on his face.

"You know Alan, next week is your birthday. Leila and I thought it would be good for you to go halibut fishing that day, how about it?"

"I think my halibut fishing days are over, Partner. I can't crank a reel any longer." There was sadness on his face.

"You give up too easily. Leila and I bought you a birthday gift. Wait here and I'll go get it," said Bill as he walked toward the boat. He climbed on the trailer fender and reached inside the craft. He came back carrying Alan's favorite halibut rod with a new reel on the butt. "I'll bet you can crank this one," he said, handing the rod to Pulis.

"What in the heck is that?" asked Alan.

"That's your rod with a new electric reel. We had a sturdier rod holder put on the boat, too. When you get a bite all you have to do is push the button. The meter on the top tells you how much line is out. It looks so good I may get one for myself."

At this point Leila stepped up to hand Alan an envelope.

"Oh yeah, Alan, we spent all our money on the reel so we made the card ourselves." At this point Bill and Leila broke into the Happy Birthday song.

"I'm going to have to go inside and sit down to read the card," Alan was becoming weak from the activity.

"Can I get you some coffee or a soda or something?" asked Leila.

"No, I'm fine. I want to read the card." He struggled to open the envelope with his one good hand, but finally managed. He took out the sheet of paper with the verse printed on it and read. Suddenly he began to smile and shake his head. Looking up he said, "You two aren't going to feel sorry for me, are you?"

"Why should we, Alan? You and I have been partners for too long to quit now."

Alan sat in his recliner and read the poem again. "Leila, get me a beer." Alan Pulis was home again.

In Newark things were busy. Woodbury had come back with bad news about Vito Roma. He had been denied bail and the feds were now entering the case. Woodbury had hired a local attorney to defend Roma, but neither of them had any hope of winning. The new attorney hated Roma and the way he treated his lawyer. This would be one case he didn't care if he won or lost and it looked like he was going to lose. It didn't make any difference to the new attorney he would be paid either way.

Roselli had received word by way of his informant in the FBI office that a raid was about to take place. Woodbury advised him to put together as much cash as he could gather and run. Roselli contacted his New York rival and asked him what he would give to own the New Jersey operation.

"How much?" asked Lou "Waterboy" Zena. He had acquired his nickname as a teenager when he was on the high school swim team and was considered for the Olympic Swim Team.

"I'll take a hundred million, cash. The feds are about to try to arrest me and I have to liquidate."

"Let's meet, Roselli. I think we can work out a deal." Zena would offer a quarter of what Roselli had wanted, but time and an impending arrest were on his side. "Where do you want to meet?"

Sal thought for a moment, it had to be somewhere neutral. Somewhere Zena would be as vulnerable as he now was. "Stamford, Connecticut, that little seafood restaurant on the east side, do you remember it. It's where we had a meeting three years ago."

"Yeah, I remember. Be there at eight tonight, you and a driver, no one else. I'll call and make reservations." Lou Zena was uncomfortable with the arrangement, but knew Sal was also out of his kingdom. It would take until eight for the driver to get him there. He knew Sal would be short of time to set up a double cross. It would be perfect.

The two men met in the parking lot of the upscale restaurant. Inside the hostess was waiting for the two men and seated them at once.

"I heard you're about to have a bad day, Sal," reported Lou.

"Yeah, I expected it today, but the feds couldn't get the warrants signed by the judge in time. I have until tomorrow morning to be out of town." Sal's eyes darted around the room as he spoke. He didn't spot any of Zena's men.

"You said you wanted a hundred million, Sal. That's a little steep, how about I offer you twenty five. I'll give you five mil cash and wire transfer the rest."

The waiter came to the table, "Can I get you men something to drink?" he asked.

"Tell Vinnie a bottle of old wine for my friend and me." Old wine is personal, made by the owner and his family. It is only served to special customers, select friends and close family, of course.

"Of course, Sir," the waiter knew this was someone the owner knew well and respected. He spun on his heels and quickly walked to the kitchen.

"That's impossible, Lou. The equipment and property are worth more than that. Remember, you've been trying to get my operation for a long time. This way you'll have it and you won't have to spend any money trying to find out what I'm doing over there across the river." Sal chuckled, letting Zena know he had been aware of his spying.

"You're a clever man, Sal. But it seems to me you're in a very tight spot and must sell today. I have the advantage here. I'll up my offer to five cash and thirty five by wire."

The waiter was back with an unopened black bottle of wine. He pulled the cork and offered Lou a taste. Lou knew the ritual and approved the wine. He offered Sal a taste before ordering the waiter to pour their glasses full. "And what would you like for dinner, Sir?"

"Tell Vinnie it's for Sal and me, he'll fix me something."

"Thank you, Sir," said the waiter, knowing this would lead to a very large tip.

As the waiter walked to the kitchen Sal sat shaking his head, "Make it five cash and forty five by wire and we'll deal."

"Because we're such good friends, I'll give you what you want, but you have to pay for dinner. When do you want the cash? I'll have the wire sent to any numbers you say first thing when the banks open."

"I'll need the cash tonight. Sorry for the rush, but I think the raid is on for early tomorrow."

"I'll make the call as soon as I get to my car. It'll be delivered by the time you arrive back in Newark. Will you tell me where you'll be going?" asked Zena, showing an innocent face.

"Yeah, Right!" said Sal, raising his wine glass to toast the deal.

"You'll have to give me the account numbers you wish me to send the rest of the money to." He raised his own glass to consummate the deal.

The old enemies were now friends at a leisurely meal without hostility. Both men had done what they had come for. In the parking lot Zena shook hands with Sal. "It's been a good rivalry for all these years, Sal. I'm going to miss you."

"And I you, my friend," said Sal. "When I arrange for a telephone I can trust, I will call you. I have friends and if I hear of anything I'll call you. If you can keep any of my employees they'll do a fine job for you. Vito is in jail in Alaska and I can't get him out. Rinaldi is dead, killed on a job in Alaska. The men at the warehouse are mostly union and do honest work. They'll be worth keeping. If you can find a place for Marco Cidella, it would be good. He can run the operation in Newark if you need someone. Say the word and I'll tell him to do the job for you."

"Tell Marco I'll call him when I know how I'm going to operate on that side of the river. I'll see you back in Newark tonight, Sal"

Sal sat in the front seat as Marco drove the Lincoln back toward Newark. "I think I have it set up for you to run the operation when I'm gone, Marco. I'm sorry you can't come with me, but I understand your family comes first. Tonight may be goodbye for you and me, Marco, but I have to tell you there's only one other man I ever trusted like I trust you. I don't know where I'll land, but when I am settled I'll call you and see how things are going. I love you my son."

"The feeling is mutual, Mr. Roselli. Thank you."

"After we meet Zena I want you to drive me to that private airport to meet with the Gulfstream Pilot. The title for the Lincoln is in the jockey box. I've signed it off and it's yours. Have a good life, Marco."

Back in the Ace Trucking Company parking lot a limo was waiting for them. A large man in a dark suit stepped out to pull two large metal suitcases from the rear seat of the limo. Marco stepped out to open the rear door of his new car. The man set the bags inside and turned back to his car without saying a word. As the limo pulled away Marco opened one of the bags to see they were full of cash. He sat behind the wheel again and nodded to his boss. The trip to the airport was silent and quick.

Chapter 28

Captain Caswell called Bill Gant to come into the office to meet with Agent Greer. In had been two weeks since Pulis had been released from the hospital. Gant and Leila had done little but help with his rehabilitation. The muscles, tendons and nerves as well as the shoulder joint had been destroyed. The therapist gave them exercises to perform to enable him to regain some function of his left hand, however the arm was useless. It was a frustrating process for both Pulis and his aides. Leila and Bill worked well together and between them had improved Alan's attitude and outlook. The three were looking forward to a weekend halibut fishing trip; their first since Alan had been released.

This would be Bill's first official day of duty since the shooting. He was looking forward to it. He wanted to get back into the action. There were personal scores to settle now. Agent Greer was sitting in the captain's office when he arrived.

When Bill entered the office Agent Greer instantly stood and offered a handshake. "Good to see you again, Bill," said the FBI man.

"I'll second that," said Rollin Caswell.

"Thanks, it's good to be back. I'm not sure I can wrestle drunks yet, but I think I can investigate, if the hours aren't too long."

The three men laughed together.

"How is Alan doing?" asked Ed Greer.

"He's getting stronger every day. He'll never be able to use his left arm again, but he's working hard to learn new ways to cope with the handicap. We had a new electric reel put on his halibut rod and he's anxious to try it out."

"That's good news, Bill. Have a seat and I'll fill you in on the results of the raid on Roselli's place in Newark. Do you want a soda or coffee?" asked Greer.

"No thanks, I'm fine. Tell what happened to Roselli?"

"The New York office had a time getting the warrants signed. The judges were out of the city for a full day at some legal convention at Yale University. We know we have a leak in the New York office and the word got back to Roselli. He met with Lou Zena, the head of New York organized crime, and sold his New Jersey interests to Zena. That lawyer, Woodbury, wrote a bill of sale, signed by Roselli, for all Roselli's holdings. Zena bought it all. The price was said to be One Dollar and Other Considerations. This whole deal was done in the middle of the night. By morning Roselli had skipped, nobody seems to know where he went. We did the raid anyway and took down more than a hundred enforcers and runners. The officers found a small amount of cash in the office, but Roselli had emptied the safe of cash and destroyed all the records he had on hand. We served two murder warrants and 105 racketeering warrants. There are active warrants for Roselli for murder, conspiracy to commit murder and racketeering: if he ever shows up."

"You managed to get all that from the books I brought you?" asked Gant.

"Yes, we had the cases worked but lacked having documentation. You gave us the proof we needed to act on these cases." Greer wore a broad grin, "You're a genuine hero, Bill."

Caswell was smiling too, "I've had a call from Emilio Perez, Director of East Coast Operations for the FBI. He's writing a commendation for you and Alan, but somehow I felt he wasn't impressed with Alan; something about insulting remarks. The commendations will go directly to the Governor and the Commissioner of Public Safety."

"Can I trade it for another tank of boat gas?" asked Gant.

"I don't know if you had heard, but Roma is still in jail. The judge denied bail and set a trial date for late next month. Roma has a new attorney. He is out of Anchorage. He's a high-dollar criminal lawyer. Woodbury made the arrangements and paid the fee. As it stands now the DA thinks he will get about 200 years on the charges. Shooting a cop is still against the law in Alaska." Caswell had kept a close eye on the case. He conferred regularly with the District Attorney on the matter.

"I guess I can expect to get a subpoena any day now," said Gant.

"I would guess so," said Caswell. "How soon will it be before you come back to work?"

"I suppose I can start anytime. Leila and I have been busy doing the therapy for Alan's arm. I think she can handle it now."

"Is she still living with you?" asked Caswell.

"At my house, but not with me," explained Gant. "We've spent most of our time with Alan at his place.

"Sorry, Bill, I didn't mean to imply anything improper was going on."

"It's OK, Cap, under any other circumstances they probably would."

"Would it be permissible for me to stop and see Alan on my way back to Anchorage?" asked Greer.

"I'm going back there when I leave here, Ed. You can follow me to the house if you care to."

"Let me know when you want to officially start back on the payroll, Bill. There's a lot of reports to be filed. The investigation seems to be at an end and this will wind it up. I'm trying to get the commissioner to approve compensation for both you and Alan because of your job-related injuries. I still haven't had word from the office about that."

"See ya, Cap." Gant stood and walked out of the office with Greer following.

It was a ten minute drive from the office to Alan Pulis' house near Sterling. When they arrived Leila came out onto the front porch to greet them. Introductions were made and everyone went inside. Alan was seated on the couch in the living room.

"I brought you a visitor, Alan," said Bill.

"Agent Greer. Good to see you, what brings you to the fringes of civilization like this?"

"I was down for a meeting with the captain and asked Bill if I could stop by and say hello to you. You're looking good, for a shot-up old man." Greer knew Pulis would not take kindly to sympathy.

The men visited for more than an hour. Most of the time was spent talking about Roma and Roselli and what they expected to happen to the East Coast Crooks. Leila tired of the shop talk and went into the kitchen to fix lunch. Minutes later Bill followed. In the privacy of the kitchen he wrapped his arms around the tall waitress and held her tight.

When he loosened his hold she said, "A girl could get used to that."

"I hope so, Leila. This case is about to close and I'll be able to hold you legally. That is if you want to be held by me. I haven't had much luck with permanent relationships in my life."

She smiled a pretty smile, "Maybe I can help you with that."

"If this is going to turn serious we have a lot of things to discuss."

"Like what," she asked.

"First of all, you're a very rich lady and all I have to offer is a pension. You can go anywhere in the world you want. I can only take you fishing. I just have to know you can be satisfied with a slow-pace lifestyle with peace and quiet the main ingredient. You'd better think hard about that."

"I have thought about it. You and Alan have been friends for a lifetime and I'm a recent interloper in the equation. I see you wanting to keep an eye on him for at least the near future. I hope I can be part of that life with you. I like peace and quiet. I've had enough excitement to last me a lifetime. I thought

I'd like excitement, but it ain't what it's cracked up to be. Somehow I'd rather not have people running around trying to kill me all the time."

"I'm glad you feel like that," he stepped close to her again and, for the first time, kissed her. "I don't know what happened to Roselli and I don't know if he has given up on you, but he'll have to come through me to get to you." Gant snickered, "You'll have to learn to bait hooks and clean the boat."

"I already know how to bait a hook. I caught you, didn't I?" Now she was chuckling, "We have to get Alan well and he can clean the boat."

"I like the way you think, Lady." He kissed her again and walked back to the living room.

Greer was standing at the door. "Thanks for allowing me to come by to see Alan. I'll come back again, if you'll let me. I'm glad to see you're feeling better, Alan. Keep up the good work."

After Greer left Bill sat to talk with Alan. "The captain wants me to come back to work for a while. I have to write all the reports and get Roma's case ready for the DA. I doubt it'll take more than a couple of weeks. Leila will be here to help you with your exercises. From what Greer says the case is wrapped up. I don't know if the crime lab will be able to connect Roma with the evidence I found in the bombed out car, but he's going away for a long time for what he did to you and me."

"When are you planning to let me in on the situation between you and Leila?" asked Alan.

"Is it that obvious?"

"Not to everyone, but it is to me. I'm proud of you, Bill. You could do a lot worse, in fact, you have done worse. Don't let this one get away, Partner."

"I just had a talk with her about it. I learned she can bait a hook. I have to keep her." Both men laughed.

Pulis became serious, "Bill, I don't want to be a factor for you. Take Leila and make a life for yourself. I can manage just fine. I'm glad you have someone to share your life with."

"Don't get all misty on me, Alan. We've discussed it and you're in this with us. We'll be here for you as long as you want us around."

"Can I come with you on the honeymoon?"

"You're a pervert, Alan."

"I know. It slips out now and then." Again both men were laughing.

Salvatore Roselli, now residing in Costa Rica where there is no extradition, was on the telephone with Marco Cidella who was reporting the raid. "Did the feds arrest you, Marco?"

"Yeah, but I wasn't on any of the warrants so they had to release me. Woodbury threatened to sue them for false arrest, it was kinda funny. The drivers and the dock hands never got arrested. The union had stewards on the dock to see they were treated OK. Your accountant and all the office personnel were booked, though. They took every scrap of paper in the office as well as all the computers. Lou Zena came down and raised cane with the feds. He said he had bought the business and they were to get out and leave him alone. He told them he was just an honest businessman trying to make a go of it."

Roselli broke into hysterical laughter. When he was able to speak again he became somber. "Marco, I want that girlfriend of Steven Collier. I think she was the one who had all the evidence the feds used. It looks like Vito will go to jail, too. If he is convicted I want him iced. He knows too much about me. But first I want that girl found and put away. She's the cause of all my problems. Once you find her have one of Zena's men finish her. I want it ugly. I want everyone to know. You can't screw with Salvatore Roselli and get away with it."

"I'll get it done, Boss." There was a long pause. "Hey, Boss, are you ever coming home?" asked Marco.

"It doesn't look like it right now, Marco, someday, perhaps, but not soon."

"I'll call you as soon as I know anything, Boss. Enjoy the sunshine and palm trees." Marco didn't like the assignment, but Mr. Roselli was still the boss.

Chapter 29

Early the following morning the trio set off on the first fishing trip in recent weeks. The days were beginning to lose hours of daylight at a rate of two minutes a day now. As the days grow shorter the weather in July and August remain warm and calm. Wildflowers bloom everywhere making the landscape a colorful sight. Cow moose are now bringing the new calves out to browse with them, making the drive to Anchor Point a perilous adventure.

Alan had been in a very good mood in recent days having resigned himself to his condition. He was learning to cope with his disabled left arm, but still had moments of frustration when he had trouble managing some task. Bill drove the truck to the launch site and paid for the launch and take-out. They had loaded all the gear in the boat before leaving home so there was nothing to do but climb aboard and wait for the tractor to push them into the water. Pulis climbed into the captain's chair. "I'm driving," he announced.

Bill and Leila watched Alan as he piloted the boat the 26 miles to the fishing spot they had agreed upon today. The water was calm and the tide slowed. The air was warm allowing them to be on the back deck without a coat or rain slicker. Bill went to the back of the boat to prepare the bait and attach hooks and leaders to the rods. It felt good to be relaxed and fishing once again.

Leila sat in the cabin with Alan, watching his satisfied expression as he steered the boat toward the little X indicated on the GPS. Minutes later he slowed the boat as the arrow moved closer to the little X. Bill climbed to the top of the side rail and made his way to the bow. When Alan called out "OK" Bill dropped the anchor. They were to fish in 180 feet of water, but it required about 500 feet of anchor line. When the anchor bit into the bottom and the boat stretched the anchor line tight Alan cut the engine.

"Come on Leila, let's try that new reel," urged Pulis, stepping out of his chair, holding on with his good hand to maintain balance in the small waves.

Bill had made his way to the back and baited a rod for Leila. "Go ahead and fish. It'll take a minute or two to set up his rod."

Pulis was inspecting the power port where the reel would be plugged into the boat's power. He held the rod in one hand and was able to turn the chrome star drag wheel on the side of the new reel while Bill tugged on the line. It was important to set the drag because they expected to catch large fish today. Too loose a drag and the fish would have the advantage and run a long way. Too tight and it could break the 80 pound test line or damage the rod. It didn't take long to accomplish the adjustment and bait the hook. Bill put the rod in the new beefed up rod holder and left Alan to fend for himself while he baited his own rod and dropped the weight.

Bill and Leila gazed at each other like a couple of teenagers. Leila got the first bite and began to reel. Bill set his rod in one of the rod holders and prepared to help Leila bring her fish into the boat. It was a small one, only about 25 pounds or so. They decided to turn it back and try for a larger one. Bill was baiting her hook again when Alan called out.

"I've got a bite," he said as he reached for the button that would bring the fish to the surface. Once sure the fish was on the line he began to bring it up. It came easily at first, but then took a run for the bottom. Alan was giggling like a child. The fish would come up a while then return to the bottom. Alan won for a while and then the fish. Finally the fish began to tire and inch by inch he was hoisted to the surface. It looked to weigh more than 60 pounds. Bill reached for a gaff with which to hook the fish and hoist him into the boat where he would stick a knife in the base of its head to dispatch it. Alan did a little jig when the fish slid into the fish box and was laughing when he said, "I have to go sit down a while." As he entered the cabin he turned to say, "Now, that was fun." He went inside the cabin to sit a while.

Both Bill and Leila were pleased at the result of the day. Now Bill had a bite. The trio fished a while, ate lunch and fished some more. It was a good day and they had tossed many smaller halibut back into the inlet. Alan had come back to the rear deck after resting a while and eating lunch.

"How many fish do we have, Partner?" asked Alan.

"Leila and I are done. You need one more. I'll clean up the deck while you fish." Bill busied himself with the chores of stowing the rods, putting away hooks and gaffs. He was nearly finished when Alan hooked another fish. This one seemed to be as large as the last one, but the new reel was doing its job well. Alan was able to hold on to the reel and balance himself against the rocking of the boat while fighting the large fish with the electric reel. Bill delighted in watching his old friend getting back into life. When the fish came to the surface it was larger than the first. This one was nearly a hundred pounds.

"Don't gaff her, Bill. She is a large female and I'm going to turn her loose."

It didn't take long to release the fish and to re-bait the hook. The tide had turned and the fish were having one last snack before hiding on the bottom again. The rod began to move at the tip. Alan waited for the fish to take the bait before he started reeling. This one came up without stripping line very much. On the surface it looked to be about 40 pounds.

"Let's keep this one, Bill. I'm getting tired."

Once the fish was in the box Bill made his way to the front of the boat. Anchor pulling is a unique experience among halibut fishermen. A large buoy is attached to the anchor line with a stainless steel ring. The boat is put into gear and the line slides through the ring hoisting the anchor from the bottom. When the anchor chain is pulled through the ring the weight keeps the anchor from dropping back to the bottom. The boat is then turned and the deck hand pulls the line aboard the vessel until he has the chain and anchor aboard.

When Bill returned to the cabin Alan stepped out of the captain's chair. "I guess you can drive back to the beach, Bill. I'm worn out," he was grinning, "and it feels good."

"This case is about wrapped up, Alan. When it's finished we can do this every day, but now there will likely be three of us. I'm thinking a new deck hand has just signed on"

Alan turned to Leila, "Welcome aboard, deck hand." He raised his coffee cup in a mock salute.

Back at Alan's home Bill drug the heavy fish from the fish box and tossed them out on the grass. He would have to filet all six huge halibut and cut the filets into dinner size portions. Once set up and ready to cut the job doesn't take long, but disposing of the carcasses and packaging the meat will take a while. Bill helped Alan get a hose into the boat in order for him to hose the salt from the aluminum boat and to be sure no blood or slime remained on the rear deck. Once it dries it is difficult to remove and the smell attracts bears to the boat. Alan washed the boat and Bill cut up the fish while Leila was in the house putting the finishing touches on dinner. Tonight she was fixing Idiot Burgers; two burger patties with slices of onion, tomato, cheese and green bell pepper inside cooked on a barbecue grill. They're too much to put on a bun, but are delicious with a little ketchup. She had prepared potato salad before they left this morning. By the time the boat was clean and the fish filleted she had the meal on the table.

All three fishermen were tired by the time they finished eating. Bill had yet to vacuum pack the fish and after eating he went back to his chore. Alan was exhausted and readied for bed. Leila finished the dishes and cleaning the kitchen before joining Bill at the fish table. She helped him package the last of the halibut while he ran the machine sealing the fish in plastic bags ready for the freezer.

The sun was low in the western sky, but would be up for several hours yet. Bill sat on a picnic bench with his back to the table holding a cup of hot, fresh coffee. Leila joined him and sat close. There were birds of all descriptions flying around the trees and the house. It was peaceful.

"Do you think we can always live like this, Bill?" asked Leila in a quiet voice.

"I hope so Leila, it's been a long time since I've felt this good. I should finish at the troopers in a couple of weeks and we should be able to be together then. You know, I've been alone for a lot of years and never kept company with anyone I wanted to live my life with, until now. After spending this short time with you I can't imagine going on without you at my side. Do you think you could consider making it a long-term contract?"

"At first I thought I was feeling close to you because you were protecting my life, but that's not it at all. I'm in love with you, Bill. You're stuck with me. I'll learn to bait a halibut hook, I promise." They both laughed and Gant put his arm around her.

"We'd better go to town, I have to work tomorrow. The sooner I get the paperwork done the sooner we can do this again." Bill kissed her on the cheek. "I'll go say good night to Alan."

At six the following morning, Eastern Daylight Saving Time, Marco Cidella drove two men to the airport in Newark. Their tickets said they were headed to Anchorage, Alaska. The men were heavy lifters sent by Marco. They worked for Lou Zena, but took orders from Marco. "Vito told me she works at a restaurant at the first intersection in town. I don't know the name of it, but in a town that size it shouldn't be hard to find. Don't get cocky up there. We had dealings with a couple of those Alaska State Troopers, and they know how to take care of business. Just get to town, find the girl, ice her and get out. Don't fail; I don't have anyone else to send up there."

Mickey Blue and Arnold "Arney" Gordon had both worked for Sal Roselli and were still loyal to the wages he was paying them. "We know our job, Marco, we'll find her and once we do she'll be history in a matter of hours. We'll drive to that town, Soldotna, and be out by nightfall. We've done this before."

"Get it done and I'll see you get a bonus for the job." Marco knew Vito had taken the job and failed, and Marco considered Vito Roma the best in the business.

Bill Gant had two meetings with the DA and worked on one report after the other. He had spent the entire day up to his neck in procedural paperwork. By six in the evening he was worn out and had a headache. It was time to go home and indulge in something more pleasant.

Chapter 30

The two newcomers to Alaska had failed to realize how gigantic the state really is. When they arrived in Anchorage it was late afternoon. The men had failed to make reservations at a hotel, thinking they would rent a car and drive to Soldotna not knowing it was 150 miles of wild country with few fuel stops. They also noted the attire worn by most people here did not include a sports coat and tie. The men picked up their rental car and a map of Anchorage and Alaska. That was when the distances began to concern them. They began looking for a hotel. Their third try was the West Coast International Inn, close to the airport. The Inn had a room at a summer rate of $340. Since it was on the expense account they took it. Their next stop was the new Cabela's store where they outfitted themselves with Khaki pants, flannel shirts and running shoes.

It had been a very long day for Mickey Blue and Arney Gordon. They returned to the hotel where they ate dinner in the nice dining room of the hotel. Blue drank iced tea, but Gordon drank three single malt scotches. It was approaching 10 PM when they made it to the room. Gordon, sleepy from the drinks, went directly to bed. Blue watched the news and studied the maps directing him to the Kenai Peninsula. He was amazed to find there were few side roads once they left Anchorage. It would be a simple navigation exercise to find Soldotna. He could not imagine what they would find once they arrived in the small town.

They ate breakfast in the hotel before checking out. Blue sat behind the wheel, remembering the maps he had studied. His first intersection would be a mile or so from the hotel. He turned on Minnesota Drive, the same street they had used to find the Cabela's store. He followed the road to the New Seward Highway and turned right. This turned out to be a modern four lane freeway, wide and busy with traffic flowing at a 65 mile per hour pace. The road soon pinched down to two lanes, traffic clogged road with a 55 mile per hour posted speed. Passing was impossible. Mickey fell into line with the motorhomes, boats and campers all headed for the famous fishing spots of the Kenai Peninsula. It took three hours, without a stop, to reach Soldotna. They had seen moose feeding in ponds and at the Russian River a huge brown bear crossed in front of their car.

Mickey had learned from the experience the day before and set out to find a hotel room. The first hotel, the Aspen, had no vacancies. The second, the Soldotna Inn had a cancellation which Mickey Blue took without inspecting the room. Between the two hotels Blue had seen the restaurant where Marco said the quarry was working. They settled into the room before going to the restaurant for lunch. Arney asked the waitress serving them about a tall waitress who worked there.

"Oh, you mean Leila. Leila Hunter. She's been off for a while. I don't know why, but she isn't here. Can I get you some more iced tea?" she asked.

"Do you know where she lives?" asked Gordon.

"Yeah, she has an apartment up on the other end of Redoubt Street. I don't know if she's in town, I haven't seen her in a week."

When the waitress went on about her business Mickey looked at Arney, "It looks like we have our work cut out for us. When we finish lunch we'll find Redoubt Street and begin canvassing the apartment houses for Leila Hunter."

Both men were surprised to find the large number of apartment buildings in the area they were searching. It was going to take some time to find her. Mickey Blue wondered if the prison would allow them to visit Vito Roma. He could possibly have some information that would be helpful in the search. He and Vito had once been good friends and he would surely like to see them.

Bill Gant had been in the office since six. His desk was piled high with files and forms. Twice the captain had come to the office to confer with him on information being sent to the District Attorney. Gant was doing his best to finish the work he had been assigned. A task that began with two officers was now down to one. The one thought keeping him tied to the desk was the reward at the end; Leila Hunter.

Leila was at Alan's house helping him with his exercises. It was important to stretch the muscles in his left arm. Without use his arm would atrophy and shrivel to a useless lump. With exercise he was able to regain a little movement of the fingers on his left hand. They had no strength, but the hope was that he could regain enough power and control of the fingers to be able to assist his strong right hand. She and Alan talked about Bill and what kind of future they would have together. Alan assured her she was getting a good man who was totally in love with her. She liked hearing this kind of news.

"You're not trying very hard today, Mr. Pulis. Are you going to concentrate or are you just going to sit here and gossip?"

Mickey and Arney found directions to the Kenai Jail Facility. Both men walked inside and met with a correctional officer to ask if it was possible to visit Vito Roma. The floor officer said he would check with the shift supervisor. A minute later he returned and showed them the door to the visiting area. He asked them to sign the guest book before going to the back to bring Roma to the other side of the glass. The entire area is glass allowing the officers to see what is taking place, but unable to hear the conversations. The two visitors waited for several minutes for Roma to be brought in. The officers took off the handcuffs and allowed him to be alone in the room with a thick glass separating the visitors from the prisoner. A telephone is used to visit.

"How are you doing, Vito," asked Mickey.

"I've had better days, Mickey. What are you doing here?"

"We were sent to take care of the girl. Sal has a thing about it."

Vito checked the window in the door to see if a guard was listening, "I got some bad news for you. Those two cops are still alive. I can't believe it, but they are. I hit them with three loads of 00 buck at eight feet and they survived. I don't know how, but they survived. Their body armor must have stopped the shots. I ain't ever had anyone live through that." Vito was shaking his head in disgust.

"We'll try to remedy that mistake for you, Vito," said Mickey Blue. "We're having some trouble locating the girl; do you know where she could be?"

"I'm only guessing, but those two cops were taking care of her. She may be with them now.

"We'll find her. Is there anything you need?" asked Arney.

"Yeah, I need out. I have to go to court tomorrow, some kind of evidentiary hearing or something. I hate it in here. Usually they take me to the courthouse in a van with a bunch of others all chained together, but tomorrow I'll be going alone and the troopers will take me over in a regular car. My lawyer is from Anchorage and he'll meet me there. I'm really tired of this crap."

"What time are you scheduled to go to court?" asked Mickey.

"The hearing is scheduled for one o'clock so they'll be here to pick me up around noon."

"Don't get your hopes up, Vito, but let me see what we can do. In any case we'll be seeing you tomorrow."

"Thanks for coming by, Mickey. I appreciate it. You too, Arney, thanks." Vito stood up, letting the guard know he was ready to go back to his cell. The door on the visitor side was unlocked and the two men on that side left as they had come. They stopped in the entry way to write down the time they departed the building.

Gant had worked late again and didn't get back to Pulis' place until after seven in the evening. Leila met him at the door with a smile and a kiss. Dinner was ready and Alan was seated at the table.

"I hope you like fresh halibut, Partner. I'm disabled now and we have to live a subsistence lifestyle around here." Alan was making a big joke, knowing halibut was Bill's favorite meal.

"I'll get by if that's all you have. I didn't stop for lunch today and I'm hungry." Bill reached for a baked potato and winked at Leila. "What did you get done today Alan?"

"This slave driver worked me to a nub. She let me stop once for a glass of water, but that was all." Alan chuckled a little. "You'd better hang on to this one, Bill, if you don't, I'm going to marry her myself."

"Is that what you two have been doing all day? Taking about my future?"

"I told you it'd been a boring day, Partner. How's the fish?"

"Perfect, Alan, so I know you didn't cook it." He turned to Leila, "Great job Kiddo."

"Tough day?" asked Alan.

"Not tough, just long. The DA keeps wanting more and more. I'm really glad this is my final case. I don't like doing this anymore." Bill pushed his plate back, rubbing his stomach. "Oh, that was good, Leila."

"Thank you Sir," said Leila, getting up to clear the table. "How about a piece of fresh apple pie and ice cream?" she asked.

"You talked me right into it," Said Gant, turning to Pulis, "I hate to eat and run, Alan, but it's been a long day and I'm really tired. I need to get some sleep."

Leila came back with three plates of pie and ice cream.

"You see there, Leila. You'd better think about getting hooked up with an old man like this one. All he wants to do is sleep." Alan dug into his pie.

"Oh, I think I can teach him a few new things. But up until now he wouldn't let me." She gave Bill a sarcastic grin.

They all had coffee before leaving the table. "I'm taking Leila out of here before you ruin her completely. See you tomorrow, Alan."

"See you tomorrow, Partner. You too, Leila, thanks for everything." Alan waved with his good arm as the two left for home.

Bill was in the office early again the next morning working on the files he had left the night before. Caswell stopped by the office once to tell him the DA had called to confirm Vito Roma was scheduled for court at 1:15. Bill nodded and kept on working.

Just before noon Mickey Blue and Arney Gordon were cruising in a neighborhood near the jail. They rounded a corner to First Street when Mickey stopped the car. Ahead on the right facing traffic was a large plumber's van. The side door was open. Blue drove slowly to the van.

"If the key is in it you jump out and start it up. Take it to the side road I showed you and park down in the trailer park. I'll call you when they bring Vito out of the jail." He pulled the car next to the open door on the van; the key was in the ignition.

Arney stepped out, climbed into the van and started the engine. He drove straight ahead to leave the area before the plumber realized his van was missing. Mickey drove the other direction toward some maintenance buildings up the street from the jail. He watched the gate, waiting for the trooper to arrive to transport Vito to the courthouse. A short time later the car came to the jail and was let into the secure yard to load his prisoner. Two minutes later he was backing out of the gate and turning toward town. Mickey called Arney.

"They're coming your way, get ready."

Outside the entry gate to the prison grounds it was a short drive to the main street back to town. Arney had the van running and could see up the street. He waited as the trooper car approached, revving the engine. When the police car was very close Arney sped the van up the driveway and into the street. The van struck the police car in the left front fender and driver's door. The force tipped the car on its side with the driver strapped in the seat, unconscious. Arney jumped out of the van with a large pair of bolt cutters in his hand. By now Mickey was on the scene helping to open the rear door of the police car. Once opened, Vito thrust his handcuffed wrists out of the opening. Arney cut the chains with the bolt cutters and Vito climbed out.

The three men clambered into the waiting car and fled the area. They were out of sight by the time the Judicial Services officer regained his senses.

He picked up the mic and called dispatch. "5D41, I've been attacked. My car is wrecked and I'm hurt. My prisoner is gone." He was about to ask for backup when he passed out again.

Chapter 31

The three attackers sped from the scene a few hundred feet to the intersection with the Kenai Spur Highway. Traffic was moderate and Marco had no trouble making a left turn toward the city of Kenai. Once on the Spur Highway he slowed his pace. He was sure no one had seen them nor would anyone identify their car. He was careful to obey the speed limits and traffic lights through Kenai. As they entered the main part of the city two Trooper vehicles sped by toward the scene on Wildwood Drive. Marco pulled to the side of the road to let the emergency vehicles pass, but before he could go again another set of red lights came into view. This one was an ambulance from the city of Kenai. When it passed the three men breathed a sigh of relief and they continued to the motel in Soldotna eleven miles to the east.

Once the injured JS officer was pulled from the car and loaded into the ambulance one of the Troopers went on to the Kenai Jail Facility. The other trooper began taking notes and pictures at the scene. The officer called a wrecker to take both the plumbers van and the patrol car to headquarters. The plumbers van would be checked for fingerprints and other evidence.

The second trooper learned the exact time the JS officer made his exit through the double entry gate with his prisoner in the back seat. There are few windows in the jail building and the Correctional Officers had seen nothing. It was beginning to look like a dead end. Vito Roma had been taken from custody by a person or persons unknown.

Bill Gant was in his office when the call came in. He had not been told of the incident until the captain came to his office and the other officers were on the scene. When he heard the news he wanted to join the search, but the captain had said no. "Finish what you're working on, Bill. I have several other officers searching. They can't go far. All the officers know what Vito Roma looks like, but none of us, including you, know who his friends are. I'll let you know if we learn anything."

By the end of the day there had still been no word of Roma or his accomplices. Bill worried all afternoon about the safety of his partner Alan and his original charge in this case, Leila Hunter. His designated quitting time, which he usually ignored, came around and he closed the office and drove home. He checked the battery in his cell phone and loaded a 12 gauge shotgun which he tossed into the trunk of his patrol car. Gant worried as he drove to the Sterling home of his partner, Alan Pulis. He was relieved to see the white Ford Taurus parked in front of the house. Leila stepped out onto the front porch when she heard his car in the drive.

Bill had a stern look on his face when he stepped out of his car, "Go back inside. I'll be right along." She went inside while Gant went to the trunk of his car to retrieve the shotgun he had just placed there. It startled both Leila and Alan when Bill came through the door with a handgun in one hand and a shotgun in the other.

"What's going on Bill?" asked Pulis.

"Vito Roma was going to court today. Someone drove a big van into the side of the Judicial Services car and took Vito. Captain Caswell had the entire detachment looking for him all afternoon, but nobody spotted him. He has to be holed up somewhere in Soldotna or Kenai."

"Can't you come home with some good news once in a while?" asked Pulis.

"What are we going to do, Bill?" asked Leila with a touch of fright in her voice.

"We're going to get ready for them. I think they came here to get the three of us, not to get Roma out of jail. But Roma knows us by sight and I think we're going to be attacked as soon as they find out where we are." He turned to Pulis, "Alan, where's your holster and weapon? And we'll need another shotgun."

"Left drawer in that cabinet, Bill, ammunition is in the next drawer down. The shotgun's in the cabinet in my office," he said, pointing in a new direction. "Ammunition for the 12 gauge is in the bottom of the gun cabinet. Bring me the .357 Smith and Wesson while you're back there. Ammo is with the shotgun shells. I won't be any good with a shotgun, but I can still handle a revolver and some speed loaders." Alan looked at Leila, "Go to that drawer," he said, pointing to another cupboard, "There are extra magazines for my automatic. Bring them over here to me."

She watched the men prepare. They knew what to do, which eased her mind some, and were preparing like an army preparing to defend itself from an attack. Bill came back with the shotgun and the Smith and Wesson along with an arm load of ammunition. He placed his load on the coffee table in front of Alan and set off on another chore.

"Make some coffee, Leila, and fill some pots and pans with fresh water. Find a first aid kit and some flashlights, Alan will tell you where to look. If and when they come they'll want to cut off the phone and the power. I'm going to get some tools and reinforce the back door. Except for the front, the windows are pretty high off the ground and will be hard for them to reach. When you finish I want you to help me get a couple of mattresses into the living room. We can use them and a table for a barricade." He turned to Pulis, "Can you think of anything else, Alan?"

"Yeah, one thing," he said, writing on a small piece of paper. "Here," he said handing Bill the small slip of paper, "go down into the basement and find the gun safe, this is the combination for it. There's a metal ammo box in the bottom. Bring it up here. There're four hand grenades in the box; souvenirs. We might need them."

"What in the world are you doing with hand grenades, Alan?"

"I thought I might need them someday and it looks like today's the day."

"You'd better get us something to eat, Leila. We'd better eat while we have the chance. Then we wait."

At the Soldotna Inn Mickey Blue and Arney Gordon were eating wonderful dinner. Mickey ate a New York Steak while Arney ordered a rare Prime Rib. Both men drank coffee. There was little conversation during the meal. Both men were relaxed after eating. They ordered a New York Steak to go and drank another cup of strong black coffee. There was a coffee maker in the room and Vito could make a pot if he wanted it. The two men were in a quiet booth and thought it was safe to discuss the problem of finding their next victims.

"Nobody's going to tell us where those troopers live. How're we going to find them? For that matter where's the girl? I went by where Vito said she lived and it looks like she's been gone for quite a while. We don't have any assets working for us in this town. It won't be easy." Arney Gordon was summarizing the situation. "Yeah, you're right, but Vito can recognize them. Maybe if we stake out the parking lot at the trooper headquarters Vito can pick them out if they're coming and going there. I just don't know what else to do."

"I'm glad we got Vito out. We need him and what he knows on this job. I guess I'd better let Cidella know we have him. "Mickey drank the last of his coffee and dug into his wallet for cash to pay the waitress. Minutes later she was back with the order to go and the tab. Mickey paid the bill and gave her a sizable tip. The two men went upstairs with the tray for Vito who was delighted to be eating restaurant food again. And this was good restaurant food.

Mickey left Vito to his meal and went out on the balcony overlooking the parking area in front of the restaurant and bar to make his call to Marco Cidella. Marco answered on the second ring.

"Mickey! How ya doin'? I've been waiting for your call."

"We've had a pretty good day, Marco. We got Vito out of jail when they were taking him to court today. He's happy and ready to work with us. He's in eating his dinner now."

"Good job Mickey. What about the other problems?" Cidella asked.

"Those aren't so easy. We can't seem to find them. We plan to watch the trooper headquarters building tomorrow to see if they show up there. The girl hasn't been to work in a couple of weeks. Her car is still in town. We can't find her, but we will. It's a small town," there was little hope in his voice.

"If you need anything, call me," said Marco. "Tell Vito he is to keep a low profile. Every cop in Alaska will be looking for him and in a small town he'll be easy to spot."

"Yeah, we've been keeping him out of sight, said Mickey. "I'll let you know if we find them. I'll call in a couple of days."

Leila and Bill spent the night at the home of their friend, Alan. Alan had installed a driveway alarm a year ago but had never used it. Now seemed like a good time to turn it on. They all slept restlessly, but they did sleep. In the morning Bill readied for work while Leila cleaned the kitchen. Before leaving the house Gant spoke with Pulis.

"I'm going to the office. Keep your cell phone handy and don't let Leila out of your sight. I'll learn more about the search if I'm in the office and close to the radio. If anyone shows up here, anyone at all, call me. I'll come on the double. I'll see you tonight, Old Buddy." Gant seldom wore a backup gun, but Alan noticed the one on his ankle as he walked to the door.

The three hoods sat in their car drinking coffee from a paper cup and eating a sack full of Egg McMuffins. It was warm and the parking area at the rodeo grounds was busy. No one seemed to notice the men sitting in the car eating breakfast. The three took turns walking to the portable toilets to relieve themselves. One at a time they walked around the car to cool off and get some fresh air. It was noon when Vito sat up straight in the seat.

"That's him! That's one of the cops. Follow him," said Vito, excited they had found one of their targets.

Mickey started the car to follow the trooper. Gant turned left on Kalifornsky Beach Road, in the direction of Kenai. He drove directly to the courthouse and walked inside. The men waited outside. With the new courthouse security post inside the door they didn't dare chance following him.

Gant met an assistant DA inside and the two went to a private attorney room to do their business. Bill was bringing more forms and statements regarding the case against Vito Roma.

"Have they found him yet?" asked the DA.

"Not yet, but he can't stay hidden forever. Worse, I don't think he'll leave until he finished what he came for," said Gant.

"Do you mean you think he'll try again to kill you and Alan?"

"That's exactly what I mean. These guys are professional hit men and mobsters from the east coast. They came here to do a job and won't give up until it's finished or they're caught or killed." Gant stared at the floor before continuing, "Alan and I had a run-in with them in New Jersey when we were back there on our investigation. We met with the secretary to the mob boss. We invited her to dinner, just being friendly. Vito and his partner followed us and saw her. When she went home that night they followed her to her apartment and threw her off a balcony seven floors up. These are ruthless men."

"I'm sorry to hear about that, Bill. I didn't know about it. You might as well give me the files and let me go to court on another case. With the prisoner on the loose there doesn't seem to be any hurry now. Thanks for bringing them though," the DA knew it was a low point for Gant.

Back in his car he checked the time and decided to eat lunch. He drove the several blocks from the courthouse to a place hidden on a side street. It was an old school bus painted blue and a small canopy added to the side. He ordered Fish and Chips for lunch. When his order was ready he found one of the picnic tables and ate. It was delicious. He relaxed, drinking a Coke, before returning to the office.

Mickey and his companions returned to the parking lot at the rodeo grounds to wait and watch, thinking they would have been well advised to have lunch with the trooper. The afternoon dragged on with the same routine as the morning continuing for hours. They watched and waited. A refreshment stand opened near the baseball field next to them. Arney walked over to purchase three Cokes and three hot dogs. The men leaned on the front fender to eat the snack, and still they waited. It was 4:45 in the afternoon when Vito said, "OK, boys. There he goes. Follow him, but not too close."

At last things were going their way. Vito checked the cartridges in the clip of the .40 Smith and Wesson they had taken from the JS Officer.

Chapter 32

Traffic was heavy this time of day in Soldotna. Bill Gant was anxious to get back to Alan's place to check on Alan and Leila. As was his habit, he checked the rear view mirror while driving. Nothing unusual appeared until he was nearly into Sterling and he turned off the main highway to the side road leading past Alan Pulis' drive. The car behind him had not gone on, but turned onto the side road behind him. It was a red Ford, clean, looking like a rental. Bill drove to the turn into the driveway to Alan's place. The drive is long and curved to keep out traffic noise and lights. The red car stopped on the street behind him. Bill eased his car a little further into the driveway and waited. Soon the red car followed. Bill sped up and drove into the yard. He parked on the side of the house close to the back. He stepped quickly from his car and ran to the back door of the house.

Alan had heard the driveway alarm beep and thought it must be Bill, but was concerned when it beeped again a moment later. Leila was in the kitchen when Bill came through the back door.

"Leila, get into the living room and on the floor. We have company." He turned to Alan, "I think they followed me home. Call the captain and have him send us some help."

Bill cautiously crept to the front window. He peered outside and could see the front end of the red car parked at the edge of the clearing where the driveway came out of the trees. He stepped back and drew his weapon, jacking the slide to chamber a round. Alan was just terminating his call to the Captain Caswell.

"Help is on the way. The closest is two miles. Hand me my .45, Bill," said Alan as he slid into a chair he had prepared for this confrontation.

Bill peeked through the curtain again. Two men stepped from the car, one moving to the left and the other to the right. Neither of them was Vito Roma.

"Here they come, they're flanking us. I locked the back door, but they may just lay a volley into the house, so stay close to the floor. One of them went behind the woodshed and the tractor barn. The other went around the garage. I don't see either of them now. Vito must still be in the car. If they don't start shooting in the next couple of minutes the backup will be here."

"They'd better hurry," said Alan. "I showed Leila how to operate the shotgun and she can keep an eye on the back door from where she is now. Unless they have some high power weapons, the rock facing on the house should keep the bullets from penetrating to the inside, but don't get near the windows."

"I just saw one of them peeking out from behind the garage. I can't see the other one," said Bill. "OH, OH! Vito just got out of the car. He has a hand gun. It looks like one of our Smiths. I wonder where he got that!"

"Keep your head down, Bill. Don't give them a target."

"Don't worry, Alan, I was shot once recently and don't care to repeat the experience." He turned around to look at Leila. "Stay on the floor and behind that other mattress, Leila. Just watch the back door in case someone breaks it down," he instructed.

Vito motioned to one of the men with him, the one on his right behind the wood shed, to move toward the house. He was now behind the red car aiming his gun at the front of the house. Bill stepped back from the window, causing the curtain to move. Vito saw the movement and thought it was one of the men on the inside in front of the window and fired. The bullet and broken glass caused the curtain to move violently. It had been a single shot, but it was the signal the war had begun.

Alan and Bill raised their weapons in preparation for an assault on the front door. Bill saw movement as Vito dove to the ground. At that instant the driveway alarm beeped again. The cavalry had arrived. Bill could see two uniformed officers working toward the red car. Vito had crouched and ran behind the tractor shed on his right.

The uniformed officers were now in place, "Alaska State Troopers; drop your weapons and come out with your hands raised," one of them shouted.

This order was met with a shot from behind the woodshed and another from the other side of the yard near the garage. Bill watched out the window, but couldn't see either of the shooters. Now another trooper was behind the red car and a siren could be heard in the distance. The newest policeman was carrying a shotgun as he moved up to talk with the trooper behind the car in the driveway. The driveway alarm beeped again and two more troopers appeared in the drive each carrying assault rifles.

"You don't have a chance," a trooper again shouted to the shooters. "Come out with your hands in the air."

This order was met with a volley of shots from the direction of the garage. When the shooter stepped out from behind the garage wall in order to fire again he was cut down by the riflemen. Vito saw the man go down and assessed the futility of the fight. He threw his .40 Smith and Wesson into the yard in front of the house.

"Don't shoot," called Vito. "I'm coming out."

"Come out with your hands in the air," shouted a trooper.

Vito stepped out from behind the tractor shed. "Come on out, Mickey," he shouted to the other shooter. The trooper riflemen watched as another handgun was flung into the grass and a second man stepped out from behind the building with his hands raised. Two troopers with guns at the ready approached the two and ordered them to the ground where they were handcuffed. Another trooper walked to the downed shooter on the other side of the house. He held a rifle on the man while his partner handcuffed the lifeless body. His weapon was retrieved as evidence.

Inside the house Alan's phone rang. It was the captain. "It's OK Alan. They have all three of them. You can come out now. Be careful, everyone is armed and edgy."

"Thanks, Cap. Bill's going outside now."

"I'm on my way there now, Alan. I'll be there in about three minutes."

Alan turned to Leila, "It's alright, Leila. Put the shotgun on safety. They've got the bad guys."

She snapped the safety on and laid the gun on the floor. Bill was now up on his feet and at the front door. He holstered his weapon before he opened the door. One of the troopers was now at the porch, his weapon still in his hands, as Bill stepped out onto the front porch. The trooper immediately recognized Gant and lowered his weapon.

"Are you OK, Bill?" he asked.

"Yeah, we're fine. We might not've been if you hadn't showed up when you did. Thanks for the help."

Leila stepped out the door and the trooper asked, "Are you OK, too?"

"Yes, thank you. I'm still shaking, though," she said.

At that moment Alan appeared at the door, "She did all right for her first gunfight."

"The captain is on the way and will be here in a minute, and I have prisoners to take care of. I just wanted to be sure all of you were safe."

"Tell the captain we'll be inside when he gets here," instructed Bill.

Before going inside he watched as the troopers were taking pictures and gathering evidence. The man on the ground had been declared dead at the scene by officers. This meant an investigation was to be conducted and all evidence would be scrutinized by the FBI and the Attorney General for the State of Alaska.

The patrol cars and the rental were moved into the yard to allow traffic to move in and out of the driveway. The prisoners were being loaded into a patrol car when the captain arrived. He spoke to one of the officers, and then walked to the house. He knocked on the door and shouted to the occupants who asked him to come inside.

"How about coffee, Captain?" asked Leila.

"You bet, thanks," he replied. "Are you all OK?"

"We're alright, Captain," said Alan. "The state owes me a front window, though. It was your escapee who shot it out."

"Take it out of the outrageous settlement you're planning to get from me for being shot."

"C'mon, Cap, it's not like we hit you up for another tank of boat gas," remarked Alan.

"I'm just glad you're all safe. I'll tell you what I'll do. Since you need to repair your window to keep the mosquitos out tonight, I'll buy dinner for the four of us at Mykel's. I have to wait for the crew to get the prisoners booked and the paperwork done before I call the Colonel to report this mess. He loves for me to call him late at night and report a shooting involving an officer. I'll have someone stand by here at the scene until they appoint an investigator to look at it. They usually use the FBI in these cases. How about it? Do you want a free dinner?"

"Let me wash up and we'll follow you to town. Thanks for caring, Cap," said Bill.

Four of the arresting troopers in two cars drove the prisoners to the jail in Kenai. Two troopers stood by during the booking process while the other two composed a list of charges for the remand slip. The list was long including; aiding an escape, assaulting an officer, theft of a firearm, attempted murder and several other charges. The DA would undoubtedly amend and add to the charges when the reports were submitted.

Vito was booked first and once done he demanded a call to his lawyer. Mickey Blue submitted to the booking without saying anything. He was trying to figure out how to call Marco Cidella for instructions and to report the mission was a failure. It wouldn't be a pleasant conversation.

Vito used his phone call to notify the Anchorage lawyer Woodbury had hired. The lawyer said he would be down to see him tomorrow. Vito was sent to the same segregation cell he had occupied before the escape. Mickey had the second cell down from Vito.

At Mykel's Restaurant the patrons enjoyed a delicious dinner. The captain ate halibut while the others had grilled King Salmon. This dining room was filled with tourists and fishermen every night during the summer months and for good reason. The service is superb, the food is prepared well and the atmosphere is Five Star. During dinner the captain asked the three of them to come to the office to make an official report of the events of the evening. During the course of the dinner Captain Caswell took a phone call from Agent Greer of the FBI. He had been appointed to investigate the shooting incident involving troopers and would be down in the morning to begin his investigation.

With dinner concluded, and the captain picked up the check. The trio set out for Alan's home to repair the window with a piece of plywood screwed to the broken window frame. They would call a repairman in the morning.

"I wonder if I'm insured against windows broken by gunfire?" asked Alan as they drove back to his home.

"If it's alright with you, Alan, I'll wait until morning to sweep up the broken glass. I've had all the excitement I can handle for one day," Leila said in a tired voice.

"I think Leila and I will be going back to my place tonight, Alan. You should be safe with the shooters in jail again. Leila can come back in the morning and the two of you will need to come to the office for the report. I'll see you there. I'm going to sleep really well tonight."

Bill Gant knew the case wasn't over, but the immediate danger was gone. He tried to determine if the danger would ever be completely gone as long as Roselli was still out there somewhere. It was too much for him to ponder tonight.

Chapter 33

Though it involved the same names, Gant was not allowed to be a part of the new investigation. His personal involvement precluded his participation. He continued to go to the office every day to work on the original case, being certain all the information was in place prior to his resignation from the list of active troopers. He had mixed feelings about this act. On the one hand he had enjoyed being a part of the investigation, but on the other he missed the relaxed lifestyle he and Alan had enjoyed before all this began. Leila had been the one bright spot of the entire case. If, indeed, he was finished he could now pursue a personal relationship with her without jeopardizing his position as the investigator in the case. It had been difficult to stay on the professional side of the line, but that no longer was a factor. It would be her decision to allow the relationship to grow or to end, but he wanted to give it a chance.

Two more days elapsed before the captain asked Bill to return his badge and weapon thus ending his current term of employment with the Alaska State Troopers. "I hate to see you go, Bill," said Captain Rollin Caswell. "I'm truly sorry for the injuries you and your partner suffered during this investigation. You have no idea how much guilt I feel for the injuries done to Alan. The three of us have been friends for a very long time and it saddens me deeply to see the disability Alan Pulis is suffering. I wish I could change it, but I can't. I plan to be in this office for a few more years. I want you to know that as long as I'm here you and Alan have a friend in this office. I'm going to miss the two of you." Caswell held his hand out across the office desk where it was met with the hand of his longtime friend, Bill Gant. "I'll have one of the Duty Officers drive you home."

"It's been fun, Cap. When Alan was hurt I thought he'd never recover from it, but he's doing well. Working on this case has been good for both of us.

Thanks for allowing us to participate. I plan to help Alan as much as he'll let me. We'll both be in your office to make life miserable whenever we can. I hope I don't have to tell you that if you need anything in the future we'll be here to help." The finality of this meeting was beginning to strike Gant.

"The same goes for me and my office, Bill."

"There's one more thing, Cap."

Caswell had a startled look, "What would that be, Bill?"

"Do you suppose you could get us a purchase order for one more tank of boat gas?"

"Get out of my office, Gant," shouted the captain, still laughing as Bill walked away.

Bill had taken his and Alan's personal things from the office they had shared, placed them in a box and taken them home with him. It had been quite a while since he had started his own vehicle, but it started right up. Leila had driven her own car to Alan's house for his daily therapy treatment and Bill noted how very lonely his house seemed without her in it. It was with a mixed feeling of relief and sadness he drove to Sterling to visit Alan. At the Alan's home he picked the box of items from the rear seat of his car and carried it to the house. He found the front door open and the screen door unlocked. He stepped inside.

"Anybody home?" he shouted.

A moment later Leila came through the back door, rushed across the kitchen floor and wrapped her arms around him. She planted a kiss lightly on his lips and backed away, "Are you unemployed?" she asked.

He placed the box containing Alan's stuff on the kitchen table, "Yes, I am, and it feels good. Where's Alan?"

"In the back yard," said Leila. "Go talk to him and I'll bring some iced tea."

"How're you doing today, Alan?" he asked as the stepped out onto the back porch.

"Strong enough to whip you, Partner. Are we out of the police business now?"

"Yes, we are, I brought your stuff from the office. I put it on the kitchen table. You can sort it out when you have time." Gant stared at his feet for a moment, "Let's go up on the porch, Alan. There's something I want to discuss with you and Leila."

Leila came out of the house with a tray of glasses and a pitcher of golden iced tea which she placed on the table on the porch. She poured the tea as the men sat. Once done she, too, sat at the table. She took a sip before commenting, "You have a serious look on your face, Bill. What's up?"

"I'm glad you're here for this, Leila, it concerns you and I want you in on the final decision."

"What decision is that, Bill?" asked Alan.

"Yes, Bill, what are you talking about?" asked Leila.

"OK, here goes. When I'm done tell me if I'm crazy." He took a long drink of tea before beginning. He appeared nervous and edgy. "I've been giving our situation a lot of thought. Up until now we've been so busy thinking about the goons chasing us we've forgotten about the man who hired them. I've talked with Agent Greer about this and he agrees with me. The point being that Sal Roselli is the one who hired the killers we've been dealing with. Greer says Roselli sold his holdings in New Jersey to a New York mobster by the name of Lou Zena and he's running it as Roselli had and making a lot of money as well as enemies. Roselli skipped the country. The FBI has information that he went to Costa Rica in order to take advantage of the extradition policies in that little country. Roselli's right hand man is now Marco Cidella. Cidella took over after Vito Roma went to jail here in Kenai. Marco works for Zena, but is still loyal to Roselli. Roselli's the one who had Marco send this Mickey Blue and Arnold Gordon here to get us, all three of us. They broke Vito out of jail and came after Alan and me. You were next on the list, Leila."

Bill Gant took another drink of iced tea. "The whole point of this is I don't believe the threat's over. I think Roselli will send someone else. The law can't touch him as long as he stays in Costa Rica, but I think we can lure him out of the country to where we can get our hands on him."

"Are you nuts?" asked Alan. "This is a number one mobster you're talking about. He has a lot of ears in the law world and a lot of guns on his side. You and I only have you and me, Partner. We make a pretty small army."

"That's where my plan comes in. Do you want to hear it?"

"Will it get me killed?" asked Pulis.

"It could," replied Gant.

Leila was attempting to grasp this entire conversation without success. "What's the plan, Bill?"

"A question for you first, Leila," answered Bill. "You're a very rich woman, nearly ten million bucks in the bank. How much of it are you willing to spend to be able to keep the rest?"

"That's a strange question, Bill, you know I don't know what to do with all that money; keep it, give it back, turn it over to the FBI or blow it on lottery tickets, I just don't know. Let's hear your plan."

"OK, you two, what do you think of this?" began Gant. "In order to arrest Roselli and stop him as a threat to of us, we have to get him out of Costa Rica. I think if we dangle a ten million dollar bait in front of him he'll bite." He looked at the two puzzled partners, "My plan is this. We get a message to Roselli telling him he can have the money if he leaves us alone from now on. He won't be able to resist almost ten million dollars in free money. We lure him to the Bahamas to make the deal. We lease a big yacht and have him meet us there on the boat. We tell him he has to come to the bank to take personal control of the account. I think he'll go along with it up to this point, but once the account is transferred it'll change. I think he'll have Marco Cidella kill us and throw us to the sharks. I plan to cheat before he can. I've spoken with Kinney and Greer they think it can be done. Roselli likes a private wine made by a restaurateur up in Connecticut. Kinney will get a couple of bottles of that wine. After we make the deal with Roselli we toast the contract with a glass of this wine. Greer will have it drugged. When Roselli passes out we have the skipper weigh anchor and take him back to Florida where Greer and Kinney are waiting. Then we go back to the Bahamas and wait for the smoke to clear."

"This plan of yours sounds like a trip to Disneyland, Partner." Pulis was skeptical as was Leila, "What do you think Marco Cidella will be doing all this time?"

"I think he'll meet with Roselli in the Bahamas before he meets with us. Roselli may bring him with him when we make the deal." Gant was being as candid as possible.

"Don't you see him as a threat here?" asked Alan.

"Yes I do, and that's why Kinney will supply the skipper and mate on the boat." Gant was smiling now.

"So we'd have some kind of backup, right?" Pulis was still not convinced.

"Leila, the cost of this caper would have to be paid out of the money in the Bahamas account. It'll take the travel expenses, the boat lease and the additional help we'll need in the Bahamas; like a boat and skipper to shuttle everyone back and forth to the yacht. I estimate it'll cost $150 thousand to $200 thousand dollars. I can't afford to pay it myself or I would." He looked at her and smiled, "Are you in?"

She shrugged her wide shoulders and tossed her shoulder length hair. "I don't know what to say, Bill, I thought we were all done with the danger and now we're planning to start it all over again. I guess if it'll end it forever it'll be worth it, but I'm scared. These past weeks I've learned I don't like being shot at and chased all over the countryside. If this will end it, then, yes, I'm in."

Alan had been sitting quietly, rubbing his wounded shoulder. "I won't be much good in a fight, Partner, but count me in. What do you want from me?"

"I want you to be the coordinator for the entire operation. It's something you're good at. You know Greer and Kinney and you'll be the one to hire the assets we'll need when we get there. I don't want you in the line of fire. I want you to stay out of sight and do all of our liaison work during the entire time we're there. You and I know the feds like to take over, but they'll have no jurisdiction down there. It'll be our job to get Roselli back to U.S. waters and turn him over to the FBI. Marco will be the wild card. There'll be no telling what he'll be doing. You'll have to keep an eye on him."

"Well, if that's all I have to do I guess I'm in. What about you Leila?" asked Pulis, both men waiting for her answer.

With a huge sigh she answered, "OK, but if you get me killed I won't marry you."

Gant was so startled he jumped, "When did I say anything about marriage?"

"You don't think I'm going to go off with you for this length of time, staying in small hotel rooms together, sleeping on a boat together and probably getting killed together, without some kind of reasonable commitment from you?" she was laying on thick and fitting in well.

"Will there be a trial period to get used to the idea?" asked Bill.

"Yes," she said, "The same one you're giving me and Alan."

The three spent the rest of the evening writing questions and making notes as well as compiling a list of things they would need on this adventure. They were all excited, especially Bill, who wondered if the marriage proposal was a good idea. He would have to give this more thought.

Chapter 34

The next several days were spent preparing for the trip. Leila needed a wardrobe suitable to the southern climate. She had her hair trimmed and permed, her nails done. More than a week was needed to make her ready for this adventure. Any thought of this possibly being her last adventure were dismissed. She could only think of this as a beginning. Once Roselli was finished she could get on with her life. More than once she found herself thinking about her future. Most of those thoughts included Bill Gant.

Alan was in charge of airline reservations as well as hotels in Florida. He made reservations for himself in a small beach hotel in Nassau. He would fly directly from Miami to Nassau while Bill and Leila would be travelling by yacht; the lucky devils.

Bill Gant was busy every day. He and Greer had been on the phone with Kinney making lease arrangements for a yacht. Kinney had found one in Miami belonging to one of his old clients. He was able to get the 93 foot vessel for no money. It was a ten-year-old favor being collected upon by Kinney.

Kinney agreed to pay all expenses and repair any damage incurred while he had the boat. Kinney would be a crewman on the vessel, the skipper, however, was the owner's skipper and would be in charge of the boat and its uses during the trip. Kinney offered to reveal the destination, but the owner wanted no part of it. "The less I know the less I will worry," the owner had said. Kinney travelled to Miami and began the chore of stocking the boat with supplies; food, fuel, liquor, water and two bottles of special wine from a small restaurant in Connecticut.

Greer had men from the New York office contact Marco Cidella. They would tell him to contact Roselli and deliver a message. The message was from Lucile Mc Dermot. She was in possession of nearly ten million dollars stolen from Roselli by Steven Collier. He was to meet her in Nassau where she would make the transfer of the cash to an account with his name on it. He was to meet them on their boat in the harbor in Nassau one week from this Thursday. If he wasn't there the deal was off and the he would never see the money. In exchange she wanted a guarantee of safety for herself and the two troopers.

Marco, of course, denied knowing where Roselli was now located and could not deliver the message. The FBI agent from New York shrugged his shoulders and said, "Then, I guess Sal will be out ten million dollars." The officers left the meeting knowing Marco would deliver the message.

Once the officers had gone, Marco called his old boss, Salvatore Roselli. He delivered the message as the agents had given it to him.

"That's interesting, Marco. What do you think?" asked Sal.

"Don't do it, Boss. I think they're just trying to get you out of Costa Rica so they can arrest you. It ain't worth it, Boss."

"You could be right, Marco. Let me check on some things and I'll get back to you. If I go, I want you in Nassau to keep an eye on things. You could be right, but I'm not going to lose ten million bucks without checking it out. I'll be getting back with you by tomorrow."

Alan Pulis had done an excellent job of booking first class seats with only one short lay-over in Atlanta. Leila, Bill and Alan arrived in Miami two days later. Kinney met them at the airport to drive them to their hotel. Greer arrived the next morning after flying all night. Kinney had picked him up at the airport, too. They met at the hotel where Leila ordered a room service breakfast for the entire crew. Once the meal had been disposed of they got down to business.

"Where do we stand, David?" Greer asked Kinney.

"The boat, a really nice yacht belonging to a friend of mine, is ready to go. We'll be sailing tomorrow afternoon. I'll go on the boat with Leila and Bill. They'll look like a couple of rich folks on holiday. I'll be part of the crew. The crew will be me, the regular skipper and a crewman to maintain the boat." Kinney was explaining his part in this caper. "One piece of good news for you Bill, the boat will cost nothing except upkeep and supplies. The owner loaned me the boat without a lease fee. He owed me one from a long time ago."

Bill and Leila smiled, "Thanks, David. That cuts the overhead by a lot," said Gant.

"Greer, you and Alan will fly to Nassau tomorrow morning. Keep an eye out when you get there. I'll bet you a Mai Tai Marco will be there somewhere. He's dangerous, watch out for him. Alan has made all the reservations for you, as well as a rental car. All the tickets and rental agreements are in the packet on the table. We probably have a couple of days to relax, but Sal will be suspicious and Marco is always dangerous. When we get to Nassau Bill and Leila will take in the sights like a couple of tourists. She'll have to go to the bank to get some money for expenses. If Marco is watching the bank and sees Leila entering he'll think the money is in that bank." Kinney was reviewing his notes.

"I don't suppose you'll tell us where the money really is deposited, will you Leila?" asked Greer, knowing she had no intention of giving it to the FBI.

"What money?" she asked, smiling.

The entire group laughed. As a universal rule in public cops are stoic and serious, usually quiet and unemotional. Privately they have a weird sense of humor and joke amongst each other about things most citizens would consider tragic or horrifying. It's this sense of camaraderie that cements friendships within the fraternity and is seldom seen outside the band of 'brothers of the badge.'

"Remember," mentioned Gant, "Marco's our wild card. We can't predict what he'll do. We know he's loyal to Roselli, we know he's capable of murder, but we can't be certain how he'll react when he learns his boss has gone missing. It's going to be a slow boat trip back to U.S. waters and I expect Marco to get on the first plane back to Florida. Greer and Alan will be in the line of fire if he gets violent in Nassau and we'll have no way to protect them."

"Don't you worry about us, Bill, you do your job and we'll do ours. I got shot in the arm and neck, not the head." Alan was being a little defensive about his condition, but he was right about one thing, he was a good cop who used his head. "Besides, I have FBI Agent Greer with me. That's as good as a bullet proof shield. I'll just keep him between Marco and me."

Kinney looked around the room, "Anyone have a question or an idea?" he asked.

There were no comments from anyone. Everyone knew the plan and, as skeletal as the plan was, seemed ready to carry it out.

Alan volunteered to buy dinner for the group. They discussed at length where to go. Some wanted one of the well-known places in Miami, others wanted to experience the down home, down south type of cuisine they could never find elsewhere. The local flavor won out. A call to the Concierge gave them the answer. The hotel provided them with reservations for dinner and a limo to take them there.

The café was in the Cuban section of town. It was small and crowded. As promised they were taken to a reserved table and provided with menus. A Hispanic looking waitress came to take their orders for drinks. A local beer was on the list and all ordered a glass. Soon she was back with a tray of glasses filled to the rim with bubbling, golden brew. They sipped the beer and looked at the menu trying to decide what to order.

She was back soon to take their order. "What will you have tonight," she asked.

Alan was seated next to her and asked, "Do you have a specialty of some kind? We're from out of town, you see, and have no idea what to order."

"I will fix that for you. First, how spicy do you like your food? I warn you 'Hot' means 'Really Hot', if you are not from this area."

The patrons looked at each other and Bill asked them, "How about Upper Medium Hot?" All members of the group nodded in agreement.

"Would you like another beer with dinner?" she asked.

The two FBI men ordered another beer while the three Alaskans ordered iced tea, sweet.

The dinner was outstanding. Much of it didn't have a name, but the main course was a fish plate cooked with mango sauce. All five patrons enjoyed the dinner and the unique flavors it had presented. As promised, Alan bought the dinner and provided the waitress with a healthy tip. She came back to have him sign the credit card slip and asked, "Would you like me to call your limo?"

"Thank you that would be nice."

They sat at the table until the waitress again came to tell them the car had arrived. Again they thanked her. In the car Kinney asked the driver to take them to a private marina. He knew the place and took a leisurely drive through an elegant neighborhood to where their yacht was moored. It was impressive in both size and design. All of them were impressed with what they saw.

"You U.S. Marshals have some ritzy friends," commented FBI agent Greer.

"Too bad you won't be able to go along and enjoy it with us," replied Kinney.

"I get seasick," Greer replied, gruffly.

Back in the hotel they all retired early. Alan and Greer would be taken to the airport in the morning and the rest would take their belongings to the boat to ready for the luxury transport to Nassau.

Kinney was dressed in a white uniform matching the ones worn by the skipper and the other crewman. As the rest of the crew managed the duties of untying the yacht and motoring out of the marina area into open water, Kinney brought fresh lemonade to the two VIPs seated on the rear deck.

"Ms. Mc Dermot, I might suggest some sunscreen, and the same for you, Mr. Gant. The sun along with the reflection from the water can be hazards for people from the northern climates," advised Kinney. "I'll bring some from the salon, if you like."

"That would be kind of you, thank you." Leila replied to his offer. "How long will it take to reach Nassau?"

"The skipper is at cruise speed, but I can ask him to increase the speed if you'd like."

"No, the present speed is very nice. I'm sure he knows our timetable," Gant said, enjoying the ride with Leila at his side. "If he knows a good spot we might catch a couple of fish for dinner when we get close to shore."

"I'll mention it to the skipper, will there be anything else, Sir?" asked Kinney.

"No, leave us alone so we can neck," Gant teased Kinney.

When they were alone Bill turned to Leila, "Kinney's right. We look like beached belugas. Our legs and arms are pretty white. I wonder if they have some lotion with fake suntan mixed in."

"Sit here, I'll go check." Gant watched with pleasure as Leila stood and walked to the door leading to the salon.

The trip was relaxing and pleasurable. In late afternoon Kinney returned to the rear deck to advise the pair they were approaching a good fishing spot and the other crewman would bring a couple of rods and bait for them to use to catch dinner.

"A nice Grouper would do nicely, Sir," commented Kinney.

Leila caught a very nice Grouper only minutes after dropping her bait into the water. A crewman dressed the fish and took the rods back to be stored. An hour later they were dropping the anchor in the harbor offshore from the City of Nassau. A Nassau customs agent came out to the boat to inspect the papers of all passengers and crew and inspect the boat for contraband. He was a polite man. As he departed he wished them a pleasant stay in Nassau.

Once the customs inspector was gone Kinney fished a watertight plastic bag from the bait well on the transom of the yacht next to the exit gate to the rear and the swim ladder below. In the bag were three .40 Smith and Wesson handguns and a supply of ammunition. Kinney gave one of the Smiths to Gant and kept one in his own belt. The third would be delivered to Agent Greer when he came to the boat in the morning.

After dinner they turned in for a much needed night's sleep. The motion of the boat, the motion of the ocean and the warmth of the southern sun had taken its toll. They were relaxed and tired. It was time to turn in for the night. A crewman would be on duty all night to watch over them.

Bill and Leila had separate suites, but walked down the passageway together. He turned to her at her door and said, "I'm beginning to enjoy life with you. Perhaps a permanent arrangement would be a good idea after all."

She gave him a long hard kiss and stepped back, "I like the idea, too. Good night."

Chapter 35

Early the following morning Greer had taken a morning run on the beach. He was walking back to the hotel when he stopped at a small street vendor stand to buy a glass of fresh orange juice. He paid the vendor, who gladly accepted U.S. currency, and began his walk back to the hotel. He had gone only a half block when he spotted a face he knew well from his photo. Greer stopped to peer into a shop window.

Marco Cidella was strolling down the far sidewalk whistling a tune. Two men were following him. They looked to Greer to be street punks. It was likely Marco had hired them for extra muscle. Marco and his companions continued down the street toward the pier. When they were out of sight Greer continued his walk to the hotel.

On the way to his room he tapped on Alan's door. When it opened he said, "I just spotted Marco Cidella headed toward the beach. He had a couple of locals with him."

Alan smiled, "He's right on time, Ed. It means Roselli has taken the bait."

"Right," said Greer, smiling. "Keep your guard up, Buddy. I'm going to take a shower then I'll be ready to get some breakfast."

Half an hour later he called Alan and met him in the hallway. They said little as they made their way to the coffee shop in the hotel. Both men ordered the lobster omelet with toast and coffee. Outside the sun was shining, promising another beautiful day in the Bahamas. Alan had made arrangements with a local fisherman to charter his boat for the next three days. He was to be available to transport individuals to and from the big, white yacht anchored off-shore. The fisherman owned a cell phone and promised to stay close to the beach to be available whenever he was needed.

It was mid-morning when Gant called to say he and Leila were ready to come to the beach and go to the bank. While he was on the phone Alan passed on the news of Marco's arrival. The two agreed things were now on schedule.

At the appointed time the fisherman had his open boat alongside the ladder on the stern of the luxurious boat. Leila was the first down the ladder, wearing white slacks, a white tank top and sandals. Gant followed wearing tan slacks, a flowered short sleeve shirt, deck shoes and a straw hat with a wide brim.

The fisherman looked, but saw no one else on the rear deck.

"Are you the only ones going ashore?" inquired the fisherman with a hint of British accent.

"Yes, we have some business in town," said Leila. "Will you be available to bring us back to the boat in about three hours?"

"Of course," said the fisherman, holding out his hand. "Take my card. I'll come when you call. Your friends are waiting for you. They said to tell you they will see you when you finish your business. They want to meet at a local café. I'll show you which one."

The trip to the pier was short and uneventful. Fish were seen darting from under the boat as they neared shore. A small floating dock alongside the pier allowed them to step out of the small boat without difficulty. They appeared to be two successful tourists visiting Nassau.

Every male eye on the pier was gazing at Leila as she walked up the pier to the sandy shore. When the two reached the street there was a car waiting for them. Alan had done his job well. The car took them to the bank branch close to the beach. Inside they went to a teller's window to ask for the branch manager who came out of his office to greet them.

"Mr. Jarreau called and said to expect you. I am Edwin Goodard. Please follow me to my office where we can conduct our business in private." They followed him to a nicely appointed office where he offered them seats.

"Mr. Goodard, I'm Lucile Mc Dermot and this is my friend, Bill Gant, from Alaska. I suppose Mr. Jarreau told you what I wanted?"

"Yes he did, and I have the amount in my safe. I can furnish you a metal briefcase, if you like."

"Normally I wouldn't care to have this much in cash, but there's some business I must take care of while I'm here in Nassau. We'll be here for a few days, if I need anything further would it be alright if I called you?" asked Lucile Mc Dermot.

"Of course, we pride ourselves on our customer service. You may call me anytime."

"Then, I suppose we should complete our business in order that I may take care of my other matter."

"Of course, please wait here and I'll have the briefcase filled and brought to my office where you can count it and take possession. Would you like something to drink while we wait?" offered Goodard.

"No, thank you, Mr. Goodard, my schedule is rather tight today."

Goodard picked up the phone to give orders to a clerk on the other end. Ten minutes later the clerk entered the office with a metal briefcase in her hand. She passed it to Goodard who gave it to Lucile Mc Dermot. "I suggest you count it before sign the receipt," he said, handing her the metal case.

She thumbed through the stacks of bills, quickly multiplying the number of packets, coming to the agreed upon total. "Where would you like me to sign Mr. Goodard?"

He handed a sheet of paper across his desk. "If you're satisfied, just sign on the line at the bottom of the page and I'll notarize the signature which will complete our business."

She signed the paper and Goodard notarized it. Leila and Gant thanked him for his time and left the bank. The car was waiting at the curb when they came out. The driver seemed to know where to take them and dropped them at the cafe pointed out by the fisherman who had brought them to shore. Inside Alan and Greer were waiting. After sitting and saying their hellos Greer began the conversation.

"Marco Cidella is in town. I saw him this morning. He had two men with him, they looked to be locals. It's time we became cautious, folks. Roselli can't be far behind."

"Leila said she has some business of her own to do this morning, so if the two of you can stand it, I'll go with you for a while." Gant didn't like leaving Leila on her own, but she had insisted.

"Will it be all right if I use the car and driver?" she asked.

"Sure, just give us a call when you come back. And keep an eye on the rearview mirror. Marco may be following us." Greer was not at all certain this was a good idea. "I'll be glad when tomorrow comes and we can be done with the sneaking around."

"Me too, Ed," Said Leila as she stood to leave.

They watched her walk out the door carrying the briefcase. Gant was worried about who was out there and concerned for her safety. She's a big girl and can take care of herself, he thought, but not convinced.

Alan was first to speak, "I think we're ready here, Bill. Greer is going to the airport to watch for Roselli and I'm keeping an eye on the pier for any sign of Marco. The two of you will have Kinney on the boat as well as the skipper and crewman. You should be able to take care of Roselli no matter how your end works out. The unknown is Marco. We have no way to know how he's going to react. All I can tell you is I think whatever he does will be violent. Ed and I will have to deal with that. If your plan works Roselli will be sleeping like a baby when you leave Nassau. I can only think of two things Marco might do. ONE: find a boat and chase you down, or TWO: get on a plane and beat you back to Miami. If he takes a plane he'll have access to a lot of help. That would mean a shooting war. If he hires a boat we're ready for him. That fisherman you met has a reputation for getting things done. I hope he goes for the boat option."

"Stay on the phone and let me know which option he selects so we can be ready for him." Gant didn't like either of these scenarios. "And whatever you decide to do; don't get killed. I wouldn't like that. I may be in need of a bridegroom when all this is settled."

"Congratulations, Partner. It's about time someone took you off the market," said Pulis. "The rest of us single guys will have a chance with you out of the market."

Gant laughed, "Don't run out to buy a wedding gift just yet. There're still some things we have to iron out."

Greer laughed at the two ex-partners, "You'll have to settle this without me. I should be getting to the airport and watch for Sal Roselli."

Pulis nodded, "I'll hang out here and watch for Marco. This could be a long afternoon."

"I'll stay here until Leila gets back. Keep your head down, Ed."

Gant and Pulis passed the next two hours talking about what to expect after this case was done. Alan quizzed his partner about the upcoming marriage, but got no hint of a date. They talked about Leila and agreed she was nearly perfect for Gant.

When Leila returned to meet with the men she ordered an ice tea. "I'm done," she told the two ex-troopers. "We can go back to the boat now. I think I need a swim and a Mai Tai. Do you know if Kinney can make me one?"

"I'll bet he can," Bill commented.

Pulis sat, watching and was about to burst, "OK Leila, tell me about the wedding."

She looked at Bill and giggled, "I guess the cat's out of the bag."

"I told Bill you were too good for him, but he asked me not to tell you. You know, of course, the only reason he's interested in you is your ability to bait a halibut hook."

"I suspected that, but he won't be so cocky when I show him I can out-fish him any old time." Leila was enjoying the thought of making Bill uncomfortable.

"I've heard enough about this wedding deal. Let's go back to the boat and have some lunch." Gant turned to Pulis, "Take care Partner; there're dangerous people hanging around down here."

"I will. You two go back to the boat and don't worry about this old cripple. I'll just sit on the sand and watch out for those killers."

"Nice try Alan, but I can't feel sorry for you having to sit in the sunshine on a beach in Nassau. In fact I didn't feel sorry for you when you had to sit on a snow berm in Fairbanks at fifty below. Stay in touch. See you tomorrow if we can. If not we'll see you in Florida."

Bill and Leila made their way back to the pier and called the fisherman. His boat was at the floating dock, but he was nowhere to be seen. He answered his phone and they saw him stand up. He had been sleeping in a huge pile of mooring lines coiled on the little pier.

Back on the yacht Leila took the briefcase to her cabin, changed into a rather skimpy swim suit and returned to the open deck. Kinney brought her a towel and a Mai Tai. Bill had changed from slacks to a pair of walking shorts and followed her to the swim plate on the back of the boat. They swam and frolicked in the water for an hour before climbing out to dry in the sun.

When they climbed back onto the open rear deck, Kinney brought her another Mai Tai. "Something for you sir?" asked Kinney.

"Iced tea, please, I have some thinking to do," replied Gant as he flopped into a padded deck chair. "About the wedding?" inquired Federal Marshal Kinney?

"Word sure gets around, doesn't it?" Gant knew it was no longer his secret.

Chapter 36

Kinney had gone inside the cabin leaving Bill and Leila alone on the open rear deck. She was sipping her Mai Tai while he tasted the sweet iced tea.

"Tomorrow's the big day, Leila. Things could still go wrong. If Roselli comes to the boat alone for this meeting, we should be safe. If Marco tries to get aboard we could be in trouble. It'll be up to Kinney to watch for him. I just want to get this over with so we can make some real plans," Bill spoke quietly, but with apprehension in his voice.

"I have a surprise for you, Bill," said Leila, giving him a coquettish look.

"What kind of surprise," he asked. "I know you aren't pregnant."

She laughed aloud, "No, I'm not pregnant, I haven't been exposed. No, this surprise should please you."

"Are you going to tell me what it is?" asked Bill.

"I was going to save it until we finish, but I can't wait," she moved closer to him. "Do you remember the first trip to Nassau, the time we took a long walk on the beach? And do you remember the beautiful home on the bluff overlooking the beach?"

"Yes, I do. Gosh that's a beautiful place."

"I bought it today. It is now our home. Yours and mine," she was rocking back and forth with joy. "I hope you're as happy about it as I am."

"You did what?" he nearly shouted.

"I bought it. I took some of the money from the bank and made a deposit. I looked inside and around the grounds. It's even more wonderful than I imagined. You'll love it." She was excited when telling about the house. "I want us to come here often and have a place of our own to live in. We can lease it out when we're not here if you want, but it's ours and we can do what we want. I just love you so much and we have all that money we can't take back with us, it seemed a natural thing to do. Are you happy with me?"

"I don't know what to say, Leila, I really don't," Bill was stunned by her announcement. "So that was your secret mission today?"

"Yes, the property managers didn't want to sell, but I made them an offer they couldn't refuse. Oh, Bill, tell me you're happy with what I've done.

"It is going to take me a while to get used to the idea, but, yes, I do like the idea. Right or wrong, I like it."

"Tomorrow we'll be done with Roselli, you'll be done with the troopers and we can start a new life together. I want it to be perfect for us. There's a guest house on the property. A really nice guest house, I thought Alan could come live there when he wanted to get away." Again she was squirming and wiggling with excitement.

"We'd better keep this between us for now, Leila. I don't want Greer and Kinney to get wind of this. They'll get too curious about where the money came from. When we finish with Roselli and Cidella and are done with Greer and Kinney, then we can relax, but until then we'll have to keep it a secret between us."

"OK, but I had to tell you."

Kinney came out of the cabin to announce dinner, and asked, "Can I make you another Mai Tai, Leila?"

"No thank you, David, I think I've had enough for tonight."

Meanwhile, on the beach Greer and Alan had sighted Marco and his two new local helpers sitting at a table outside a small café near the sand. They appeared to be discussing serious business as they watched the foot traffic coming and going around them. At dusk the two locals left the area, but Marco sat at the table for another hour. Finally he gave up and walked up the street. Greer and Pulis walked down to the same café Marco had just left and sat. Each had a light dinner before retiring for the night.

The following morning Marco drove to the Nassau Airport to meet Salvatore Roselli. He waited in the car near the arrival gate ignoring the no parking signs. Minutes later Roselli came from the terminal building carrying a sizable carry-on bag. Marco stepped out of the car to motion to his boss. Roselli spotted the waving hand and came to the car.

"Good to see you, Marco," said Sal.

"Good to see you, too, Boss."

As Cidella drove away Roselli asked, "What have you seen, Marco?"

"Not much, Boss, I did spot a crippled guy hanging out with another tourist. They've been hanging around the beach and pier for the past couple of days. I think the other guy is a cop. I don't know for sure, but he has the look. One morning a guy and a woman came from the big yacht in the bay and went to the bank. They were there a long time and came out carrying a briefcase. She took off by herself for a couple of hours and then met him again at a restaurant near the beach. I think these are the people you're meeting today. How do you want me to handle it?" asked Cidella as he drove toward the pier.

"I've been thinking about that, Marco. I don't want anything to stop this deal. Leave everything to me for now. After I go to the bank with them to sign some papers I'll let you know what I want done. I'm going to call them when I get to the pier. I expect them to meet on the boat and try to make a deal to get off my hit list. I plan to agree to most everything and be friendly until they sign over the cash. Once they do that, all bets are off. I want them taken out. I'll leave that part up to you, but I don't want any loose ends. If the men on the beach are cops, I want them eliminated. I don't want anyone to know I was even here, Capiche?"

"Sure, Boss, I have a pair of locals to help me, but we'll stay back until you give the word. After I let you out at the pier I'll stay out of sight, but I won't be far away, in case you need me," said Marco.

"You are a good man, Marco. I can trust you. I'll call you as soon as I'm finished with them. Wait until I call you." Sal stepped out of the car and opened his cell phone. It was time to call Lucile Mc Dermot. Marco drove away to find a place to wait and watch.

Sal dialed the number his contact had given him. It rang four times before a female voice came on the line.

"Hello," said a friendly voice.

"This is Sal," he replied.

"It is good to hear from you. You're right on schedule. I'm sending a boat for you. We're waiting on the large white boat anchored off-shore. You'll be safe here. The boatman will deliver you to our yacht. Wait on the pier. He'll contact you in a minute." The voice was still friendly. Sal had difficulty with doing something unknown. But he agreed.

The fisherman stepped from behind the large stack of mooring lines and spoke to Sal with a slight British accent. "Do you wish a water taxi, Sir?" he asked.

"Are you my transport to the yacht," asked Sal.

"Yes, Sir, I was just now called."

"Come back at noon," ordered Sal.

"I was told to pick you up now," said the fisherman.

"And I said come back at noon." Sal wanted the ones on the boat to know he was still in charge of the situation.

The fisherman retrieved his cell phone and punched a button. He waited for it to be answered and when it was he said, "He wants me to come back for him at noon." The fisherman listened, then closed his phone and spoke to Roselli, "I will return for you at noon."

Roselli turned around and walked to the small beach side café where he took a table and waited. He sat and drank iced tea, watching the bay and the boat until the fisherman returned at noon.

The fisherman showed his passenger the ramp down to the floating dock and his small boat. "It is only a short ride to the big boat, the ride will be pleasant. Have a seat and I will untie my boat."

Sal watched for activity on the yacht as he climbed to a center seat on the taxi. The fisherman tossed the mooring line into the front of the boat and stepped into the fiberglass craft. "That's a very nice boat you're going to, Sir. I'd like to own one like that someday," said the driver.

Sal did not answer, but sat silently during the ride to the beautiful white luxury yacht. When they arrived at the small floating dock alongside the big boat the fisherman jumped out to hold the small boat while Sal stepped out. The fisherman stepped back into the craft and started the motor. "I'll be back to pick you up later, Sir."

As he idled away from the little dock, Sal looked up at the face above him. It was Kinney.

"Would you like me to assist you on the ladder, Mr. Roselli?"

"No, I'll make it," he replied, wondering who else was on the deck above him.

He climbed slowly to the rear deck of the big boat. Once he was at deck level Kinney opened the gate on the rear of the yacht to allow him to come on board at the open rear deck. Gant and Leila were seated in the shade of the cabin having a glass of orange juice when he arrived. Bill stood and walked into the sunshine to greet the visitor.

"How do you do, Mr. Roselli, you probably remember me. My partner and I met you in your office in Newark." Bill put out his hand to shake, but Roselli ignored the gesture.

"Yeah, I remember you. You and that other nosey cop came to my office. Where is he, by the way?"

"I'm sorry, he couldn't make it. The only ones on board are yourself, me, Leila; you know her as Lucile Mc Dermot and the crew of three. There's no reason for you to feel threatened here. That's why we chose this place to meet. You can look around first if you want to be sure."

"That won't be necessary, but be advised, I have people watching. If there's any sign of funny business I'll give the signal and they'll sink this tub." It was a bluff, but a believable threat. Sal wanted them to know he was still in charge.

"I understand you're no longer in business in Newark," said Leila from her seat in the shade.

"That's none of your business," said Sal, "I came to discuss the property you possess, which rightfully belongs to me. What's the total value of this property right now?"

"As of yesterday it was \$9.4 million." Leila was speaking again, "But I wish to correct your statement, Mr. Roselli. The amount is in a local bank in my name, not yours."

"The money was taken from me by your criminal boyfriend. It is my money," snarled Sal.

"If we can come to an agreement the money can be yours," explained Leila. "Please, have a seat and we'll discuss this like reasonable adults."

Roselli moved to a chair at the table in the center of the deck and sat. "What is it you want in return for my money and how much of it are you keeping?"

Leila stood and walked to the table and sat across from Sal. Bill Gant sat next to her. "You can have it all, Mr. Roselli. I don't want any of it. The only thing I want from you is your promise to forget about me, Bill and his trooper friend Alan Pulis. We know you were behind the attempt on their lives and we know your goons are in jail in Alaska. You may think Alaska is full of dumb hillbillies, but we have many talented prosecutors. Your men will be going to jail for a very long time. I'd be willing to bet they're talking right now in order to reduce their sentences. They won't be around to help you. You've given up your kingdom in New Jersey to another member of the organized crime community, a man you should fear much more than the three of us."

"I fear no one, least of all you and your friends." Sal's bluster had not shaken Leila.

"You have a win-win situation here," said Bill Gant, "we'll sign over almost \$9 ½ million dollars to you with nothing in return but your promise to forget about us. You risk nothing and gain a lot of cash. You can take possession today and go home. You can live happily ever after and we can do the same."

"That's it?" asked Roselli. "You don't want any of the money? You just want me to leave you to live your lives?"

"That's it. If you agree I'll have the crewman bring us a bottle of your favorite wine from the little Italian restaurant up in Connecticut," said Gant.

"You're a very convincing salesman, Mr. Gant. It's hard for me to believe I'll get almost ten million dollars while you get nothing of substance." Now Roselli was nibbling at the bait.

"We'll get what we want, Mr. Roselli; freedom from worry. That's all we want."

Salvatore Roselli sat rubbing his chin, thinking. He finally looked up at the two, "I think I'll drink a glass of wine with you to seal the deal. You can call the boat to take me to shore and I'll meet you this afternoon to sign the papers at the bank." He stood up and extended his hand. "Now I'll shake hands," he said.

Chapter 37

With a sigh of relief Bill Gant reached out to take the hand of Sal Roselli. "You won't regret this decision, Mr. Roselli. It may be the most profitable one you ever made. You give up nothing of value and keep a very large sum of money. We'll go to the bank together this afternoon and finalize the papers. I do have one word of caution for you, though. Don't renege on your part of the deal. You tried to have me and my partner killed once and I survived. This time I'm paying you to leave us alone. If there's a next time I'll personally come for you no matter where you live." Bill smiled at Roselli, nodding his head. "Now, to more pleasant things: Mr. Kinney," he called, "Bring us the wine and some glasses. We're celebrating."

"At once, Sir," said Kinney as he disappeared into the cabin. When he reappeared he was carrying a tray with three glasses and a black bottle of wine. It was unopened. Kinney placed the tray on a small table next to the one being used by the three negotiators. He placed the three glasses on the larger table and showed the old black bottle to Roselli who recognized it as one from the old stock in his friend's restaurant.

"How did you know?" asked Roselli, inspecting the bottle.

"We know many things about you, Sal," said Gant.

Roselli chuckled a little, "You have nothing to fear from me, Mr. Gant. I'm out of the business these days. Open the wine."

Kinney took the bottle and removed the cork. He poured a small taste into Roselli's glass for him to approve. He smelled, tasted and inspected the color of the liquid in the glass. After a long moment he nodded his approval. Kinney filled all three glasses and reached to set the bottle in the center of the large table. In doing so he slipped on something unseen on the deck tipping the bottle. He reached and held the shoulder of the guest to steady himself as she caught the black bottle before it tipped and spilled. Kinney stepped back and apologized for his error.

"Forgive me, Mr. Roselli, something caused me to trip as I was setting the bottle back on the table. I didn't mean to grab you like that. I'm sorry."

"It's alright, Mr. Kinney. We'll be fine. We'll call you when we've finished. You can call the water taxi for Mr. Roselli, though"

"I'll take care of it, Mr. Gant," said Kinney as he picked up his tray and went back into the cabin.

"Are you OK Sal?" asked Gant.

"Yes, yes, no harm done. It would have been a shame to spill this good wine." Roselli took another sip from his glass as did Bill and Leila. "I have another bottle of this wine in the locker. I'll send it with you when you leave," continued Gant.

"The wine is good and the sun is warm. I think it's affecting me. Thank you for the gift of wine. It's the thing I've missed the most since I left Newark." Roselli rubbed his forehead with the back of his hand, "Ooh, the wine is beginning to get to me. Call the taxi and I'll go to shore to rest a while."

"You're welcome to rest here if you like." Leila spoke softly, watching Roselli's eyes. She could see he was becoming disoriented, his head bobbing from side to side and his eyes beginning to droop. Moments later he was asleep.

Kinney returned from the cabin. "I got him when I grabbed his shoulder." Dave held out his hand to show the two the tool he had used. "This is on loan from the CIA. It slips on your finger with the stinger inside the palm." He held it closer for them to inspect. "It's a small hypodermic needle and the flat base is the syringe containing the sedative. I've never used one before, but it sure worked."

"How long will he be out?" asked Gant.

"Several hours, according to my friend at the CIA," Kinney said as he gathered the glasses from the table.

"Tell the Captain we'd better get under way before this stuff wears off." Gant didn't want to take any chances with their prisoner.

The skipper started the engines to warm the oil while the other crewman made the boat ready to sail. The sea was calm and the air warm and moist. It was a good day to sail to Florida.

Gant found his cell phone to call Alan. He and Greer were sitting under an umbrella at a table on the beach watching Marco and his friends at the little outdoor café a city block away. Alan answered the call, "How did it go?" he asked.

"Perfectly," said Gant, "Roselli is wrapped tightly in the arms of Morpheus as we speak. How are things on the beach?"

"Marco and his friends are across the beach at the restaurant drinking coffee. They've been watching the boat with binoculars. I haven't seen any sign they know what is happening."

"Keep watching, Alan, the Skipper just started the engines. We'll be pulling the anchor in a few minutes. We'll need to know if he gets a boat and chases us or goes to the airport to beat us to Florida."

"I just thought of another possibility, Bill. What if he goes to the airport and sends his flunkies to chase you in the yacht?"

"I hadn't thought of that. You could be right. Let me know if they head out to sea," said Gant. "Oh, oh, they're pulling the anchor right now."

"Stay on the line, Bill, and I'll let you know what they plan to do." Alan watched in silence as Marco used his binoculars to scan the bay. Suddenly Marco stood up, field glasses at his eyes. The boat was moving and Marco was giving orders. The two locals ran away from the beach, returning minutes later with Marco's rental car. Marco was still focused on the departing yacht.

As the yacht motored toward the open ocean Marco could read the name of the boat on the transom. The name on the yacht was *BYE BYE BABY*. Marco was furious. He threw his binoculars in the sand and ran to the waiting car, departing in the direction of the municipal airport.

"OK, Bill. It looks like Marco is headed to the airport. I think you can relax, at least for now," said Alan. "Enjoy the trip."

"That's good news, Alan. We'll see you in Miami tomorrow. I think we'll stay on the boat tonight and settle up with the owner and the crew in the morning. We'll need to fuel the tanks and help with the cleaning. Why don't you and Greer take the rest of the day off and enjoy the sights? Come back in the morning and we'll pick you up at the Miami Airport."

"I'll talk it over with Greer and see what he wants to do. I've never been to Nassau. I'd like to see what the town looks like. I might want to trade my place in Sterling for a place here. I haven't swatted a mosquito since I got here."

"We'll talk about that when you get over there. See you tomorrow, Alan."

On the yacht, Kinney came to sit with Bill and Leila. She was now in her bikini and he in his walking shorts and open shirt. Kinney was still in his crewman's uniform.

"The skipper told me we would be in U.S. waters in three hours. The Coast Guard will have a boat meet us shortly after that. A helicopter will transport Roselli to the Coast Guard boat in a Stokes litter. I'll go over in a small launch to ride in with the prisoner. It's been a real pleasure working with all of you. I can't remember ever having this much fun on a case. Thanks for inviting me along."

"I'm proud to have been working with you, Dave. If you ever get to Alaska look us up. We'll go fishing and I'll have Leila bait your hook." Both men laughed while Leila scowled at them.

"Don't forget to invite me to the wedding, Leila," said Kinney.

"You'll be at the top of the list, David. Come visit."

Leila's tan was beginning to look good. She lay in the sun soaking up the warm rays, working on her tan. Bill watched her for a long time as he sat in the padded chair in the shade. "What'll happen now," he wondered, "after all the excitement dies down?" He considered his future with Leila, wondering how Alan would fit into the picture. He and Alan had been partners and friends for most of his life. He couldn't leave him without help, but would Leila understand? This case was nearly over and he would have to make some decisions soon. "She's sure good to look at and she can catch fish," thought Gant. He shook off his thoughts to go inside and talk with the captain of the boat.

Soon a large Coast Guard craft came into sight and contacted the skipper on the UHF radio. Kinney was in the wheelhouse and heard the call. He went to his cabin to change his clothing. Leila had heard the engine slow and came inside to watch. As the Coast Guard boat stopped alongside Kinney came on deck. Roselli was brought outside on a stretcher, still sleeping. A small boat came to the yacht carrying the Stokes litter and two sailors. They lifted the Stokes to the deck and strapped Roselli into it for the ride. A helicopter lifted off the aft deck of the larger boat and hovered over the rear deck of the yacht. A line was dropped and attached to the Stokes litter. A sailor gave some signals and the litter was lifted from the yacht.

Kinney waved goodbye to the skipper and the crewman, shaking Gant's hand as he passed. He kissed Leila on the cheek before walking to the little gate in the transom to board the launch for the ride to the Coast Guard Cutter a quarter mile away. The helicopter had now landed there and Roselli taken to the medical bay.

The skipper put the engines in gear and motored toward his home base near Miami. It had been a relaxing trip for him, but he was still at a loss as to what all this was about. Once the *BYE BYE BABY* was tied to the home dock and the engines shut down. Leila came up from her cabin to say goodbye.

She had two envelopes in her hand, one for the captain and one for the crewman. Each contained ten thousand dollars in cash. "We can never thank you enough for what you did for us. I know you want to know what's going on, but we can't tell you at this time. You will, however, be reading about it in the papers soon. Bill and I will be staying on board tonight and will go with you to get fuel in the morning. If there is anything we can do for you, help you clean the boat or anything, please ask."

"The owner pays us well and a gratuity is not necessary, Ms. Hunter. We've enjoyed this voyage with you. Your friend Kinney made a very good cabin boy," they all laughed.

"The crew and I will be on board with you tonight. You'll be my guest for dinner, no need for formal dress. If you wish to go somewhere I'll have the limo brought around."

"Thank you again for everything," said Leila.

"You are most welcome. Oh, one piece of advice, Ms. Hunter. There are many alligators in this canal. I would advise you not to swim here." With that he went about his duties.

Chapter 38

The following day Bill and Leila packed their belongings and moved out of the boat. They had called the limo to take them to the hotel once again. They had just checked in when Alan called them to say he and Greer were at the airport. Greer had called the previous day to ask a local FBI agent to watch for Marco and find where he was staying. He was in another hotel across town. Bill said he would pick them up as soon as he had a rental car.

Two hours later he and Leila were on the way to the airport. Leila called Alan and advised him they would soon be at the arrival gates to pick them up. Greer and Pulis were waiting at the curb when Bill arrived. Both men sat in the rear of the rental with their bags on their laps.

"We reserved rooms for you both at our hotel. How was the flight?" asked Bill.

"The flight was great. Even better was the evening off last night. We had a nice dinner and some drinks. We sat on the beach and enjoyed the tropical air. I didn't realize normal people lived like this all the time."

Greer added his two cents worth, "I agree. It was nice to sit in the open air without someone wanting to shoot at me. I'll be glad when I'm done with the two of you and this life of danger is at an end." Everyone laughed. "How did your trip go after leaving us?"

"You'd have been proud of Bill. He schmoozed poor old Roselli all the way. Sal wasn't buying any of it at first, but then Bill convinced him he was getting all the money in the bank and had to give up nothing except us. He thought about it a little, but went for the deal. Dave brought out the wine and, of course, Sal couldn't resist his favorite. You should have seen the pratfall Dave did, nearly spilling the wine. It was worth an academy award. He reached out and grabbed Sal by the arm to keep from falling. Old Sal didn't even know he had been stuck. Three minutes later it was over, Roselli was asleep." Leila was excited when telling the story.

"I assume Kinney went with Roselli?" asked Greer.

"Yes, they hauled Sal to the cutter by helicopter and Kinney went over on the launch. We haven't heard from him since then." Bill was now talking. "I'll bet Roselli was one mad Italian when he woke up."

"I'll bet he'll make the papers by tomorrow."

"What do you want to do about Marco?" asked Alan.

"I don't know, Alan. There are no warrants for him, as far as I know. Unless he comes after us we can't arrest him. He's totally loyal to Sal and probably will come after us simply for revenge. We'll have to keep an eye on him." It was this comment by Greer that set Gant to thinking.

"Why don't we bait him, too? How about we go to his hotel and let him spot us. He can make the choice: come after us or go back to Newark to be with his boss."

"That might be a good idea, Bill. Swing by the federal building where I can pick up some firepower." Greer knew he could check out some weapons from the local FBI office.

On the route to their hotel Greer went into the federal building. He was inside for almost an hour before emerging with what looked like a computer bag in his hand. In the bag were three Glocks and extra magazines.

Gant drove to the hotel where the new residents checked into their rooms. They met for lunch in the hotel coffee shop. Afterward Pulis said he was tired and needed to lie down for a while. His injuries were fatiguing him. Leila abandoned the other two at the hotel also, saying she had some shopping to do. Gant and Greer drove across town to find the hotel Marco where was living.

Greer went to the desk and asked if Mr. Cidella was in his room. He wasn't, but Greer didn't leave a message. They found an open parking spot a half-block away and waited. They waited all afternoon and into the evening. At seven Leila called to check on the stakeout crew.

"Are you two alright," she asked.

"Yeah," said Gant, "We're getting tired and haven't seen Marco come out of or go into the hotel. I think we'll give it up if he doesn't show soon. Are you ready for dinner?"

"I'm famished," she said. "I'm worried about Alan. I haven't seen or heard from him since you left. Do you suppose he's alright?"

"We'll check on him when we get there."

They were about to drive back to their own hotel when Greer spotted something.

"That car going into the parking garage, I think it's Marco. The window was down and I got a good look at him."

"Good," said Bill, "what room number did you say was his?"

"541, fifth floor, at the back," replied Greer,

"Why don't we go up and welcome him to Miami?"

"That's a wonderful idea."

Both men checked their weapons before exiting the vehicle. Checking traffic they walked across the street and into the hotel. Greer checked the desk but there was no sign of Cidella. They went to the elevator to ride to the fifth floor. Greer stepped out first, his hand near his weapon.

"Clear," he said.

"541 will I be to the left, toward the end." Both men cautiously moved down the hall. At 541 Greer knocked on the door. They heard movement inside the room.

"Who is it?" asked a voice from the other side.

"Bellman, Sir. I have a message for you."

They heard the lock being moved and the door opened a crack. An eye appeared in the open slit. "What the--," said the voice under the eye. He didn't finish. Gant hit the door with his shoulder, forcing the occupant of the room to be pushed aside. The two lawmen stepped inside before Marco could regain his footing.

"Who are you?" asked a flustered Cidella.

Greer produced his FBI identification, "I'm Agent Greer and this is my friend, Alaska State Trooper Bill Gant. Are you Marco Cidella?"

"Yeah, why do you want to know? I'm not wanted for anything."

Greer ignored the question, "How was your flight from Nassau, Marco?"

"What makes you think I was in Nassau?"

"C'mon, Marco, we saw you there with those two local tuffs. We saw you deliver Sal Roselli to the beach. We know you, Marco. Where have you been all day?" asked a smiling Agent Greer.

"You know so much, suppose you tell me?" bluffed Cidella.

"I can't be sure, but my guess is that you have been looking for your boss. Have you heard from him?"

"I ain't heard from nobody. I'm on holiday. I'm the manager of Ace Trucking Company in Newark. Mr. Roselli used to own the company, but now it's owned by Mr. Zena, from New York. I'm an honest businessman on vacation and you two come busting in here like Elliot Ness. Get out of my room or I'm calling the cops."

Gant chuckled, "I don't suppose you've heard from a lawyer by the name of Lawrence Woodbury, either?"

The question made Marco stop for an instant, "Get out, I'm calling Miami PD." He turned to reach for the telephone.

"Go ahead, Marco. Call the PD. But before you do I thought you might want to know where your - former, boss is right now."

"What do you know about Mr. Roselli, Agent Greer?"

"I know where he is. I know his name will be in the headlines in the morning papers. I know he called you to come to Nassau. I know you were pretty upset when that big white yacht pulled anchor and left Nassau with your boss aboard. I just came up here to relieve your anxiety over the whereabouts of Sal Roselli. I'm just here doing you a favor."

Marco was surprised, "What do you mean he'll be in the headlines tomorrow?"

"Just what I said," repeated Greer. "His name will be in every paper on the East Coast. He may even appear in court to be read his rights and hear the charges cited on the stack of arrest warrants he is appearing for."

Marco regained some of his composure, "Mr. Roselli and I are old friends. I do a favor for him now and then, that's all."

Gant spoke, "You're an old friend of Vito Roma, also, aren't you?"

"Sure, I got his job when he didn't come back from Alaska."

"And you know why he was sent to Alaska, don't you, Marco?" Gant was enjoying this part.

"No, I don't know anything about that. Who are you anyway?" asked Marco.

"I'm surprised you don' know me, Marco. I'm one of the two officers Vito tried to kill."

"I told you, I don't know anything about all that?"

"That's all right, Marco, just as long as you don't decide to take up the torch and finish the job Roma started," Gant was giving a gentle warning, but the ice in his eyes told Marco he was deadly serious.

"I don't do that kind of work," said Marco. "Get out of my room," he ordered, reaching for the telephone.

"We're going, Marco. We just thought you should know the whereabouts of your boss, excuse me, ex-boss. You have a nice day now, you hear?" Gant was moving toward the door before Greer finished speaking.

Marco slammed the door behind them and marched to the telephone to call Lawrence Woodbury. Woodbury answered his cell phone number.

"Mr. Woodbury, I just had a visit from an FBI agent and a trooper from Alaska. They said Sal was in jail. Is that true?"

"I just finished talking with the federal prosecutor myself. Sal will be sent to court this afternoon. I'll be there to represent him."

"How can they do that? We were in Nassau and he went to a big yacht to do some business with them and he never came back. I watched and waited for him, but the boat just sailed out of the bay with him on board. He never called me or nothing."

"That is interesting, Mr. Cidella. Give me your number and I will call you after I meet with Mr. Roselli. I'm going down there now."

Marco gave Woodbury his cell phone number. After the call he sat on the edge of the bed wondering what to do next. Sal had wanted the two Alaska cops done along with the tall woman Steven Collier used to date. Marco pondered the question and decided he should do what the boss had asked him to do, take care of the three. This could be even more important now; they could possibly be witnesses against him. The Newark gangster had a few contacts in Miami and would enlist their help to find the cops and the girl. Marco thought he might erase the FBI agent as well, for personal reasons.

Back at the hotel Gant knocked on Leila's door and asked her to go with him to Alan's room. He was concerned for his partner. They walked down the hall to the room Pulis was renting. They knocked several times before a sickly-looking Alan Pulis answered.

Bill was horrified at his partner's appearance. "What's the matter with you, Alan? You look terrible."

"I was sick all night and I still don't feel too good. Just let me rest and I'll be better tomorrow."

Leila stepped forward and placed a palm on the forehead of the sickly Pulis. "You're burning up, Alan. I think we should call a doctor."

Gant didn't stop to ask, but picked up the hotel phone and asked the desk clerk to send a doctor to Alan's room. Leila ordered the patient back to bed. It took only a few minutes for the doctor to arrive. He thrust a thermometer in Alan's mouth, pulled it out and read it. He took a pulse and noted the injuries to the left arm, shoulder and neck of the patient.

"This man needs to be in the hospital. He may have an infection inside his body. I am giving him some antibiotics and calling an ambulance. These injuries look recent and I think they may be the cause of this infection." The doctor called the desk and ordered an ambulance for Pulis.

"He was shot a few weeks ago, doctor, but he's been just fine. What happened?"

"It looks to me like he was healing pretty well, but sometime in the last few days, three or four, he pulled something loose and it became infected. Judging from the scarring he's fortunate to be alive at all. The doctors at the hospital will examine him and look for the source of the infection. If you know him and what happened to him, I think you should go to the hospital and talk with the doctors. They'll need all the information you can provide. He's very ill."

The paramedics came to take Pulis to the ambulance and on to the hospital. Leila went down the hall to Greer's room and asked him to drive them to the hospital. Pulis was in the Emergency Room when they arrived. It was three hours later when a doctor came out to the waiting room to speak with them. He sat in one of the chairs opposite the three friends, took off his cap and wiped his face and head of sweat.

"You're the friends of Alan Pulis?" he asked.

"Yes," answered Gant.

"First of all I want you to know he's a very sick man. You won't be able to see him tonight. We've just sent him to ICU where they'll try to stabilize him. His infection is out of control and, quite honestly, I don't know if he'll be able to fight it off. He's been getting worse for several days and apparently not saying anything to anyone. We've done everything we can do tonight. It'll be up to him and his own body to do the rest. Please leave your phone number and where we can reach you. Get some rest and check with us tomorrow. We'll contact you if there's any change." The doctor stood to leave.

"Thanks Doc," said Gant.

Tears were flowing down the cheeks of Leila Hunter.

"Come on, let's go back to the hotel and get some dinner. There's nothing we can do here tonight." Greer was having difficulty maintaining his professional demeanor.

The three said nothing as they walked across the parking lot to their car.

Chapter 39

Early the following morning Marco called an old friend living in Miami. Camden Dalton was an ex-gangster from Newark. He retired after he was badly burned in an arson fire he had set. He was hired to torch a warehouse in Newark at the request of Salvatore Roselli, but while he was inside something or someone had closed his escape route door and after setting the fire he was unable to exit the building. Firefighters found him inside the building, badly burned and suffering smoke inhalation. He was rescued and taken to the hospital where he survived, but never regained his health. He retired to Miami after he was released from prison. He now owned a car wash and walked with a cane.

"I need your help, Cam," said Marco.

"You got it, whatever you need, Marco. It's good to hear from you."

"Thanks, Cam. Things are getting bad. The boss has been busted and is in federal jail in New York. Woodbury says he'll go to court today. It don't look good for him, Cam. Before he got arrested he gave me a job and I need your help finding them."

"Locals or tourists?" asked Dalton.

"There are actually four people, three men and a woman. I got their names here, and what they look like. All of them are from out of town."

"I might be able to help you. A lot of the cabbies in town use my carwash. Some of them owe me for favors. Give me their descriptions and names and I'll see what I can do."

Marco gave his friend the information he needed as well as his cell phone number, "Thanks, Cam. I'll be waiting for your call."

Cidella then went to the hotel coffee shop for breakfast and was returning to his room when Lawrence Woodbury called.

"Marco. It's Larry Woodbury. I've just come from talking with Sal. I acquired a copy of the charges from the court. It's bad Marco, it's really bad. There must be fifty charges, all major felonies and all federal charges. I don't think I can get him out on this one. I talked to him this morning and he's completely irrational. He's screaming and telling me to get him out. He even told me to hit the judge. I don't want to know anything about those things, Marco. Even so, I don't believe the judge will grant bail today. I'll try, but it'll be out of my hands. Our only chance is to challenge the arrest as unconstitutional. From what he told me he was kidnapped in Nassau and brought to the U.S. and handed over to the U.S. Marshals. He doesn't remember much of how he got here, but he says it was against his will."

"Do the best you can, Larry. I'm trying to locate the people who brought him back here. They're in Miami and I'm looking for them now. Sal asked me to take care of them when we were in Nassau, but they left on a boat before I could take care of it. We have to get him out of jail and back to Costa Rica."

"Easily said, Marco, but not so easily done." Woodbury was being candid with Marco Cidella, but not offering much hope for success. "I have to go now. It is almost time for court. I'll call you and let you know how it goes. I'll tell Sal you are working on the other problem."

"Thanks, Mr. Woodbury. Tell Sal I'm with him all the way." Cidella was disappointed in the news. He closed his phone and sat in the hotel room waiting for word from Camden Dalton.

Greer, Gant and Leila met for breakfast in the hotel. There had been no news about Alan during the night. After a quiet breakfast they drove to the hospital to check on Alan's condition. They waited while the doctor was in the ICU room with Pulis. The nurses wouldn't give them any information so they waited. For almost an hour they waited, impatiently. Finally the doctor came from the restricted area to confer with the visitors.

"How do you do, I'm Doctor Abbott, I specialize in infectious injuries. It's my understanding you brought Mr. Pulis here last night."

"Yes, Doctor, how is he?" asked Bill Gant.

"I wish I had better news for you, but he's in critical condition. He's deteriorated since last night. We're doing the best we can, but he's developed a deep infection of the bone. I've examined his injuries and I'm amazed he survived the initial trauma. We found some impurities in the wounds. We removed two small shards of glass and one lead pellet. These were lodged in the damaged shoulder bone, causing the infection which has now progressed into the upper shoulder and neck as well as the blood stream. We've removed the cause, but his general condition due to the infection is extremely grave. If he improves during the next 24 hours he might have a chance, but don't get your hopes up just yet. I'm sorry I don't have better news for you."

The doctor returned to the ICU while the three friends remained in the waiting room. Leila was sobbing, her eyes red and swollen. Gant choked back tears of his own. Greer, too, was feeling deep sadness for his friend. "I'll call Kinney," said Greer.

The three drank coffee, worked the crossword puzzle in the morning paper, drank more coffee and waited and waited. It was close to noon when the doctor returned. "I'm sorry," he said as he approached. "We've lost him. The infection was overwhelming and his heart just couldn't take it any longer. I understand he was a policeman and his injuries were in the line of duty. I am truly sorry. We have a chaplain here in the hospital. Would you like for me to notify him for you?"

His eyes red and tears running down his cheeks, Gant said, "No, that won't be necessary. He and I were partners. I'll be making arrangements to take him home to Alaska."

"We'll try to make this as easy as possible for you, Mr. Gant. I'll send a nurse to help you with the arrangements."

After speaking with the nurse the trio drove back to the hotel where Gant called Captain Rollin Caswell to deliver the news. Caswell immediately called the DA to amend the charges against Vito Roma from Attempted Murder to Murder One.

Greer contacted Kinney to give him the news. Kinney said he had just come from the court where the judge refused to grant bail to Salvatore Roselli. Roselli's lawyer, Lawrence Woodbury, protested and claimed the arrest was illegal. The judge said that was a point for another court to determine. Roselli had screamed and threatened the judge during the proceeding. He was taken back to jail by the U.S. Marshals.

Greer had been in his room and was about to return to Gant's room. He opened the door to see a man standing across the hall, it was Marco Cidella. He closed the door and called Bill. "Get on the floor behind the bed. Marco is at the door." He chambered a round in the borrowed Glock and again opened the door a little. Marco was now holding a handgun and about to knock on Bill's door.

"Drop the weapon," shouted Greer.

Surprised by the voice from across the hall and behind him, Marco spun around to face his challenger. As Marco was raising his weapon to fire, Greer touched the trigger of his Glock twice, striking Marco in center chest.

Gant heard the shots and opened the door, his Glock at the ready. Marco laid face down, bleeding, on the floor in front of the hotel room door. Greer stepped into the hall to kick the pistol on the floor away from Marco's lifeless hand. Heads began to stick out from hotel room doors, a strange response to gunshots. Greer was checking for a pulse when hotel security came down the hall, guns in hand. Greer dropped his weapon and produced his FBI identification. Gant stepped back into his room to leave his Glock on the dresser.

Miami police and local FBI agents came to the hotel to investigate the shooting. Statements were taken along with pictures of the scene. The body was taken from the hotel hallway and the blood cleaned from the carpet. The hotel manager politely asked Greer and Gant to refrain from shooting anyone else during their stay—"It is bad for business, you know," he had said.

The rest of the day and much of the next was spent talking with police. Leila had stopped crying, but clung tightly to Bill Gant. It was two more days before all the papers were completed and arrangements made to take Alan Pulis back to Alaska. Greer returned to Alaska with Leila and Bill. They were met at the Anchorage Airport by a black hearse. The three friends stood by as the casket was loaded into the black Cadillac.

The Governor had sent a trooper aircraft to transport Leila and Bill back to Kenai. Captain Caswell met the plane in Kenai and drove them home. It was a sad homecoming for all involved.

Bill Gant spent the next several days finishing the reports of the floating body case and finalizing his last days as a trooper investigator. Rollin Caswell was sorry to see his old friend leave.

Leila had been cleaning up Alan's house to make ready for the memorial service to be held there. In the process she came across a document in his desk addressed to Bill Gant. It was sealed, but looked important, as all thick envelopes do. She gave it to Bill when he came to pick her up that evening.

Bill opened the envelope and read the cover letter.

Bill:

If you are reading this it is because I didn't make it through. You and I have been through a lot in the past 30 years. I have enjoyed most of it. I can't think of another person I could have enjoyed it with more, except my wife. As you read this I will be with her and watching over you. Someone has to keep you from hurting yourself.

I want to thank you for being a friend all those years and especially in the months following Cybil's death. If not for you I never would have survived those days. I can never thank you enough.

> *Enclosed with this letter is my Will. In it I give you everything I own. I have no relatives who want to come to Alaska, so I am leaving it to you. There isn't much cash left, but you only need money enough to buy bait.*
>
> *Always think kindly of me, Bill, and I will put in a word for you when I get where I am going.*
>
> *May you live a long and happy life.*
>
> *Your friend and partner,*
> *Alan Pulis.*

It was signed by Alan.

"What does it say?" asked Leila.

He didn't answer, but handed her the letter. She sat at the table and read. When she finished she was weeping and handed the letter back to Bill.

She wiped her eyes and looked across the table at Gant. "I hope I live long enough to have a friend like that. He loved you, Bill."

"I loved him, too. We were closer than brothers. There will never be another Alan Pulis."

"What do you want to do now, Bill, since it all belongs to you?" she asked.

"What do you think WE should do now? I think it's time we decided if we should make this a permanent relationship. I was married once and never felt about her the way I feel about you now. I think I understand how Alan felt about his wife. She was a wonderful lady and was devoted to Alan. I hope we can have the same kind of relationship. Do you think it could work that way?"

Leila laughed, "Little boys need little girls to play with and to keep them out of trouble. The answer is yes, it will work. How soon do you want to start?"

"Right now," he walked around the table and lifted her from the chair to kiss her.

"As soon as the memorial service is done and those emotions out of the way we can set a date. Is that alright with you?" she asked.

"Perfect," he replied, and kissed her again. "You know, I haven't seen you sneaking out for a smoke in recent weeks."

"No, it's too much trouble to stop what I'm doing with you and have a smoke. I've quit. I feel better, too."

"How do you feel about moving out here instead of my little house in town?"

"I'd like it. There are more closets for my clothes," she giggled. "We can rent the house in town. The rent would be enough to buy bait."

"I think this new partnership is going to work out just fine," said Bill Gant. "Yes, just fine.

Other Books by Ron Walden

Flying Blind: Alaska Adventure and International Intrigue

Alaska Fish Wars: Nobody Wins

Wyatt Earp V: Alaska Bush Guardian

Cinch Knot: Pigs, Politics, and Petroleum. The Multinational Plot to Nuke the Trans Alaska Pipeline

Devil's Heart: Native American Lore and Modern Police Work

Ice Blue Eyes: An Alaska Story of Greed, Live, and Revenge

Blue Sky and Green Grass: Murder, Money Laundering, and Winter Farming in Alaska

Poacher's Paradise: An Alaska Wildlife Trooper Novel

Easy Come Easy Go: Alaska Gold Fever

Getting Even: What Goes Around in Alaska, Comes Around in Florida

Penny Files: Alaska State Troopers..Unfinished Business

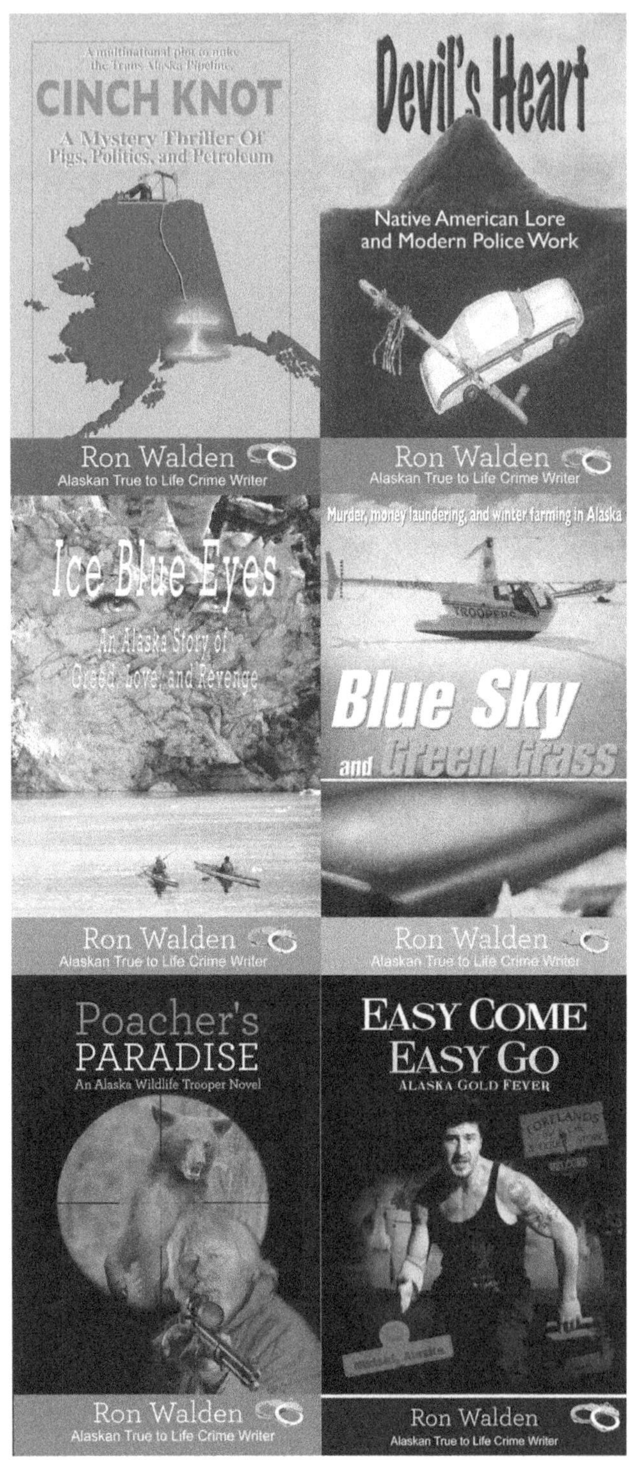
A multinational plot to make
the Trans-Alaska Pipeline
CINCH KNOT
A Mystery Thriller Of
Pigs, Politics, and Petroleum
Ron Walden
Alaskan True to Life Crime Writer

Devil's Heart
Native American Lore
and Modern Police Work
Ron Walden
Alaskan True to Life Crime Writer

Ice Blue Eyes
An Alaska Story of
Greed, Love, and Revenge
Ron Walden
Alaskan True to Life Crime Writer

Murder, money laundering, and winter farming in Alaska
TROOPER
Blue Sky
and Green Grass
Ron Walden
Alaskan True to Life Crime Writer

Poacher's
PARADISE
An Alaska Wildlife Trooper Novel
Ron Walden
Alaskan True to Life Crime Writer

EASY COME
EASY GO
ALASKA GOLD FEVER
Ron Walden
Alaskan True to Life Crime Writer